PRAISE FOR

"...a riveting tale told with humor and compassion. Treat yourself to a fine read and then go back and listen to The Band's song, 'The W.S. Walcott Medicine Show'".

—**STEVEN PHILLIP SMITH**, author of American Boys and writer/producer of TV's *New York Undercover, The Long Riders, Tour of Duty, Reasonable Doubts'* and *Hack*.

"...an enjoyable and engaging trip, full of humor, perceptive observations, period details, diverse characters—and a complete-the-circle surprise at the end."

—**GARY M. LEPPER**, mystery writer and author of *A Deadly Game*

"...Brittain has written a marvelous historical novel richly capturing the best and worst of the human experience. This story will stay with you long after its extraordinary ending."

—**RICHARD S. JAFFE**, author of *Quest For Justice: Defending the Damned and When Night Sets In*.

"Written with an easy grace and wit. Let's hope that Brittain gives us more like this. It's a charming journey with unique characters set in another time in the American midwest."

—**DALE DAUTEN**, King Features syndicated columnist and author of *The Weary Optimist*.

Brother Daniel's Good News Revival
by Bruce Joel Brittain
© Copyright 2017 Bruce Joel Brittain

ISBN 978-1-63393-508-2

All rights reserved. No part of this publication may be reproduced, stored in a retrieval system, or transmitted in any form or by any means – electronic, mechanical, photocopy, recording, or any other – except for brief quotations in printed reviews, without the prior written permission of the author.

This is a work of fiction. The characters are both actual and fictitious. With the exception of verified historical events and persons, all incidents, descriptions, dialogue and opinions expressed are the products of the author's imagination and are not to be construed as real.

Published by

◤ köehlerbooks™

210 60th Street
Virginia Beach, VA 23451
800-435-4811
www.koehlerbooks.com

Brother Daniel's Good News Revival

By
Bruce Joel Brittain

Bruce J Brittain

Dedication

This book is dedicated to the memory of my mother, Elizabeth Kirk Brittain (1915-2000), and to my father Byron R.T. Brittain (1919—). Both grew to adulthood during the Great Depression, lived in the heart and fury of the Dust Bowl, and served their country during World War II. They were, and are, bona fide members of the Greatest Generation.

Chapter One
Summer of '33

HEADING SOUTH WAS heading home. The caravan had come to Indiana from Kentucky early that summer. But now, more than three months later, the little band of travelers was seeking geography where the evening temperatures of fall were better suited to outdoor worship.

Once again they would strike the tents, stow the wooden chairs, load the piano, box the frayed hymnals, and drive to the next town in their two trucks and one Lincoln sedan. It was the occasional evening chill as much as the calendar that suggested the migration; like a small flock of geese turning their heads south, anticipating the cold seeping in from behind.

In early September, however, the Midwest heat was often still in command. It was a warm night when Mother Daniel quietly asked Michael to rub mayonnaise on her breasts. And so he did. But, there is much to tell of the journey to this Indiana evening and of the events that came after.

Michael had joined the group in Guffie, Kentucky, just south of the Indiana line. He had attended Brother Daniel's Good News Revival there in late May. He went with his Aunt Elizabeth and her kids. The four of them lived eight miles south in Calhoun.

They had gone up to Guffie on a Wednesday evening. Michael and his young cousins rode in the back of Mr. Berryman's hay truck. Aunt Elizabeth sat up front with Mr. Berryman. Then, on Sunday evening, they all went back for the evening service by the same hard ride. Given that Aunt Elizabeth had been known to walk Highway 815 up to Guffie to attend the revival, it could have been worse.

Brother Daniel's Good News Revival had been coming to this corner of Kentucky since the spring of '28, and Aunt Elizabeth had gone each and every time, five years running. This was Michael's third year. The members of the revival troop always seemed to recognize everyone who came to the services, and made a big show of being delighted to see them again—but Michael suspected that "show" was more the reality.

His cousins, too young to complain about being herded here or there by their mom, seemed to enjoy the music and could sing along with several of the hymns Sister Ruth banged out on the almost-in-tune upright. Many of the songs were the same ones that the children sang twice a week at the Second Coming Pentecostal Church in Calhoun.

Michael had moved in with his father's sister in the summer of 1930. That was the year his parents, desperate for work, had taken baby Nelle and Michael's twelve-year-old brother, Matthew, and headed for Oregon, where there was supposed to be farm work. There wasn't. Now, his parents and siblings were somewhere in the central California valley, working crops when there was any work at all. The last letter from his mom was postmarked Porterville, California.

Michael's lot, as explained by his father when he and Michael packed the old Ford for the trip to Oregon, was to "finish your schoolin', help Lizzie with the young'uns and the farm." Michael was nearly sixteen when they left. Three years on, and the sharp pain that was his ache of abandonment was now a low thrum.

Aunt Elizabeth's husband—of whom few spoke, at least not in her presence—had gone looking for work in '27 and stayed gone. Aunt Elizabeth claimed that he had evaporated into the Smoky Mountains. A Second Coming Pentecostal Church lady swore that she had seen the man in Atlanta in the winter of 1930, but no one followed up. Michael guessed that Aunt Elizabeth wasn't much interested in wherever the hell he was. By then, she had taken up with Mr. Berryman, although she would deny it for several years. After Mr. Berryman's bed-ridden wife passed in '38, Aunt Elizabeth became the second Mrs. Berryman, and not too long after the first one was declared permanently cold.

"Truck driver/stagehand needed," a hand-lettered sign was tacked to a tent pole at the rear entrance of the revival venue. Below those letters was scrawled, "See Mother Daniel after the service."

Aunt Elizabeth raised her chin toward the sign and observed that it might be Michael's "ticket outta here." He could drive a commercial truck, had just graduated high school the weekend before, and the prospects in Calhoun were something worse than bleak. She wasn't trying to get rid of the boy, but she knew what was what. It was certain that Michael had no means for college. Roosevelt had promised jobs during the campaign of '32, but jobs had not magically appeared after his inauguration in March of 1933.

And so, after the final call for sinners to "Come down front and accept Jesus as your Lord and Savior," and after the final ringing notes of "Nearer My God To Thee," and after the last Brother Daniel "Amen and come back next year to celebrate what God hath wrought," Michael worked his way against the small tide of believers who were headed for the rear tent flap and the warm Kentucky night.

The main revival tent was forty-five feet, front to back and thirty feet wide. Three main tent poles, each twenty feet tall, held the peaked roof aloft. Strung between these poles down the center aisle and about ten feet above the ground, was an electric wire with a dozen bare lightbulbs to illuminate the evening services. The side walls of the tent were eight feet tall, braced with a half-dozen wooden poles per side, each one connected to a large exterior metal stake by a one-inch diameter sisal rope.

The canvas sides could be rolled up or down depending on the weather. They were put down when it was rainy or cool, or up for hot weather ventilation. Even when rolled up, however, the summer Midwest heat often caused the worshippers to break out their paper fans, most of which had been compliments of some local funeral parlor.

At the front of the tent was a low wooden riser, twenty feet across and six feet deep. It was just big enough to accommodate an upright piano and a small, somewhat unsteady pulpit, although Brother Daniel rarely stood behind it, preferring to pace the riser as he delivered the Word.

As Michael had learned from his Aunt Elizabeth, Mother Daniel was Brother Daniel's wife, a confusion of titles that didn't bother most, and an irony that didn't occur to Michael until some years later. Sisters Ruth Grace and Rebecca Joy were Mother and Brother Daniel's daughters. The couple's youngest, a boy, a nine-year old called Petey, although his full name was Peter Paul Daniel, a moniker that gave him the coveted all-biblical-names prize. Mother Daniel's given names were Annie Maypearl, but Brother Daniel was the only one to call her "Annie," and then only when speaking to her, not about her. Brother Daniel was actually Harlow Eugene Daniel but no one, except the occasional sheriff or constable, addressed Brother Daniel except as "Brother Daniel" and that included his wife and children.

There, surrounded by the modest bustle of her children gathering hymnals and sheet music, plus the oaky thwack of folding chairs being stacked by two fellows in bib overalls, Michael found Mother Daniel at a small table behind the piano.

Mother Daniel, whose only revival role seemed to be sure that the collection plate was passed to everyone in the tent, and then to tally the money after the service, was a slender woman of average height, and her hair was pecan-shell brown. She was a mature woman—Michael guessed at least thirty-five, maybe older—but still very pretty. Mr. Berryman had commented to Michael once that he didn't mind coming to these services because she was a "looker."

At the small table she was carefully ruffling through the dollar bills looking for anything larger. There wasn't. All of what she called the "noisy money"—half dollars, quarters, dimes, nickels, and pennies—was pushed to the side for later tabulation. A few silver dollars were placed on top of the quarter-inch pile of ones. Michael could see that there was serious money in the revival business.

After a silence that seemed inappropriately long and certainly uncomfortable for him, Michael said, "Excuse me Ma'am but is there still a driver job?"

"And stagehand," said Mother Daniel. "It's two jobs for one person." Her eyes never left the money.

"Yes, Ma'am, and stagehand. Are they still available?" Michael noticed a small rubber tip slipped over the end of Mother Daniel's right thumb. She used it to fan the bills as she counted. It occurred to Michael that this was likely a more sophisticated operation than he had envisioned.

"Depends," said Mother Daniel. "Can you drive a truck?"

"Yes'um."

"Got any education?" her eyes on the table.

"High school graduate, Ma'am; last weekend."

"Congratulations."

She wrote some figures into a small cardboard-bound ledger, slipped the folding money and silver dollars into a cracked leather portfolio, and zipped it shut. Only then did she lean back in the chair and raise her eyes to look at Michael. Unlike Michael's very dark eyes, hers were pale blue and they seemed to take his measure in a piercing instant.

"Ever live away from home?"

"No Ma'am."

"You'll just want your momma in a few days and then we'll be lookin' for another driver." Mother Daniel turned her attention to the task of counting the noisy money.

"I haven't seen my parents since three summers ago," said Michael, "So I doubt that I'll miss my momma any stronger on the road than I have already."

Mother Daniel sat back, looked at Michael and pursed her lips. "Who will you miss?"

"I guess I'll miss my cousins and aunt some—that's who I live with now—but likely not enough to leave a payin' job." Michael shifted his weight and drew a deep breath.

"Sit down, boy, you're making me lose count with all your fidgitin'." Mother Daniel corralled the half dollars into a group, swept them off the edge of the table into her left hand and set the stacked coins back on the table. Michael did a quick take and figured it was maybe a five-dollar stack. He'd saved five dollars last summer doing yard work and odd jobs for The Second Coming Pentecostal Church. He used all of that to help

Aunt Elizabeth buy books, school supplies, and a few clothes for himself and his cousins. Money just didn't go as far as it had when he was a little boy.

"How old are you, boy?"

"Comin' up on nineteen in July. My name is Michael, Michael Boone."

Michael, a shade over six feet tall, had inherited his mother's tangle of hair, except his was dark brown while hers was reddish, a trait that suggested her Irish roots. He was lean from hard work and a diet that featured farm vegetables and fruits, fresh and canned, depending on the season. He didn't have his mother's freckles but he did have his father's ruddy cheeks that easily turned red when he was embarrassed or angry.

"Well, Michael Boone, the job pays eighteen dollars a week, we feed you, there's two bedrolls per truck. You get half a day off on Sunday mornings and if you get in trouble with the law, you're on your own." Mother Daniel isolated the quarters and made three small stacks.

Michael sat forward in the wooden chair. "When would I start?"

"Tonight, if you're ready; tomorrow noon at the latest. We're headed up to Boonville as soon as we're packed. Monday is always travel day." Mother Daniel riffled through the dimes, nickels, and pennies on the table making small islands of each.

"I'll have to come back tomorrow," said Michael, standing up. "I'll have to get some extra clothes and all."

"You won't be needin' nothin' fancy, just blue jeans, overalls, a hat and such. If you have work boots, I recommend 'em and a pair of leather gloves. Of course we won't pay you for a full day if you get here at noon. The heavy lifting will be done by then. Get here by 7:00 if you want a full day's credit,"

Mother Daniel brushed some stray hair back from her eyes. She reached down to retrieve a small metal box from the floor. Michael could see down the gap at the top of her blouse. He knew that he should politely look away but he didn't. The view was quite remarkable, completely free of foundation garments.

"I'll be here before 7:00, Ma'am." Michael said, looking up and waiting for some sign of dismissal.

"Good," she said, without looking up from the money. "We'll

plan on it."

Michael turned and headed for the back of the tent, which was now quickly losing its interior form as the chairs were becoming stacks instead of rows. The two men in bib overalls paid him no mind as they worked.

"Mr. Boone," Mother Daniel called out. "Are you a Christian?"

He stopped and turned halfway. She was now standing behind the table.

"I guess I am, Ma'am."

"Well good, but it's not a requirement. Right, Mr. Gilbert?"

One of the workmen stopped in mid-stack, looked at Michael, looked back at Mother Daniel and replied, "That's for sure, Ma'am."

When Michael told everyone at the hay truck that he got the job and had to be back here at 7:00 in the morning, Aunt Elizabeth gave Michael a long hug, cried a little and then shooed Michael and her children into the back for the ride home. Mr. Berryman agreed to bring Michael back in the morning.

The next morning at 6:00 am, when Michael climbed into the cab of Mr. Berryman's truck, he had no idea when he would see Aunt Elizabeth or his cousins—the little ones were still soundly asleep in the house—again.

"Send me a card or letter, Michael, and let me know how to send you mail." His aunt was standing beside the Dodge. She leaned in and pecked him on the cheek. "I'll let your folks know about the job."

Michael and Mr. Berryman rode up to Guffie without much conversation. When they arrived at the revival tent it was half past 6:00, and there was no activity except for some chickens that had crossed the parking lot looking for whatever it is that chickens find to eat on apparently bare ground.

"Here, Michael, you can use these," said Mr. Berryman, handing Michael a pair of work gloves that he pulled from behind the seat. "I've got another pair and I figured that it would be awhile before you could buy a pair. You can give 'em back when you get home."

"I don't know when that'll be," said Michael.

"Whenever," said Mr. Berryman.

"Thanks. And thanks for the ride."

Mr. Berryman nodded. Michael retrieved his small canvas duffel from the back, and then Mr. Berryman edged the truck out of the gravel lot. Michael watched as it grew smaller down toward the south curve. Bits of hay scattered from the truck's bed mixing with the faint hint of blue exhaust from the tailpipe.

Michael went under the open-sided revival tent and sat on a short stack of folded wooden chairs. He was there several minutes before he heard smoky coughing and the moist clearing of a throat. This bit of activity seemed to come from behind or inside the nearest truck, a newish-looking Ford with a canvas covering over a rounded tent frame built on the flat bed. The back flap of the canvas covering was then tossed back and one of the men who had been stacking chairs the night before made the short drop to the ground. He spat.

He was wearing the same bib overalls but no shirt or shoes. He fished in one of the chest pockets, pulled out a flat of rolling paper, slipped his hand in another front pocket, and brought out a pudgy drawstring pouch of tobacco. Deftly, he did all the undoing, doing, and licking that produced the morning's first pleasure, a cigarette that bore an uncanny resemblance to a very white and uncircumcised penis. Striking a wooden match on the rough metal frame of the truck, the man lit up and deeply inhaled. This was followed by a spasm of coughing, hacking, and spitting that was followed with another deep draw but no further respiratory theatrics. For the next seven months, this noisy morning ritual would replace, for Michael, the rooster's crow of the farm.

He looked at Michael, raised his chin in a subdued greeting and walked slowly toward the privy that sat 100 feet or so back of the small, sturdy-looking brick church that had hosted Brother Daniel's Revival in Guffie.

"That man may be the only other, besides the Lord himself, who could raise Lazarus from the dead," Brother Daniel said to no one in particular as he emerged from the larger of two tents that were set off to one side of the main tent. These two tents were the family compound, as Michael would soon learn. They were the Daniel clan's home, the larger for Brother Daniel, Mother Daniel, and Petey. The smaller one was for Sisters Ruth and Rebecca.

Brother Daniel was wearing dark trousers, a well-worn undershirt, white socks but no shoes. A pair of grey cloth suspenders gave the impression of formality in spite of the modest ensemble.

He went back inside the tent and quickly emerged carrying a pair of brown, high-top shoes. He walked over to where Michael was sitting, pulled a chair off of nearby stack, opened it, sat down, and began putting on his shoes.

"Mr. Boone, I assume."

"Yes, sir, Michael Boone."

"Welcome to the Good News Revival, Mr. Boone," said Brother Daniel. "We are a small band of wanderers doin' the Lord's work where the Lord's work most needs doin'."

Yes, sir, I suppose you are," said Michael.

"There's no 'suppose' about it, Mr. Boone. This country's headed for Perdition and all the faster with that Democrat in charge," said Brother Daniel. "The people in America need to be re-invigorated with the good news that someone cares for them and that 'someone' is Jesus." With that, Brother Daniel stood up and extended his hand to Michael. "You'll be glad that you joined us. Mr. Gilbert, the man of a thousand coughs, will get you squared away when he returns from his morning constitutional." Brother Daniel walked over and disappeared into his tent.

The privy door opened and Mr. Gilbert, followed by a blue cloud of tobacco smoke, came out. He stopped to re-adjust the ride of the overalls, walked back to his truck, and put on a pair of sorry-looking shoes. He came over to where Michael was still seated and, with his hands in his front pockets, said, "Name's Winslow Gilbert but most call me Bert. Brother Daniel and his missus call me Mr. Gilbert, but they're about the only ones. I'd shake your hand but I haven't properly washed."

"I'm Michael Boone, Mr. Gilbert. We can shake hands later."

"It's Bert."

"Okay, Bert. Anyway, we can shake hands later."

"Boone, huh?" said Bert, "Of the Kentucky Boones?"

Michael's brow furrowed but he said nothing, trying to decipher the question.

"You know," said Bert, "Dan'l Boone; he who killed a bar."

Michael nodded in understanding. "Dad says that we

probably are. He says that even if we are, so what?"

"Sounds like a practical man, your father. I'd probably like him," Bert said as he ground the stub of his cigarette into the dirt with his shoe. "Let's get started on this packing before breakfast."

And so, with Bert's taciturn directions, Michael began the labor intensive but not mentally challenging work of dismantling, rolling up, stacking, packing away, bundling together, tying down, and otherwise preparing the hardware and necessities of a traveling Christian revival for transport via a bone-jarring, leaf-sprung commercial truck across the graveled and poorly maintained roads of middle America.

The travel day routine was much the same for every Monday going forward: Stack and tie down the folding chairs, box and tie down the hymnals, roll the piano up the incline boards and tie it down double, fold the main tent side flaps, then stack and tie them down at the very back of the flatbed. With that done, Michael's truck was ready for the road. It seemed to Michael that not an inch of space under the canvas tarp was empty.

The preparation of the first truck, the one that Michael would come to know well in the next few months, was complete by half past 8:00 and then it was time for breakfast.

Michael had been vaguely aware of the activity around the two standing tents as he and Bert went about their work. Sister Ruth and another girl who looked nearly identical—at least they did from across the gravel lot—set out fruit, bread, cheese, and a bag of wheat germ. Sister Rebecca brought a bucket of water from a hand-pumped well near the back door of the church. She prepared a coffee pot. Brother Daniel got a fire going in a small brick fireplace that was used for church cookouts. Sister Rebecca placed the pot over a portion of the fire and soon the smell of fresh coffee was drifting in the morning air.

"Mr. Gilbert, Mr. Boone, come have some breakfast," called Brother Daniel. "The Lord has sent us a beautiful travel day and some fresh pears and plums; a gift from the ladies of the Mt. Zion Baptist Church."

Bert and Michael washed their hands with a sliver of lye soap, one pumping the well handle while the other lathered and rinsed.

Closer at hand, Michael was surprised to realize that the other girl working with Sister Ruth was, in fact, Mother Daniel.

They were eerily similar including body type, height, dark blond hair tied back with a patterned bandana, and their travel day uniforms of faded dungarees, blue work shirts, and clumsy-looking work boots. The only difference from a distance of more than a few feet was Mother Daniel's bandana was red; Sister Ruth's was blue.

They gathered around the wooden picnic table where the food was arranged down the center. The metal plates and silverware—actually, just forks and spoons—were placed three to a side. The Daniel clan clasped hands and Petey, being closest to Michael reached for Michael's hand. Sister Rebecca reached across Bert and grabbed Michael's other hand. The circle, excluding Bert, was unbroken.

"Let us give thanks to the Lord," said Brother Daniel and the group, except Bert, lowered their heads.

Brother Daniel was never a man of few words, especially on the occasion of a prayer. Besides blessing the food and the ladies of the Mt. Zion Baptist Church who had delivered the fresh pears and plums, he thanked the Lord for bringing Michael to the effort of spreading the Word and finished up with kudos to the Lord for the "bright blue, cloudless miracle of the finest travel day ever delivered on the God's green earth. Amen."

It was somewhere during the mention of the "fresh pears and plums" that Michael looked up and found that he was being stared at by Sister Ruth, who was between Mother Daniel and Sister Rebecca. He quickly returned his eyes to his work boots. He took in enough in that brief glance to reinforce how similar she looked to her mother. They could have been sisters.

At prayer's end, everyone but Petey selected a seat, men on one side, ladies on the other. Mother Daniel fixed a plate for Petey who stood at her shoulder and then he took his breakfast to the back of the empty flatbed and commenced to eat standing up.

"You can have my seat, little boy," said Michael, somewhat self-conscience of his role as the new hire.

"His name is Petey," said Mother Daniel, "Anyway, he likes to get away from the adult talk around the table."

"Are we planning to have any of that this morning?" said Bert.

Ignoring Bert, Brother Daniel broke the brief and awkward

silence. "Mr. Boone, you are sitting directly across from Sister Ruth, the oldest of the Daniel girls. To her left is Sister Rebecca. You can decide for yourself whether you wish the younger members of our family to call you by your given name or your family name. Mother Daniel and I will use your family name."

"Y'all can call me Michael," he said to the group.

"How about Mike?" asked Petey; he was slicing a pear with his pocketknife.

"I'd rather be Michael."

"Gotcha," said Petey. "Mike it is." He smiled broadly, revealing a significant gap between his front teeth.

"Petey, behave yourself," said Mother Daniel as she quickly shook her head and suppressed a smile.

"Brother Daniel," Bert said while stirring a spoonful of sugar into his coffee mug, "The next time you have a word with the Lord, ask him to get us two new tires and tubes for my truck. The current ones are sure to flatten two or three times between here and Boonville."

"I don't believe the Lord works that way," Brother Daniel's voice was tight.

"Well, maybe I could steal some tires and tubes and then you could ask the Lord to forgive me," Bert rested both elbows on the tabletop and held the coffee mug near his mouth with both hands. The steam from the coffee curled up in front of his nose.

"That's quite enough, Mr. Gilbert." Neither Brother Daniel nor Bert had looked at one another during this exchange. Michael, sitting between them, kept his eyes on his own plate.

Brother Daniel continued, "Once we're packed and ready for the road, Sister Ruth will ride with Mr. Gilbert and work on her Greek studies. Sister Rebecca will ride with Mr. Boone as his navigator, in case we get separated on the road to Boonville."

Michael glanced up at Rebecca, who smiled at him briefly and then returned to her breakfast, her travel duties established.

The sun edged its way above the elm grove on the far side of the church and the remainder of the morning's work proved hotter but no harder than the pre-breakfast efforts. Bert stopped occasionally for a smoke break, and Michael took the opportunity to sit in the shade. It was during the second of these lulls that Michael asked Bert about the "Greek studies" comment.

"Oh, that," said Bert. "I'm a driver, a stagehand, and a tutor for the kids. Sister Ruth struggles some with Greek. It's hard to say why; she a whiz with Latin."

Michael pushed this information around in his head. "Latin?" "Greek?" He suddenly felt disoriented, vulnerable. He was a country rube, just another sucker primed to be fleeced by the sharpie at the ring-toss. Except there was no ring-toss, just this little group of travelers who were clearly way ahead of him.

And so, town by town, soul by soul, the caravan worked its way north, then east and south again through the summer heat of Indiana: Boonville, Jasper, Paoli, Bedford, Seymour, Morgantown, then nine or ten more. When the mayonnaise jar episode occurred, they were in a town right on the Ohio River, just north of Kentucky. Maybe it was Green Fork. No, that was in August, somewhere to the north. Or was it Brookville? That didn't seem right either. Michael couldn't keep them straight. By the time Mother Daniel came to his truck in her blue pajama top, carrying the Blue Plate mayonnaise jar, they were in a gravel parking lot in Southeast Indiana. Given the nature of the event, one would think that Michael would recall the specific location, other than it was in the back of a truck somewhere near his home state. No matter.

Of this Michael was sure, his experience with Brother Daniel's Good News Revival started with the early summer drive from Guffie, Kentucky, north to Boonville, Indiana.

As the crow flies, the distance between Guffie, Kentucky, and Boonville, Indiana, is less than forty miles. But a road traveler, not being a crow, had to cross the Ohio River at either Evansville or Owensboro. The trip, including stops for gasoline, three flat tires, and a broken tie-down strap, took almost five hours. Lunch consisted of bacon, lettuce, and tomato sandwiches, washed down with lemonade, and topped off with the last of the fresh pears. Mother Daniel handed the lunch items around while Bert was repairing the first of the flat tires, which deflated just north of Moseleyville where Panther Creek crosses under Highway 81. Bert, it was clear, knew his tires and their limits.

Petey conspired with Brother Daniel to use this break for a swim. The two of them disappeared down the embankment and under the bridge. Moments later there was a yelp from Petey and the splash of a body hitting water in an awkward way. Sister Rebecca pulled off her boots and hurried under the bridge. Soon there was splashing and laughter as the three used their cupped hands to spray water on the others from close range. At one point, Michael could see Petey on Brother Daniel's shoulders emerge from under the bridge. Petey was in his underwear. Brother Daniel, shoeless and his pants wet to mid-thigh waded to a small, flat outcrop of rock near the bank, stepped up on the rock, walked to the waterside and unceremoniously pitched Petey into five feet of calm, clear Panther Creek water. Petey came up laughing and asking for another round. This time, Petey crawled up Brother Daniel's back and put the soles of his feet on Brother Daniel's shoulders, steadied by his father's hands, stood up and jumped into the creek from his human perch.

Sister Rebecca came into view, swimming against the modest current. She had shed here dungarees and her long blue work shirt served as her swimwear. She ducked her head underwater and swam a few strokes like a tadpole, the current gently pushing her hair and work shirt back over her adolescent body. She surfaced, took a strong breath and plunged back under, turning back towards the bridge. Between each swimming stroke, the current pushed her hair forward and her shirt toward her shoulders. Michael could see the white flash of her underwear for a second or two. She disappeared back under the bridge.

Petey appeared from the opposite side of the bridge where the three had gone down.

"Hey, Mike, can you swim?"

"Yeah," said Michael.

"You ought to go have a dip. The water is warm." His smile indicated that this assessment was less than honest.

"Mr. Boone has work to do." Mother Daniel walked to Petey and handed him a towel so thin that water absorption was but a vague memory.

"Rebecca," she called out, "Come up and dry off. We're about ready to leave."

"In a minute, mother." There was brief silence and then Michael heard Rebecca say, "Don't! Let me have my pants." There was anger and a tinge of fear in her voice. Michael glanced at Sister Ruth, who was reading a Latin textbook in the shade.

She did not look up, but Michael thought he saw a slight clench of her jaw. Mother Daniel turned abruptly and walked to the far side of the car, searching for towels and dry clothes.

"Oh, don't be such a crybaby," Brother Daniel said over his shoulder as he emerged from under the bridge carrying Rebecca's dungarees and his shoes. He turned and tossed the pants into the middle of Panther Creek, and they floated on the current going under the bridge. Michael heard Rebecca splashing into the water to fetch them.

When she came up to the roadway, her face was flushed. Her soaked clothes stuck to her torso, revealing the outline of her bra and giving her young figure more contours than Michael could have expected. He turned away and fixed his attention on Bert's final repairs. Then, between the two of them, they inflated the tire with the hand pump, a pump that Michael would grow to hate.

When Rebecca joined Michael in the cab of the truck, she had put on dry clothing but her hair was wet and slicked back. Her face had lost its flush but her mood was somber. Michael concentrated on getting the truck off of the narrow dirt shoulder and back on the road while maintaining a safe distance from Bert's truck. The caravan was on the move. The Daniel's Lincoln sedan, pulling a tarp-covered trailer, was in the lead followed by Bert and Sister Ruth in the Ford truck while Michael and Sister Rebecca followed behind.

All three vehicles had signs on the driver's and passenger's side doors advertising *Brother Daniel's Good News Revival*. The lettering was professionally painted and reminded Michael of the signs on the side of a circus train that he had once seen in Louisville. For those cars and trucks unlucky enough to get stuck behind this clearly identified, slow-moving mini-parade, there were likely very few drivers who developed a more positive attitude toward salvation once they had risked life and property to hopscotch beyond this little exhaust-spewing spiritual band.

"I guess your father was having a little fun teasing you back there at the creek," said Michael after many minutes of silence.

"He's not my father." Rebecca was staring straight ahead when Michael glanced over.

"Oh," said Michael, at a loss for a more appropriate response.

The sound of the bald tires on the pavement was like the sound of light sleet in the winter.

"My daddy died when I was four," Rebecca finally offered. "A cow kicked his head in the barn. I was asleep. I don't remember him too much."

Between two more flat tire stops, one on Michael's truck and then the same tire on Bert's that they had patched near Panther Creek, Michael learned some of the history of Brother Daniel's family and the traveling revival. Rebecca offered the story up in dribs and drabs as her memories clicked into place.

Her father, Lester Foster, and her mother owned a dairy farm just southwest of the panhandle town of Perry, Florida. Ruth was six and Rebecca four when Lester died on the milking room floor. The 300-acre farm was successful, but too much for a young mother with two little girls to manage on her own. Her mother, Annie, sold the property, the livestock, and the farm equipment to a cattle rancher from Gainesville. That happened in the spring of 1924, just four months after Lester's death. With a moderate nest egg from the sale, but few prospects, Annie and the girls moved to Tallahassee.

Annie found a small house to rent, stocked it with some furniture that she hadn't sold with the farm, and began a frustrating search for work. She finally got a job in a dress shop. She got the girls into school. Rebecca went to kindergarten a year early because Annie fibbed about her daughter's age. Ever since, the sisters were one grade apart even though there was more than two years difference in their ages.

Sometime, Rebecca couldn't remember exactly when, Harlow Daniel started coming to the house for supper from time to time and then all the time. Eventually he moved in. When Rebecca had almost completed the first grade the family headed north from Tallahassee in one new truck with a trailer and one new big car with a trailer. Her mother was pregnant at the time. Annie drove the car with Rebecca and Ruth in the back seat and Harlow drove the truck. They would stop in little towns, set up the tent and hold revivals.

"So," said Michael, "Your mom married Brother Daniel and then they started traveling to preach the gospel."

"Can't say for sure they got married," replied Rebecca. "I

don't recall any wedding. The travelin' and preachin' was to make money. Momma still had some money so she bought the trucks and stuff. I think it was Brother Daniel's idea."

Michael had a lot to think about as they drove on in silence to Boonville.

Chapter Two
Early Summer in Indiana

THE TRAVEL DAY had taken them up to Owensboro, across the Ohio River, north on Highway 161, and into Boonville from the east on Highway 62. The First (and only) Nazarene Church was on the north side of town at the intersection of North 3rd Street and East North Street.

The church had a small paved parking lot so the tents would be put up in a large grassy area just to the back of the lot. Brother Daniel gathered the group together to thank the Lord for their safe arrival, and to ask that He hold off on any rain until after next weekend, given that muddy ground made for lousy camping and fewer sinners in attendance.

Michael then got instructions from Bert for where to park his truck. After a brief discussion, there was some jockeying around until both trucks were positioned for unpacking. It was a little after six, so there were still a couple of hours of daylight.

Mother Daniel and the three children took the sedan to a local grocery for provisions. Bert and Michael tucked into the work of setting up the family tents. The revival tent would go up on Tuesday. This was a process that would be repeated, with the occasional alteration, every week for the next fourteen weeks.

While Brother Daniel sat out of earshot in the cab of Bert's truck writing sermon notes so as to tailor the message to fit the Boonville faithful, Michael asked Bert some of his nagging questions.

"What happened to the other driver; the one I replaced in Guffie?" he asked.

Bert kept working at unfolding the tent. "He got a little too interested in Sister Ruth, so Mother Daniel canned him before things got sticky. Charlie is a good kid. He was only doing what comes natural. Ruth didn't seem much interested in him but he kept shadowing her, mooning over her like a fool. I only hope he makes it back to Florida with some money in his pocket. He started thumbing back to Tallahassee that night in Guffie when you were hired."

"Sister Rebecca told me that Brother Daniel is not her father," said Michael. "Is that true?"

"Very," said Bert. "She and Ruth are the daughters of a guy named Foster. He's dead. The Huns didn't get him at Verdun, but a Holstein got him in their barn. If you are into irony, that's a doozy. But, I never met the man."

"When did you start working for Brother Daniel?"

"Summer of '28."

"Are you from Florida?" asked Michael.

"Nope."

"Where's home then?"

"That truck over there," Bert nodded toward the Ford.

"No, I mean, where are you from?"

"Tell you what, boy; let's get this tent put up." Bert cut off the conversation.

Winslow Gilbert was an angular man with sharp cheekbones, a Roman nose, and lean sinewy arms. He was clean shaven when he bothered to shave, which only seemed to be once or twice a week, and his brown eyes seemed nearly black. No more than six feet tall, he and Michael could look eye to eye. His manner of speaking suggested that he was an educated man, confirmed by his role as tutor to the Daniel children. Michael figured he was pretty old, maybe forty or so. He preferred being known as Bert. As it turned out, his given name had some baggage that he wanted left behind.

By the time both tents were secure, Mother Daniel and the girls had fixed a cold cuts dinner with fresh tomatoes, cantaloupe, and some store-bought ice cream—a rare treat as it turned out. She had also stopped by the local icehouse and filled a thick wooden box, with its thick tin-covered lid, with chunks of ice.

"We'll have mostly hot suppers the rest of the week," said Mother Daniel, "when we get settled in."

Michael was glad to get into his bedroll when the dark and the hard work had pushed him toward sleep.

Tuesday morning started early, with Bert and Michael preparing to raise the revival tent. Once the tent was positioned, it took all hands to raise the heavy canvas with the thick oak main and side poles. Michael simply took directions and heaved when told and held on until told to move somewhere else and heave again. After a couple of weeks, he knew the process and it went somewhat smoother. He admitted to himself, however, that raising the main tent was a pain in the butt, even when you knew exactly what to do.

Once the tent was secure, Michael and Bert unloaded the piano, the chairs and the boxes of hymnals. Bert ran a power wire from the church basement to a pole between the revival tent and the family tents. From that central location, a string of bare bulbs down the center of the big tent would provide light for the evening services and the power for modest lighting inside the two family tents. The trucks didn't get any electrical lighting. If they wanted light at night, Michael and Bert had gas lanterns, or the one bare bulb at the central pole.

The First Nazarene had indoor plumbing, a luxury that Michael had rarely seen. Late on Tuesday afternoon, Bert suggested that he and Michael could use the men's washroom to get a "heathen's bath," as Bert called it.

"Bring some clean skivvies and get a towel from Mother Daniel," said Bert. "We need to wash up whenever we can because many of our stops don't have facilities like this."

Bert brought an empty gallon can. They both stripped down. Bert filled the can at a tap and poured it on top of Michael's head. Even though the weather was warm, the shock of cold water momentarily took Michael's breath away. Bert repeated the process for himself, and the men lathered themselves with some soap from the sink. Michael doused himself with more water and lathered up again, paying particular attention to armpits, his crotch, and his feet. The soapy water and rinse water gurgled down the drain in the cement floor.

"Good to see a fellow who knows to hit the stinky parts twice," said Bert, smiling faintly. "The ladies don't care much for stink on a man."

Michael felt himself flush.

"And," said Bert, "You'd be what we used to call a bank walker."

"What's a bank walker?"

"Well," said Bert, drying his back with one of the camp's skimpy towels, "When the boys went swimming in the creek, the ones with the short peckers all jumped in as soon as they were stripped, but the boys with an impressive member took their sweet time walking along the bank. Ergo, bank walker."

If Michael had only partially flushed at the "stinky parts" comment, he engaged his entire circulation system with this exchange.

"Oh now, don't be embarrassed," smiled Bert, "It's a good thing," and he slipped into a clean pair of boxer shorts. "Come on, get dressed or we'll miss Brother Daniel's Sermon on the Mount prayer before dinner."

Over dinner, Bert raised the issue of the truck tires again. Before Brother Daniel could respond, Mother Daniel said that the offerings from Guffie were enough for at least two new tires here in Boonville. And that, seemed to be that. Petey chimed in, insisting that he would go with Bert to the filling station to buy the tires tomorrow.

"Well, I'll need one of the Daniel's clan along to make sure I don't spend too much on 'them thar tars'." Bert's emphasis on the country folk pronunciation struck Michael as a verbal smirk.

"I believe that we can do without further sarcasm, Mr. Gilbert." Mother Daniel glared his direction. Bert shrugged his shoulders and went back to work on his half of a small fried chicken.

After the dinner, Michael pulled a folding chair underneath a lone lightbulb dangling from the tent pole. He fetched one of three books that he had brought from home and sat down to read. There were murmured bits of conversation from both of the family tents. Bert was in Sisters Ruth and Rebecca's tent providing some instruction on geometry, and Petey was in there as well, working through a vocabulary lesson. Schoolwork during the summer was a lighter load, and was mostly done during the days of Wednesday through Friday, when Bert had fewer duties. Nighttime work was usually only an hour or so.

Michael was on the third story in *Haircut* by Ring Lardner, when Sister Ruth came out of the tent and went over to the church to use the bathroom. When she came back she pulled another chair under the bulb.

"Whacha readin'?"

"Oh, just some stories by a guy. It's about sports and stuff."

"You mean Ring Lardner?" she said.

"Yeah, that's him. Have you read some of his stories?"

"Sure," said Ruth. "Bert thinks he's very good."

"Is Bert really teaching you Latin and Greek, Sister Ruth?" Michael closed the book.

"Oh yeah," she smiled. "But Latin is the much easier because of all the words that turn into recognizable English, Spanish, Italian, and German words. Greek is Greek. And Michael, just call me Ruth; 'Sister' Ruth is for the sinners and Brother Daniel."

Michael wasn't sure what she meant but didn't ask.

Ruth was tall for a girl, but not as tall as Michael. She had dark blond hair just like Mother Daniel, and the same green eyes. None of the women in the caravan could be called "striking," but their natural good looks stood out among the dowdy farm – and small-town wives who came to the services. Ruth wore her hair pulled back, often secured with a bandana. The style was utilitarian, given her role as pianist. Long hair falling over your eyes while playing hymns was a nuisance, and her hair was well past her shoulders.

Michael always wanted straight hair like Ruth's. His brown hair was all tangled and curly cued, just like his mother's who often proclaimed his tousle of hair "gorgeous" but then that was a motherly opinion.

"Is Ring Lardner your favorite?" Michael pressed the literary theme to keep the conversation going. He hadn't had a conversation with someone his own age since high school graduation, especially a pretty girl.

"Oh, I like him a lot. But Fitzgerald and Hemingway write about more serious stuff. Bert says that besides Twain, they're America's best."

"I don't know either one," said Michael, once again feeling the bumpkin, "but I have read Mark Twain."

"And there's a new guy, I think Bert said his name was Steinway or something. He has a new book to be published soon. Bert says that when we get back to Florida that we'll buy a copy." Ruth tucked a stray strand of hair behind her ear.

"Why not get it as soon as comes out?" Michael asked. "I'd like to read some new good stories."

"Well, Michael," Ruth stood up and patted his shoulder, "Look around Boonville and let me know if you see any bookshops. Good luck, especially since Boonville is one of the larger burgs on our hallelujah tour." She headed toward her tent, stopped, turned and said, "I'll dig out the Fitzgerald and Hemingway books for you tomorrow. Goodnight."

"Thanks, goodnight."

Wednesday afternoon, after more morning tent work and setting up rows of folding chairs, Bert, with Michael and Petey tagging along, drove to an American Oil filling station on West Main. Bert selected two new tires and tubes. The station manager was a fireplug of a man, with a stubby, unlit and well-chewed cigar firmly chomped between his teeth. They could mount the tires as part of the deal, he said, but they couldn't start for another hour, maybe longer. He and his mechanic were replacing a radiator in Mrs. Hawkin's Packard.

Bert said, "Well boys, why don't you go explore greater downtown Boonville? I'll be catching up on some adult social time while we wait. This gentleman has recommended a place across the street that caters to his customers." Bert motioned with his chin to a dilapidated storefront with a handmade sign: Cards, Dominos and Snooker.

"Brother Daniel won't like that," said Petey.

"Well, your daddy isn't here to like it or not, Peter, so I'll just make my own decisions." Bert turned and walked away.

Mr. Stubby Cigar told Michael and Petey that if they walked east three blocks and took a right on South 4th, there was a drug store that had magazines, a soda fountain, and a "purdy gurl" dipping ice cream.

Michael didn't have a cent, but off they went. Miller's Pharmacy was exactly where Stubby Cigar had said. It did, indeed, have a magazine rack and a soda fountain. The girl, however, turned out to be acne-faced boy of about fourteen.

Petey went straight to the fountain counter and hopped on a stool.

"How much for a chocolate soda with vanilla ice cream?" said Petey, pulling a dollar bill from his pocket

"Quarter," came a surprisingly squeaky reply.

"Sounds good," said Petey, "I'll have one."

"How about you?" the boy looked at Michael who was standing behind Petey.

"Nothing for me, thanks," Michael felt awkward. "I'll just check out the magazines."

"Can't thumb through 'em unless you're going to buy one," said Acne Boy.

There was a park bench just outside the front door. Someone had left part of a newspaper there. Michael sat down and rustled through a two-day old *Indianapolis News*. He read the sports stories, but wasn't much interested in the local sports teams. There was coverage of the St. Louis Cardinals and Chicago Cubs, but mostly it was Indianapolis high school baseball and track and field. He looked back through the pharmacy window and Petey was sucking down his second chocolate soda.

There were news stories about the sour local and state economy, news that was no longer news to the millions, like his parents, who had rendered their family in order to survive. The new administration was making bold policy moves, but in places like Indiana there was a great deal of skepticism about this new president with his odd patrician speech pattern and New York roots.

Customers came and went from the pharmacy. A few nodded, but no one spoke. Mostly, the passers-by simply ignored the young man in well-worn overalls idling on the bench.

By the time Petey had his third chocolate soda and bought two comic books with the remaining quarter, nearly ninety minutes had passed.

"We better get back to the station, Petey." Michael stuck his head in the door.

As they walked back to the station, Petey remarked on how good the chocolate sodas had been.

"Too bad you couldn't have had one, Mike," he said, "maybe next time."

When they reached the station, Stubby Cigar was just starting on the second tire. Bert was not there. Another twenty minutes and both tires were mounted and ready for the road. Bert was still not there.

"Your buddy is still across the street," Stubby Cigar said. "Round 'im up. I want my money."

"Wait in the truck," Michael said to Petey.

Petey gave Michael the finger and headed across the street.

Michael caught up with Petey, and as he opened the door to the bar, the sunlight created a bright shaft of floating dust motes. Petey peered around Michael, straining to take in the ill-lit scene.

There was a man sitting behind a small counter immediately to the left of the door. He was using what light came in through the darkened glass of the front window to read a newspaper.

"That kid can't come in here," he said to Michael. "And, unless you're over 18, neither can you bub."

"We're not planning to stay, mister; we're here to let Bert know that we're ready to go."

Michael took a couple of steps into the room and saw that it was smaller than he expected. There was one snooker table and two card tables with cheap caned chairs. Bert was nowhere to be seen. Michael gave the man a puzzled look.

"He's in the back," said the man. "I'll have to let you in. The kid stays here."

They walked to a sturdy interior door at the back of the room and the man gave a series of knocks and then unlocked the deadbolt.

Inside this room was a lengthy bar with permanent stools bolted to the floor. Three beer taps stood like silver storks just behind the center of the bar. A large bartender stood with crossed arms behind the beer taps, a cigarette dangling from the corner of his mouth. One of his ears was cauliflowered, and a jagged scar ran from his upper right cheek, straight across his mouth and ended at the lower left chin.

Michael walked back to where Bert was listing on the bar stool, his shoulder up against the wall.

"Come on, Bert. The tires are on, the guy across the street wants his money, and Brother Daniel will be wondering what took so long." Michael reached for Bert's upper arm to coax him to his feet.

"Fuck Brother Daniel and fuck you, you country hick."

With that, Bert came unsteadily to his feet and with surprising power and quickness, shoved Michael backward. Michael's foot caught the base of a captain's chair and he fell back, landing hard in another chair at the same sticky table.

"Hey," said the man behind the bar, "Get your drunk ass out of here.

"Yeah, well maybe I'll just show you what a 'drunk ass' man can do," Bert said, turning to face the bartender.

Michael stood up as Bert took two unsteady steps toward the man.

"Come on," Michael said, "Let's just go."

Bert turned to his left, caught sight of Michael behind him, and threw a right-hand roundhouse punch that missed Michael by at least a foot and caused Bert to lose what little balance he had. Bert was trying to get to his feet when Michael caught a glimpse of rapid movement over his shoulder. There was a dull "thunk," the sound of thumping a cantaloupe, and Bert collapsed, face down with a moan.

Michael looked up and the bar man was holding a round leather pouch with a braided leather handle.

"Fishin' sinkers," he said, smirking and slapping the pouch into his palm, "Pound and three quarters."

The man reached down and took Bert's wallet out of his back pocket. He took three dollars and stuffed the wallet back into Bert's overalls.

"Two bucks for the beers and one for my tip. Get his carcass out of here."

With Bert nearly immobile, it took great effort to get him on his feet and headed for the door. Michael guided him toward the light. Petey was holding the door open but made no effort to help get Bert across the street. Michael finally got Bert into the passenger seat of the truck.

"We owe the man thirty two dollars for the tires, Bert. Where's the money?" Michael's face was near Bert's in an effort to cut through the man's semi self-inflicted fog. "Is it in your wallet?"

Michael reached behind Bert to try and extract the wallet.

"No, no," Bert mumbled, "Here." He dug into his left front pocket and pulled out a forty-dollar wad, mostly ones. *Collection plate money*, thought Michael.

Michael paid Stubby Cigar. Petey got into the back of the truck, hollering "You're in trouble now," and they headed back to the First Nazarene Church.

"I sense that Mr. Gilbert has had another losing battle with his demon." Brother Daniel walked up behind Michael as he was helping Bert out of the truck cab.

"The barman whopped him on the head, too," said Petey as he hopped out of the rear of the truck.

"Come on," Michael said to Bert, "get in the back of the truck and lay down for a spell."

Michael turned to Brother Daniel, "Do we have any ice left? He could use some on that knot on his head."

"We're not wasting any ice for headache cures. Do you have a receipt for the tires?"

"The tires were thirty two, here's the other eight that was in Bert's pocket. I figure that money was what Mother Daniel gave him for the tires," said Michael.

"No receipt?" said Brother Daniel. "How do I know that the tires weren't twenty five and you put seven in your pocket?"

"I don't steal," said Michael.

"He tellin' the truth?" Brother Daniel turned to Petey who shrugged his shoulders and offered a soft, "I guess."

"Next time, Mr. Boone, get a receipt." With that he turned and strode toward his tent. He turned midway and said, "There's an evening service to prepare for, Mr. Boone, and you'll have the work of two men to do to get everything ready. Best get started." With that, he disappeared into the tent.

Michael figured out most of what had to be done before the sinners started to trickle in, which would be in about three hours or so as the light began to fade and grow summer soft. The strand of bare bulbs in the main tent would light the way to salvation.

Michael noticed a dusty black Ford parked at the church.

About twenty minutes later, Michael saw Mother Daniel, a slight man in a black suit, and a stout woman in a one – piece dress emerge from the side door. They stood by the car. Mother Daniel and the man seemed to be doing all of the talking while the woman, her dress belted at what used to be her waist, stood silently, arms folded tightly across her chest. The conversation ended, and Mother Daniel gave the man a hug and patted him on the cheek as she pulled away. The man looked sheepishly at the pavement. The woman abruptly got in the car and slammed the door. After the couple drove off, Mother Daniel stood looking their direction and shook her head.

When she turned toward her tent, Mother Daniel caught sight of Michael.

"Do we have new tires, Mr. Boone?"

"Yes Ma'am. They were thirty-two dollars installed. I gave the change to Brother Daniel."

"Well," she said, "You and Mr. Gilbert have a few things yet to do before the service. We'll need two more chairs up by the pulpit for the Pastor Grindle and his lovely wife."

"Bert's not feeling well, Ma'am. I can get everything ready by myself."

"What's wrong with Mr. Gilbert?"

"He's got a real bad headache, Ma'am," Michael said, grabbing two folding chairs from the front row to place on the stage.

"Does his 'real bad' headache have anything to do with alcohol?" Mother Daniel asked.

"Partly," said Michael. "Petey can tell you about it."

"I'll bet." She turned and walked toward her tent. "Petey!" she called.

By 5:30, Michael had the revival tent, stage, pulpit, and folding chairs in worship-worthy order. Sisters Rebecca and Ruth had prepared toasted cheese sandwiches, a green salad, boiled potatoes, and sliced tomatoes. Michael was ravenous, and took nearly double of everything.

"I'm sure that Mr. Gilbert will appreciate that you did his share of the work and ate his share of dinner," said Brother Daniel.

"I'm sorry," said Michael, "Did I eat too much?"

"Eat as much as you want, Mr. Boone," said Mother Daniel,

staring at her husband. She turned toward Michael, "You work hard so you need the fuel. Brother Daniel can afford to be a light eater, given his schedule."

An uncomfortable silence lingered over table until Petey merrily piped up, "Man, you should have seen ol' Bert go down when that bartender hit him with that bag of lead."

"That will be quite enough, Petey." Mother Daniel stood and began clearing away her dinner utensils.

"But, Mom…"

"Enough! Clear your things; wash and rinse everything in the hot pots and put them away. Our service starts in just over an hour, and the early birds will start arriving before that," said Mother Daniel.

Even though The Church of the Nazarene was becoming the largest Wesleyan-Holiness denominations in the world by 1933, the church's outpost in Boonville was very small. And, while the church was founded to "minister to the poor" and create disciples worldwide, the local members were too poor themselves to do anything but try and hold the congregation together through the economic catastrophe that engulfed them.

When the Wednesday gathering settled into their seats, the head count was probably less than thirty. Michael based his estimate on the number of empty seats. If every chair he and Bert had carefully placed in the tent had a sinner's behind in it, the gathering would be about sixty.

Pastor Grindle opened the service with a tepid prayer, his monotone droning through the obligatory call for the Lord to bless the entire group and to give "inspiration to all who brought the word." He then introduced Brother Daniel, a man, he claimed, who "Needed no introduction." He then sat down beside the rotund Mrs. Grindle.

"A man would need some serious 'inspiration' to crawl into bed with her every night," Bert's sotto-voice was gravelly over Michael's shoulder. Bert exhaled a stream of smoke as he walked up beside Michael who was taking in the scene, sitting on the bed of his truck.

"I probably owe you a major apology for whatever happened in town, but I don't recall much." Bert's voice remained a husky whisper. "I don't imagine that it was you who put this goose egg on my head; probably that son-of-a-bitch with the wet stogie."

"It was the bartender," Michael whispered.

"Well, I likely deserved it."

The Nazarenes were known for the inclusion of music in their services, and so before Brother Daniel got completely wound up, Sister Ruth accompanied the gathered flock as they sang two hymns from the hymnals that Michael had placed on every other chair earlier that afternoon. Brother Daniel, his velvet baritone cutting assuredly through the initially self-conscience congregation voices, swung his right arm through the air, leading the choral as if a concertmaster.

As the summer progressed, there emerged a clear pattern for the message of each of the daily worship services. The Wednesday service was all about Jesus as the shepherd of the world's Christian flock and how the resident pastor was doing the work of Jesus for the local faithful. It was the only service of the week where the host church's leader shared the stage with Brother Daniel.

Brother Daniel's Wednesday sermons always made frequent mention of Jesus as shepherd, quoting from *John 10* verses *14* and *16*, *First Peter 5:4* and *Hebrews 13:20*. He always finished with *Isaiah 40:11*, "He will feed his flock like a shepherd; he will gather the lambs in his arm, and carry them in his bosom, and will gently lead those that have their young." This last passage, as Bert pointed out to Michael, was from the Old Testament and didn't refer to Jesus at all, but to the Jew's ancient version of God or *Yahweh*. If any of the gathered faithful noted the disparity, it was never given voice. Bert, as Michael was discovering, was full of observations that cast a critical and often uncomfortable light on the contradictions in Brother Daniel's biblical references and onto the Good Book itself.

Thursday's messages were the "brimstoniest" according to Bert. Brother Daniel leaned heavily on the Old Testament, where God was often vengeful, bloodthirsty, mean-spirited and cruel.

"He likes to scare the bejesus out of the faithful on Thursday, and my apologies for the clever reference," Bert told Michael during one such Thursday service.

Friday services were primarily an attack on all other religions, especially the Jews and the Catholics, although the Muslims came in for their share of excoriation. Brother Daniel didn't spend much time bashing the non-Abrahamic religions—Hinduism, Buddhism, Shintoism and such—because, as Bert noted to Michael, "Brother Daniel doesn't know diddly, especially beyond his literal reading of the Bible." Clearly, however, Brother Daniel wanted the faithful to know that religions that didn't include accepting Jesus as Savior were false, a waste of time, and sure to lead their followers straight to hell.

Michael had never knowingly laid eyes on either a Catholic or a Jew. He had a vague notion that most Catholics wore fancy robes and odd hats, and that Jews loaned money at very high rates and lived in New York City. He had certainly never met a Muslim, Shinto, or Buddhist. There was a Chinese lady back in Calhoun, who was married to the plumbing supply store man, but Michael had never given her religious affiliation any thought.

That first week in Boonville, Bert reminded Michael, more than once, that he should be sure to take in the Saturday night service.

"That's baptism night," said Bert, "And the process usually has its share of spectacle."

Michael didn't fully understand Bert's observation until he saw the spectacle of it for the first time.

Saturday morning, two men in a flatbed truck drove into the parking lot. There was a horse trough secured in the back. The trough was a standard one, maybe six feet long, two feet wide, and two feet high. The ends were rounded and it looked to be new. As Michael later learned, when he and Bert carried bucket after bucket of water from the church to fill the tank, it held nearly 170 gallons.

At Mother Daniel's direction, the deliverymen placed the trough on the ground directly in front of the pulpit. She told Bert and Michael to fill it with water right away so that the "water wouldn't be ice cold" when baptism time came that evening. Even sitting inside the tent for a few hours on a summer day, that amount of water would remain bracing, especially for the first few of the faithful to be submerged.

Brother Daniel had reminded attendees at the Wednesday, Thursday, and Friday services of the opportunity to be baptized on Saturday, and so the Saturday gathering included many familiar faces from earlier in the week. Most attendees brought family members. Two of these families had teenage daughters who seemed less than enthusiastic to be there as they were to be participants in this very public ceremony.

"Ever wonder why Jesus felt it necessary to be baptized by John the Baptist?" Bert asked, as they took up their observation spots on the back of Michael's truck. "If being baptized means accepting Jesus, why would Jesus need to accept himself?"

"Never gave it a thought," said Michael.

"Most folks don't, so you are not alone. Do you always believe in Bible stories without thinking about them?" Bert rolled a smoke and sealed it shut with a quick lick.

"Mostly, I guess. I mean, it is the Bible." Michael felt uneasy and at a disadvantage. He had never been challenged about his religious beliefs, and had never questioned what he took for granted.

"Well, that's one way to take the heavy lifting out of the process. I agree with Kierkegaard, he said that having doubt is what makes faith strong," Bert exhaled two streams of blue-gray smoke through his nostrils.

Michael wondered *who* "Kearigard" was but didn't want to extend the conversation

Brother Daniel was now asking those to be baptized to repair to the family tent to be prepared by sisters Ruth and Rebecca.

The group included two boys of about nine and twelve. They looked so much alike that Michael decided that they were brothers. There was an older man with very thin white hair, a middle-aged woman of enormous girth, and the two teenaged girls who were giggly and nervous.

The woman and girls entered the tent first, and soon emerged wearing what looked to be white sheets with their heads poking through a hole in the center. Their legs were bare from mid-calf down and they were barefoot. The teens continued to fidget nervously. The covering flattered the heavyset woman.

When the two boys and the old man emerged from the tent, they were in similar attire.

Sister Ruth led the group to the side of the stage riser.

Bert joined Michael where he was perched on the back of his truck's flatbed. From where they sat, out of the direct light of the bare bulbs, they were only thirty feet away from the horse trough baptismal.

"Keep your eyes on those girls," said Bert. "Baptism night races Brother Daniel's motor."

"To be washed in the blood of the Lamb is to declare that you have accepted Jesus Christ as your Lord and Savior," Brother Daniel raised his voice and his arms as he addressed the congregation. "And Jesus came up from the city of Nazareth to be baptized in the river Jordan by the one who was called John the Baptist. Let those who would follow the Lord's path come forward to be so committed."

Each would come forward to be baptized as Brother Daniel called their name, thus did he determine the order of their salvation. Amen.

As instructed when called, the first girl approached the trough and stood beside Brother Daniel. He leaned close and said something to her. She swung a leg over the side and stepped into the clear, still-cold water. As the water soaked the fabric it immediately revealed her bare leg through the thin material. She hesitated then grasped the edge and pulled her other leg into the water. Only two feet deep, the water came to just over her knees. She knelt into the water, her hands clutching the sides of the trough. The water now came to her waist.

"He that believeth and is baptized shall be saved; but he that believeth not shall be damned. I baptize you in the name of the Father, the Son, and the Holy Spirit." With that, Brother Daniel placed his left hand behind the girl's head, put his right on her breastbone and lowered her, face up, into the water. She had quickly pinched her nose and when he finally raised her from the water, reborn, she let go of her nose and pulled the wet hair from her eyes and mouth.

Brother Daniel put his hand under her arm and helped her regain a standing position. His hand found its way to the side of her breast as he "steadied her." It lingered several seconds after she was clearly well balanced. Brother Daniel had mastered the skill of touching interesting areas of the female form in such a manner that it was unclear, to those watching, whether it was blatant fondling or merely fatherly care. Having seen Brother Daniel's technique many times, Bert was under no delusion about which of the possibilities was true.

The wet cloth revealed the distinct contours of her body. Beneath the garment, she wore white underpants but nothing more. As Brother Daniel intoned more scriptural blather, the chilled water did wondrous and quite visible things for the girl's breasts. Growing erect, the nipples pulled the cloth slightly away from areoles that were nearly the same skin tone as her modestly developed breasts. Michael had a brief flashback to last Monday's episode at Panther Creek, and Sister Rebecca's soaked work shirt.

The religious nature of the ceremony did not stop many in the tent from making a subtle shift in their chairs to get an unobstructed view of the blushing girl. From his perch on the back of the truck, Michael had a marvelous, slightly profile view. Bert gave him a quick elbow jab but said nothing. The girl climbed out of the trough and stood beside Brother Daniel. She tugged at the front of the wet gown to un-stick the fabric from her thighs and crotch and then she crossed her arms, grabbing her shoulders, a move that concealed her breasts but pulled the fabric back against her midsection. She repeated this series of moves throughout the rest of the baptism ceremony.

Brother Daniel motioned the second girl forward. She stood frozen, her eyes locked on her friend's revealed body. Sister Ruth gave her a gentle push and she slowly approached Brother Daniel, the man with the beatific smile and wandering hands.

Repeating all of the same baptismal formalities, Brother Daniel lowered the girl into the chilling water. He seemed to keep her submerged a few extra beats, his right hand firmly in place on her breast, before bringing her up for air. The girl's physical assets were far more developed than those of her friend, and there ensued more congregational shuffling for better lines of sight. Again, Brother Daniel continued to "steady" the girl for several seconds, his hand cupped around a generous portion of her generous breast. The effect of the water plus obvious embarrassment caused the girl's nipples, darker and larger than her compatriot's, to rise to the occasion. Michael was transfixed, and not in a religious way.

While Brother Daniel perfunctorily dipped the two young brothers and elderly man, Michael's attention was riveted on the squirming girls who stood witness to the transformative power of the full submersion baptism. Michael had seen many such baptisms before at the Calhoun First Pentecostal Church, but none of them had employed the sheer baptismal garment favored by Brother Daniel.

While the young boys' and the man's bodies were also revealed through the wet material, what was illustrated was that men have very practical sensibilities when it comes to underwear selection. The man's skivvies were actually long johns, cut-off mid-thigh and mid-upper arm to accommodate the summer heat. The boys wore boxer shorts, which appeared to be of rough and sensible material. No revelations about the male anatomy were provided.

Scowling, the large woman lumbered forward and with great effort swung a leg into the makeshift baptismal; getting the other leg up and over the side proved too much. The elderly man stepped forward, grabbed her ankle, and with Brother Daniel providing a steadying hand on her upper arm, pulled her leg up and into the water. Brother Daniel intoned *Mark 16:16* as he had with the others and placed his hand behind the woman's head. As his right hand moved toward her chest, she caught it at the wrist and guided it to just below her neck. She held her grip. It looked as if Brother Daniel were strangling her and that she was defending herself.

The width of her hips was far greater than that of the two-foot wide horse trough. Her hips were wedged against the topsides of the tank. She made an effort to get to a kneeling position but even with a push on her shoulders from Brother Daniel, she couldn't overcome the physics. Thus situated, her hips providing the fulcrum, her immersion was destined to be a nearly upside down, headfirst plunge. In and under she tipped, causing a great deal of water displacement. Not having a free hand with which to pinch her nose, she came up choking, snorting and spewing water and yellow snot in substantial quantities. A disgusted murmur ran through the gathered faithful as Brother Daniel and the elderly man struggled to get the stricken woman un-wedged and out of the trough.

Sister Ruth took over and led the newly reborn back to the family tent; the woman still coughing, a reflex that caused her now quite visible folds of fat to quiver and flounce. The teenage girls were last in line, their wet smocks clinging to round firm backsides. Brother Daniel, washing snot off of his sleeve, gazed after the procession with a look of a man who had just done great good.

"Saturday night often provides wonderful memories," whispered Bert as he slid to the ground and headed for his truck.

"Tomorrow morning," Mother Daniel had sought Michael in his truck after the service, "Please empty the baptismal and haul it over by the backdoor of the church. And don't tip the water out and make a mess in front of the pulpit. Empty it bucket by bucket. Have Mr. Gilbert help."

"Yes Ma'am."

The next afternoon, after the regular Nazarene church service was complete and things were relatively quiet, Michael and Bert put up a temporary canvas screen around the horse trough while Sisters Rebecca and Ruth heated large pots of water on the churches' wood-burning stove. Sunday afternoons were bath time. Between cold buckets of water from the well pump and the heated water from the stove, the trough was half-filled with lukewarm water.

The routine order of bathing was thus: Mother Daniel, Brother Daniel, Sister Ruth, Sister Rebecca, Petey, and then the hired help. There was no changing of water after each bath, just the addition of some extra hot water. When Michael entered the enclosure, the water was milky gray with a thin skim of soap residue, body oil, and more than the occasional hair.

Bert, having experienced the routine on many Sundays, had declined the opportunity, and as Michael stared at what appeared to be some sort of disgusting witches' brew, he understood why. He turned and exited the enclosure.

"You need to get cleaned up, Mr. Boone," said Brother Daniel, sitting on a folding chair by the family tent. He was pulling on a clean pair of socks.

"I had a bath earlier this week," said Michael.

"Suit yourself. You and Mr. Gilbert need to empty that tub before the evening service. And, take down the screen," Brother Daniel laced up his shoes.

That night, after the revival finale, money counting, and preliminary packing were complete, the Good News group prepared for bed. Michael noticed that Petey was sent over to sleep with his sisters.

Michael lit his lantern so he could read some more of the Hemingway book that Sister Ruth had given him. He was just a few pages into *The Sun Also Rises* when the moaning began. At first he was mystified by the sound—low, persistent, and guttural. He sat upright and strained to hear more clearly, trying to understand if there was trouble or if someone was ill. The sounds soon changed to actual words and it was clear that Brother Daniel was in the grip of some sort spiritual experience in the family tent.

"Oh yes, yes, God yes!" Brother Daniel's voice was husky and insistent. "Oh God, oh God, yes, yessssssssssssssssss!" Then silence. The entire audible moaning and spiritual episode had lasted only a minute or so.

Michael was aware of what was happening, but it caught him by surprise. He had never thought of a preacher actually having sex. He then recalled his brief glimpse, last Sunday, of Mother Daniel's lovely breasts and pictured Brother Daniel actually touching them, right over there in the family tent. He grew erect, turned out the lantern and, concentrating on the image of those breasts, masturbated.

The next morning, when he and Bert were preparing things for the travel day, Michael asked Bert if he had heard Brother Daniel last night.

"Hard to miss, eh Michael?"

"Does that happen often?" Michael loaded a stack of chairs onto the truck.

"Sunday nights, mostly" said Bert. "I think it has to do with Sunday baths. The man gets enough stink off so that Mother Daniel can endure the attention. Or, maybe it's the other way around, but I doubt it."

"You'll like this next town," said Bert, clearly changing the subject, "They have a movie theater. Tuesday night we might catch a double feature. Jasper, here we come!"

Chapter Three
Jasper to Seymour

BERT WAS CORRECT about there being a movie theater in Jasper, although it didn't look like it was destined to remain open much longer. As the caravan motored down Newton Street, the Regency Theater had a forlorn look, with taped-over cracks in the box office glass and dusty display windows where the movie posters struggled to show through the grime.

The troupe arrived at the Hallelujah Fellowship Church just after five in the afternoon, and commenced the unpacking routine. By the time Michael and Bert had the two family tents assembled, Mother Daniel and the girls had dinner prepared. After dinner, Michael and Bert worked until dark slowed their progress.

Michael washed up at the church's outside water spigot. The water ran cold but it was clean and sweet, and he splashed water over his shirtless upper body. He put his head under the flow of water, soaking his hair and then cupped hands and drank deeply. When he shut off the water and turned to walk back to his truck, Mother Daniel was right behind him with a skimpy towel.

"Here," she said, "You'll need this," and walked away.

Michael wondered how long she'd been keeping track of his clean-up routine.

He put on a clean shirt and pulled a folding chair up to

the rear of his flatbed. He lit the gas lantern, retrieved the Hemingway book, and sat down to make some progress on his goal of finishing one book every week. The style of Hemingway's writing was very different from the books he had been reading. At first, he would stop and re-read passages just to get the rhythm and flow, and soon it began to feel more natural. Hemingway's direct, no nonsense style drew him into the narrative without a second thought about the technique.

"The man has a very distinctive voice, don't you think?" Bert walked to the back of the truck and rolled a smoke.

"Sure does."

"His personal life is a little too interesting for his own good," said Bert, "But maybe that keeps the creative juices oozing."

Sister Ruth emerged from the shadows, the lantern dancing highlights off of her hair.

"Is this just 'man talk' or can I butt in?" she said, her voice indicating this wasn't really a question as much as a smart aleck opening.

"Ruthie," said Bert, "There is no gender qualification when it comes to talking about literature. Right, Mr. Boone?"

"No, no, of course not; I'll get you a chair?" Michael was already headed for the nearest stack.

"How very gallant," Sister Ruth turned and exchanged a glance with Bert.

"Not for me, Michael," Bert called after Michael, "I'm going to finish my smoke and call it a night. You two can hash out Hemingway's underlying message, if there is one. Maybe it's just a whopping good story; not a thing wrong with that." He walked back toward his truck. "Good night."

They sat in silence momentarily until Sister Ruth said, "So, how do you like it?"

"It's different. Nothing quite like I've read before but I like it. Thanks for sharing."

"I have another Hemingway. You can read it next."

"Oh, Okay, that would be great. You can borrow any of my books," said Michael, "But you probably already read the ones I brought from home."

"Maybe," said Sister Ruth. "Show me what you have beside the Ring Lardner."

Michael hopped onto the flatbed and rustled around his bedroll and came back with two books, *The Fighting Caravans* by Zane Grey, and *All Quiet on the Western Front* by Erich Remarque.

"I've read this one," she pointed to the Remarque. "Bert predicts that it will be a classic. I haven't read this one by Grey. May I?"

"Sure, sure. He writes Westerns, mostly."

"I know," said Sister Ruth.

"Bert and I are planning to go see the two Westerns showing at the movie theater tomorrow night. Hoot Gibson is in one and Tom Mix in the other. Maybe you could go. I mean, your sister and Petey too of course," Michael swallowed hard at his own brashness.

"Sounds like fun. We've been to the Regency in the past. It's looking a little run down this year. I'll talk with Mother Daniel tomorrow and let you know."

By the time Michael settled into his bedroll and turned off the lantern, he was already playing and re-playing the image of sitting next to Ruth in the darkened theater while watching the guys in white hats take on the guys in black hats. The next morning, he even recalled that he had a dream just before he woke up with that same general theme—except in the dream Ruth turned into a horse, which stuck its nose into a bag of popcorn, and caused a commotion.

"*No horses in the theater!*" a guy in a black hat yelled.

It's not my horse, dreamed Michael, *but everyone is blaming me for the popcorn-stealing horse.* "It's not my horse," he shouted out in the dream. *He had on a white hat.*

No horses in the theater!

But, it's not my horse.

Then he woke up. He shook his head at the ridiculous ways that his mind turned when dreaming. Sister Ruth, Westerns with horses, white hats, black hats, theater popcorn all mashed together in the wrong way.

The main tent went up, chairs were set in place, the riser was assembled and the pulpit, and piano were wrestled into their spots. Tuesday's schedule was dispatched without incident, and by three that afternoon, everyone found some shade and Sister

Rebecca came around with lemonade.

"Mister Gilbert," Mother Daniel found Bert sitting on the ground, his back up against the front tire of his truck rolling a smoke, "Sister Ruth tells me that you and Mr. Boone are planning to go to the Regency to see two movies. She said that you asked if she, Rebecca, and Peter would like to go as well."

"Well," said Bert, "That would be fine, although I'm not the one who did the inviting. I imagine it was Michael. He and Ruthie were talking last night after I went off to bed."

"Either way," she said, "I discussed it with Brother Daniel. He's not interested but the rest of us will be going. That doesn't mean that I'll be paying for you or Mr. Boone. You were both paid yesterday so you should have the resources."

"I'll check with my accountant," said Bert. "He has me on a short rope given that my stock portfolio took such a beating in the last couple of years. I'll bet that I can squeeze out the two bits for admission though."

Mother Daniel ignored the remark.

"I'll pack some sandwiches for all of us. The first feature at the Regency always starts at 5:00. We can easily walk there in ten minutes. Tell Mr. Boone that we will leave at four forty five." With that, Mother Daniel turned and walked back to the family tent.

"Since I'm paying my own way," called Bert, "I don't consider this a date."

Mother Daniel kept walking and shook her head just enough to acknowledge Bert's impudence.

At the appointed time, the movie group headed for downtown Jasper. Mother Daniel, the girls, and Petey in the lead, Michael and Bert following. Both of the girls were carrying small paper grocery bags in which they had stashed tomato and mayonnaise sandwiches, peaches, and saltines. Everyone had on work clothes. Mother Daniel and the girls had tidied up and pulled their hair back, secured with clean bandanas. Michael also noted the smell of lavender drifting back as they walked.

The woman in the Regency's ticket booth had a bit of a mustache but no eyebrows. A Chesterfield dangled from the corner of her mouth, which bobbed up and down as she talked.

"Twenty five cents for anyone over twelve, fifteen for the

young'un," the cigarette bouncing along with each syllable, "You can take those sacks of food in with you but no eating in the theater unless you buy it at the snack counter."

"We'll come outside at intermission and eat," said Mother Daniel, handing a dollar bill through the opening in the glass.

"Well," said Bobbing Cigarette "Make sure to keep them ticket stubs so's you can get back in." With that, she passed a dime back through the window slot along with four tickets.

Bert stepped to the window, "Two tickets, madam, one for me and one for my wife," he said, nodding toward Michael while slipping a half dollar through the slot. "We're not from around here."

The woman's mouth dropped open and the cigarette would have fallen out except it was stuck to her lower lip. She reached up and peeled it off, leaving a bit of cigarette paper stuck there.

"I'm pulling your leg, madam," Bert said, smiling, "He's not my wife, he's just my boyfriend."

The woman's browless eyes narrowed as she tore off two tickets from the roll and slid them through the slot. As Michael and Bert walked into the theater, the woman craned to watch them disappear inside.

"I could've paid my own way," said Michael.

"That woman will likely notify the local sheriff that there are some perverts lurking about," said Bert, "That could make the walk back more interesting. I like to mess with a few Midwestern heads when they seem deserving. As for the tickets, you can buy the popcorn, that'll make us even.

Michael's vision of sitting next to Sister Ruth was thwarted. Michael ended up between Bert and Petey. Michael did buy a box of popcorn, the freshness of which was more than questionable. Bert took a couple of handfuls and then declined any more. Even Petey, after bugging Michael to share the treat, wasn't much interested in eating more than a handful or two. He then began taking popcorn kernels and pitching them at the head of a preteen girl two rows ahead.

She turned after a two direct hits, "Hey, little boy, cut it out!"

"Make me," replied Petey, sticking his tongue out.

"Enough, Peter," Mother Daniel intervened.

A minute later, the girl's father came down the row with a

small boy in tow and sat down next to the girl. She leaned in and whispered to him and he turned and glared at Petey. He then looked at Bert and said, "Best keep your boy in line."

"If I had a boy," said Bert, "You can be sure that I would."

"He's my son," said Mother Daniel, leaning forward slightly, "and I have instructed him to stop teasing your daughter."

"Make sure he does."

The house lights began to dim and the screen lit up with a crackling sound from the speakers. The screen ran white for a few seconds, the flickering black spots and lines showing where the film had holes or dust had collected and stuck. Before the first movie there was a Movietone News feature. The first story was from somewhere in Kansas where dust storms were sending kids home from school, and the blowing dirt from that part of the Midwest was drifting all the way to the East Coast. The dust was dimming the skies of Washington and dusting ships in the Atlantic, a fact that finally got the attention of those in D.C. The administration and Congress were vowing to do more to stop the farms of the high plains from blowing completely away.

Even here in Indiana, there were days when the sky was brown and a fine silt of dust from Oklahoma, north Texas, and southwest Kansas settled on cars, buildings, and people. Respiratory problems became nearly epidemic in many places

The second newsreel story was about political turmoil in Germany where rampant inflation sent many citizens to the store with sacks full of nearly worthless money. The conservative government had just signed a shared governing agreement with an even more conservative politician named Adolph Hitler and his Nazi Party.

In the newsreel, Hitler was shown meeting with stiff-lipped diplomatic types. Instead of a suit, Hitler wore a military style ensemble with a brown shirt, darker brown riding jodhpurs, riding boots, and a leather belt with a leather strap running diagonally across his chest. Several men behind him, including a large bear of a man, were outfitted the same way, and they seemed pleased with events—the ones in the suits, less so.

Bert leaned toward Michael and whispered, "He reminds me of that asshole in Italy. Guys like that are bound to be trouble."

The final clip was a two – or three-minute speech by the new president. He was sitting in a garden setting. With him were Mrs. Roosevelt, two other family members and a dog. The speech was about some new building programs that the administration was going to initiate to increase employment. The president, barely fifty, looked much older.

Bert leaned in again and whispered. "If these programs don't work, the Republicans will have his head in three and half years, not that they know to do anything except sit on the money and hope that Wall Street bails us out."

Michael, who was not one to pay much attention to world events or politics of any stripe, nodded in the dark, although he didn't fully understanding the references.

The first movie featured Hoot Gibson, a Hollywood staple for westerns. The plot was familiar: Cattlemen, farmers, marauding Indians, a woman in danger, gun fights where bullets miraculously shot pistols out of the hands of the bad guys, and men on horses chased through scenery that was iconic Western, especially for anyone who had never been west of the Mississippi.

The movie audience, small as it was, cheered the hero as the movie came to a very happy and satisfactory ending. The house lights came up and a ten-minute intermission started, which encouraged patrons to go back to the snack counter for stale popcorn, candy bars, and bottles of pop.

Mother Daniel, making sure that everyone in her group had their ticket stub, led them outside and distributed the sandwiches, peaches, and crackers. The lady in the ticket window frowned a sour scowl, took a drag off of yet another Chesterfield, and would have arched a disapproving brow, if she had had one.

"Ruth, you and Rebecca take this and go to the snack counter and get six Cokes," said Mother Daniel as she handed Ruth thirty cents.

"Are you treating me to a drink?" said Bert. "Maybe it is a date after all."

"I can assure you, Mr. Gilbert, that there is no more than a Coke involved. If you had rather not have one I can change the order."

"No, no," said Bert, "I'll not look a gift Coke in the mouth."

Food and drinks consumed, the group re-entered the Regency. This time, however, the seating arrangements were altered—not on purpose, just by chance, Michael supposed. He found himself between Mother Daniel and Ruth. Rebecca was next to Ruth, and Bert was next to Rebecca. Petey was on the other side of Mother Daniel. Michael was a bit uneasy, but also a little pleased.

Tom Mix was the star of the second film, *Hidden Gold*, one of seven westerns he had made in 1932. He had successfully made the transition from silent films to talkies. Many of his characters were also named Tom or Thomas. As the plot developed, there came a scene where the leading lady—girl, actually—was in danger, but didn't know it. Blithely taking care of everyday chores in the family cabin, she was being stalked by the baddest of the bad guys. The cameras cut back and forth between her and the bad guy, a look of lust on his face while she innocently bustled about the small room. Music was used to heighten the affect. Tension filled the Regency.

As the scene neared its climax, Ruth wrapped her right arm under Michael's upper left arm and clasped her left hand to his bicep. She turned her head, pressed her forehead against his shoulder and squeezed her eyes shut. Almost at the same time, Mother Daniel reached her right arm across her chest and latched onto Michael's right bicep. Thus pinioned, Michael watched as the bad guy suddenly made his presence known to the innocent damsel. This was accompanied by a sudden music crescendo and the sound of Mother Daniel, as well as several other patrons, shrieking.

It was clear that Tom Mix would have to come to the rescue as the bad guy threw the girl on the horse and galloped away from the cabin. Within seconds, the music changed to indicate that Tom was on the case and a careening horse chase followed. The tension eased, and Mother Daniel let go of Michael's arm. Ruth did not. She turned to watch Mix ride to the rescue, rope the bad guy, and pull him from his horse—all without snaring the girl, who then expertly took control of the reins and brought the heaving steed to a stop.

For the remainder of the movie, and there wasn't much left after the climatic horse chase, Ruth maintained her grip on Michael's arm, although, he noted, she eased up a good deal on the pressure. As the credits rolled and the house lights came on, she quickly disengaged.

They filed out of the Regency and headed back to the Hallelujah Fellowship Church. Petey, Rebecca, and Mother Daniel took the lead. Petey was busy rehashing the Tom Mix movie for his mother and Rebecca as if they hadn't just seen it for themselves.

Bert, Ruth, and Michael followed along.

"Did you know that Hoot and Tom Mix were old friends from the silent picture days?" Bert asked. Without waiting for a reply he continued, "Both of them were real cowboy types who started out doing stunt work when it involved horses and such. When the talkies came along they both landed feature roles and started making big money."

"What does 'big money' come to?" said Ruth.

"I read that Fox is paying him seventy-five hundred dollars a week."

"That can't be so," said Michael.

"Believe what you want," said Bert, "But there are several people in the movie industry who make even more. Zasu Pitts lives in a house so big that it has an indoor swimming pool and an outdoor pool. It takes plenty of dough to afford that kind of thing."

"That doesn't seem right, what with so many people without jobs and all," said Michael.

"Well," said Bert, "Capitalism smiles on some more than others. A German guy named Marx has a different way and the Russians are giving it a try. So far so good."

"Communism, right?" Ruth said.

"Right," he replied. "Sounds like a good idea but whether it works in the long run remains to be seen. Theories are like that. They look good on paper, but ..." he trailed off.

"America doesn't seem to be working all that well," said Michael. "My folks and Aunt Elizabeth are hard workers, but they don't make seventy-five hundred in a year, maybe not even in three."

They walked in silence for a few minutes. Michael was doing math in his head.

"If I work for your folks for an entire year, I'll make less than a thousand dollars," said Michael, actually thinking out loud more than making conversation. This fact was a revelation to him as it related to Tom Mix's $7,500 a week.

"Tell you what, Michael." Bert said, "Let's head for Hollywood. A couple of handsome guys like us ought to get in pictures right away. Once we're rolling in dough, we'll send for Ruthie and get her into the business too."

"Oh, that sounds wonderful," said Ruth. "I'll buy a convertible and everything,"

"No, really," said Michael. "Our system stinks if someone like me works all year for less than a grand and some guy just rides a horse and makes movies and he gets paid seven or eight times that in just one week. It stinks."

"Granted," said Bert, "But then, nothing is stopping you from thumbing to California and givin' the movies a try. Nobody says that you can't. The government won't stop you. The Daniel clan won't stop you. I sure wouldn't stop you. There's something to be said for a system that at least lets you give it a try."

"Just maybe I will," said Michael, his voice revealing his continued indignation.

This was perhaps the first time, but it certainly wouldn't be the last, that Michael's introduction to the complexities of the world beyond his Kentucky roots gave him pause.

"Ah, home," said Bert as they approached their parking lot camp compound. "I see that father has stayed up to insure our return before curfew," indicating Brother Daniel sitting on a folding chair under the bare bulb, cleaning his fingernails with a pen knife.

"So," said Brother Daniel, "How was the shoot 'em up?"

Petey launched into a detailed description. Michael and Bert peeled off and retired to their trucks. Michael could hear Petey excitedly mixing the two movie plots together for his father's edification. Come to think of it, Michael reflected, the plots were very similar.

During the next three weeks, the good news was spread to believers in Jasper, Paoli, and Seymour. Michael was beginning to memorize Brother Daniel's sermons and homilies, thanks to their unwavering repetition. Michael had finished *A Farewell to Arms* and *The Sun Also Rises,* and was deep into *Great Expectations*, a book that Bert recommended. Michael, feeling the need to catch up with Ruth and her more well-read education, was keeping to a one-book-a-week self-improvement schedule, but the current read was long and slow going, compared to the Hemingway books. Charles Dickens certainly wasn't of the short and direct school of writing.

During their northward journey through rural Indiana, Michael became aware of a different smell to the summer days and nights. The dirt was darker here than the farm land of Kentucky and it had a sweeter somewhat mustier smell where it had been turned. During the days, particularly the ones where the heat became oppressive, the smell of feed grains wafted on the breeze as the Monday travel days put them on the narrow roads between ripening crops.

The nights, dryer than those of Kentucky, often smelled of distant grass fires and honeysuckle. The night sounds were also different too: more crickets, and in those places where the camp was surrounded by trees, cicadas made an awful racket until nearly midnight. The cicadas also did a fine job of masking Brother Daniel's physical, spiritual ecstasy, which occurred almost without fail each Sunday evening.

In Paoli, where the revival was hosted by The Mount Bethel Brotherhood Church, a woman overcome with emotion during Brother Daniel's inspired histrionics toppled to the ground, scattering folding chairs. Before any concerned faithful could administer the cooling breezes of their funeral home hand fans, a common sight on warm evenings, the woman had thrashed around in a spiritual frenzy and managed to expose most of her lower body, revealing a girdle of some sort that was cinched up along the side of an ample buttock.

Without breaking rhetorical stride, Brother Daniel instructed the congregation to handle the woman with care and to respect her communion with the "Holy Spirit."

Two of her family members got her to her feet and guided her toward the rear of the tent. All the while the woman was trying to raise her arms as she hoarsely repeated, "Praise be to God."

Bert referred to such collapsing worshipers, most often women, as "divers." If he was watching when one of these folks went to the ground, he would whisper-shout "Diver down," as if notifying some celestial emergency crew.

He also pointed out to Michael that such events were rare

when the revival tent was erected on a paved or graveled area. Most of the divers, he noted, went down on the grass. "Not that they are any less devout or anything; I'm just noting the distinction," he added.

Later, when the service was over and Bert and Michael had straightened chairs and collected trash from between the rows, the two of them sat down in the grass away from the family tents, their backs resting against truck tires. Bert rolled a smoke and inhaled deeply. Michael broke the peaceful silence.

"Why aren't you a Christian?"

"Who says I'm not?" Bert replied.

"No one, but the way you argue with and poke fun at Brother Daniel and speak about people like the 'divers,' I guess I just assumed that you weren't."

"Well, in fact, your assumption is correct," said Bert, smoke escaping from his mouth with every spoken word.

"So," said Michael, "you don't believe in God."

"Didn't say that," said Bert. "Lots of folks believe in God who aren't Christians."

"How is that possible?" said Michael.

"You've lived a very sheltered life," Bert said. "Jews believe in God. Muslims believe in God. In fact, it's the same God: The God of Abraham, the God of Christians. The Old Testament and the Jew's Torah are basically the same books."

"But the Jews killed Jesus, how can they believe in God?" Michael was struggling. He sat forward and clasped his arms around his knees.

"Well, first, there is some serious debate about the 'killed Jesus' part. The Romans did the official executions in that part of the world during those times. Second, even if the Jewish Temple leaders played a role in the death of Jesus, they didn't kill off their own God, at least not in their minds."

"But Jesus is God," said Michael.

Bert flicked the ash of his cigarette onto the soft ground where the truck tire had gouged out a small furrow.

"That's the Christian theology, alright. If Jesus isn't God then there is no Christianity. You can sorta see why Christians would stick to that viewpoint about Christ."

Michael sat quietly, pondering Bert's comments. He plucked

a blade of grass and stuck it in his mouth.

"How did you become a Christian, Michael?" Bert's question lingered in the evening air for several seconds.

"I just did," Michael finally replied.

"I'll need a more robust answer than that," said Bert.

"Well, mom and dad went to church, so did granddaddy before he died, and Aunt Elizabeth goes all the time. All of us went to church and bible school."

"So," said Bert, "you didn't choose to be a Christian, you just had Christianity handed to you. I assume that before you became a Christian you didn't study the other religions of the world and then make your selection."

"No, I never did that," Michael said. "I don't know much about other religions."

"So," said Bert, "your choice of religions wasn't a choice at all, it was an accident of geography. Do you suppose that you would be a Christian had you been born to Muslim parents in Cairo, or Jewish parents in Germany?"

"I guess not."

"Then, you're hanging your spiritual hat on a religion that you accept because you won the lucky sperm contest, and popped out of you mother's womb in Kentucky instead of Korea. That's a mighty wobbly hat rack in my opinion."

Michael said, "Are you a Jew or a Muslim, then?"

Bert laughed, and it turned into a smoker's cough.

"No, neither of them. The Jews have far too many rules to follow, and the revelations of Mohammad are so contradictory—much like the Bible I should add—that I can't get excited about sorting out the conclusions, if there are any."

"Do you have a religion, Bert?"

"People like me are called agnostics. I believe there is a higher being or power, 'God', if you will, that set the universe in motion. But given the enormity of that task and the complexity of the universe, I figure that I'm not nearly smart enough to understand such a power. Even the Old Testament says, 'God is unknowable'."

"Do you think that you'll go to heaven?" asked Michael.

"Probably not in the way that you've been taught to understand it," said Bert, "But I don't worry about it. Besides, I hate harps and I would be afraid to fly."

They sat there for several minutes. Bert flicked his cigarette butt into the darkness where it sparked on contact and then slowly dimmed and died.

"Look, Michael, I don't have anything against organized religion, especially Christianity. I was raised in the Episcopal Church and learned many of the same things that you have learned from the church. But, when I was younger than you, I began to question many of the beliefs, particularly those that are exclusionary. The Christians say 'do it our way and you'll go to heaven,' the Jews make the same claim as do the Muslims. Well, they can't all have it right. Each of those belief systems necessarily excludes nonbelievers in any potential rewards after death. I believe that such a notion is massive hubris."

"Massive what?" said Michael.

"Hubris," Bert smiled. "It's a great word to tuck into your vocabulary. It means unsupported prideful certainty."

The lights in the family tents flickered off, the light on the single pole was all that was left to cast shadows.

"Must be bedtime, Michael," Bert got to his feet. "That's enough basic theology for one night anyway."

"Yeah, thanks," said Michael. "Maybe I'll do more to learn about other religions."

"Always a good move for a Renaissance Man," Bert poked the bottom of Michael's boot with his shoe. "Goodnight."

* * *

Paoli didn't have a movie theater, but it did have a pool hall. Saturday evening, Michael and Bert slipped away when the service was underway. They walked the six blocks to Lulu's Billiard Room. Lulu's had three regular pocket pool tables and one snooker table.

Bert pulled the man at the counter to one side for a brief conversation. A few minutes later the man came out of the back room with what looked like a large glass of milk. It wasn't. The glass had been painted white and was filled with beer.

"Want one for yourself?" asked Bert.

"No thanks."

"Well," said Bert, "It is an acquired taste that is best not acquired."

They checked out a rack of pool balls and took over the middle table. The first table was occupied with two fellows in slacks and white shirts, their sleeves rolled up a couple of turns. Both men were using fancy-looking cues and the game they played only used a few of the fifteen balls. Their games were over very quickly and with each game done, the loser stuffed money into a corner pocket, which the winner nonchalantly retrieved as the loser racked the balls in a diamond-shaped rack. Both of them were drinking "milk."

"Eight-ball or nine-ball?" asked Bert.

Michael, not much of a pool player, admitted he didn't know how nine-ball was played. He had only ever played eight-ball.

"Okay," said Bert, "Let's play eight-ball."

As it turned out, Bert didn't seem much good at pocket pool either, and by the time Michael sank the eight ball to claim the first game, nearly half an hour and another beer for Bert were history. Michael bought a coke and downed the little familiarly shaped bottle in four or five passes.

Between games, one of the men in the white shirts invited Bert and Michael to join them in some money games. Bert allowed as how neither he nor Michael were very good and the competition wouldn't be fair. The man persisted, offering to spot the strangers four balls from the git go.

"Thanks just the same," said Bert, "But we'd prefer to play our sorry game between the two of us.

"So," said White Shirt One, "afraid of a little competition are we?"

"No, actually I have nothing against competition," said Bert, "But I'm not a fan of losing money that I don't have to lose, especially to some stranger with a custom cue in his hand."

"Are you saying that we are trying to hustle you?" said White Shirt One.

"Why, I would never think that," said Bert, "Furthest thing from my mind. Let's play," he said, turning to Michael.

Bert bought a third beer.

White Shirt One came around the table and stood directly

in front of Bert.

"Say, mister, you seem like a smart ass. I don't much care for smart asses. Maybe you need a lessons in manners."

Bert set his beer on the table rail. "Tell you what, friend," he said calmly, "Why don't you and I shoot one game of nine ball for a small wager. I promise, my manners will be impeccable. Just a friendly game between two new friends."

White Shirt One sneered and maintained eye contact with Bert. "Sure, friend, a friendly game."

He turned and retrieved his cue from the other table.

Bert put his original cue back in the rack and walked over to White Shirt Two and said evenly, "Be a good sport, Sport, and lend me your cue. That other one is crooked."

With that, Bert took the man's cue from where it was leaning against the rail. White Shirt Two said nothing.

The tension in the poolroom was evident. The manager was clearly concerned and came out from behind the counter and sat on a bar stool near the table, his upper lip beaded with perspiration.

"I don't need no trouble in here," he said.

"No trouble, Al," said White Shirt One. "Just a friendly game for ten bucks," his smile revealed no humor.

Michael was shocked at the suggestion of a ten-dollar bet, more than half a week's wages.

"Come on, Bert," Michael said, "We've got work to do. The service is likely over by now."

"Not yet," said Bert, "My new friend here won't be satisfied until he's taken my money. Right friend?" Bert turned to White Shirt One.

"Tell you what," said White Shirt One, "I'll even give you the break," a broad grin came across his slightly crooked mouth revealing a set of teeth more green than yellow.

"You're a saint," said Bert.

"I want a ten-dollar bet, too," said White Shirt Two.

Michael did a quick calculation in his head and doubted that Bert carried around twenty dollars and Michael had but two dollars in his pocket. "Holy shit," he mumbled under his breath.

"Okay," said Bert, not looking at White Shirt Two.

Bert chalked the cue, placed the cue ball a bit less than a foot in front of the rail and a bit off-center. He rested the cue on the rail, bracketed between his first two fingers. With a smooth but surprisingly powerful stroke, he broke the tight rack of nine balls into clattering, caroming jumble. The five ball and the three ball dropped into two separate leather pockets.

"Looks like I'm still shooting," he said.

Bert took aim at the one ball and banked it in, cross table. Before the cue ball came to rest, Bert was walking to where the next shot would be executed. He prowled the table, never losing his concentration. The two ball was a simple angle into a corner pocket. As the three was already down, he left the cue ball in a convenient spot to pocket the four. With the five already down, he was on to the six and the seven and the eight. The nine ball was against the rail, two feet from a corner pocket. Without hesitation, he lightly kissed it down the rail. It made a slight clicking noise when it dropped into the pocket on top of two other balls.

"That'll be twenty bucks," he looked at White Shirt One who hadn't left his perch since the break. Bert was unscrewing the two-part cue in his hand as he spoke.

"You son-of-a-bitch," growled White Shirt One, bolting from his chair, his beer glass drawn back as if he were planning to throw a fastball.

As he came toward Bert in a frontal assault, Bert, holding the small end of the butt-end of the pool cue, cracked the big end solidly across the man's left ear which split open cleanly and wouldn't begin to bleed profusely for another half minute because the blow had pinched closed all the blood vessels, temporarily.

White Shirt One was out of the pool game and the fight before he ever had a chance to show his stuff. He crumpled to the filthy oak floor and made strange gurgling noises.

Bert turned to White Shirt Two. "Twenty bucks," he said icily.

White Shirt Two held up both hands signaling that he wanted nothing to do with Bert who still held the butt of the man's cue at the ready. White Shirt Two had no interest in being maimed by his own pool cue. He fished in his pant pocket and, with trembling hands, found a ten and two fives and tossed them onto the table.

"I'll leave this part of your cue where you can find it at the end of the block," said Bert, picking up the bills. "I'm a thoughtful guy that way. Back to work, Michael."

As Michael and Bert left the poolroom, White Shirt Two and Al were helping White Shirt One to his feet. Al was pressing a sorry-looking bar towel against the man's two-part and now, very bloody, ear. White Shirt One was trying to talk but wasn't making much sense.

As they walked back to The Mount Bethel Brotherhood Church, Bert rolled a smoke. They walked in silence for several minutes.

"I hope the faithful give generously in Paoli," Bert finally said. "We need at least two new tires—four would be better—and the thermostat on your truck has been fickle ever since we left Florida. I'm surprised that your truck hasn't overheated since you've been with us."

"That's it? Now you want to talk about tires and thermostats?" said Michael. "You just win a pool game, crack a guy's head open, collect your money and go about your business as if it happens all the time."

"Not much to talk about, really," said Bert, taking a lengthy drag on his cigarette. "You were there so I don't need to explain what happened. The guy was asking for trouble and I gave him some. I get a bit prickly when I've had a beer or two."

"Or three," said Michael.

"Or three," agreed Bert.

"Your pool game got way better all of a sudden, so you must have been setting me up for a hustle."

"Oh brother," said Bert, clearly exasperated. He spit a bit of loose tobacco off of his tongue. "You don't have enough money to make that a good strategy. I pulled back on my game so you wouldn't get frustrated and want to stop, that's all."

"Are you a pool shark?" said Michael.

"Hardly," said Bert, "But I did grow up with a pool table in the house so I played a lot. It's like riding a bike, once you know how to do it, well, you know how to do it."

Bert's past dribbled out, drop by drop over the weeks. Only wealthy people had pool tables in their homes. So, in addition to being a belligerent drunk and highly educated, probably a college graduate from somewhere back east, given his accent, Bert likely came from serious money. So, why's he driving a truck for an itinerate preacher?

* * *

Seymour, Indiana, was a pleasant little town. It had a town square with a band shell where, on summer Friday nights, an ensemble of locals played marching band-type music as residents sat on blankets under the stars. Children played games of tag and hide-and-go-seek, crouching down behind parked cars, and climbing the elm trees that grew everywhere in that part of the Midwest.

Knowing that the music would stunt revival participation and thus, money collection, Brother Daniel moved the Friday service to 6:00, a full hour and a half earlier than normal. He made sure that the local sponsoring church made serious efforts to inform Seymour's faithful of the change in schedule for Friday night.

Because the music didn't usually start until 8:30 or so, Brother Daniel's Good News Revival service could be completed by then, and the attendees could enjoy the free entertainment on the square.

Michael and Bert were straightening the rows of chairs and rearranging hymnals after the service was over.

"Michael," said Sister Ruth, who had changed out of her revival service dress and into dungarees and a pale green blouse, "Do you want to go listen to the band with us?"

"Sure, I guess so, but I have to finish here first," he said.

"Well," said Ruth, "Come to the square when you are done. Mom has lemonade and we're taking two big blankets so there'll be plenty of room."

Michael and Bert were just finishing up when they heard the first John Phillip Sousa March float in on the light breeze from the south.

"You go on," said Bert, "I'm not a fan of martial music, especially when played by folks who don't spend their days practicing the French horn. Besides, I don't believe that I was formally invited. I am a man of proper formalities, as you have surely noted."

"That's how I think of you, Bert," Michael gave Bert a wide grin.

Michael washed up a bit, slicked down his non-slickable hair, and walked toward the sound of the tuba.

The grassy area around the bandstand was crowded, and

Michael was wandering around looking for a familiar face when he heard Mother Daniel stage whisper his name. There they were, Mother Daniel and the entire family—even Brother Daniel who planned to work the crowd once the concert was over, encouraging families to attend the Saturday night baptism ceremony or the Sunday night finale. Better still, both.

Sister Ruth patted the blanket beside her and Michael slipped to the ground next to her. There was a familiar lavender fragrance, but just a whiff.

The band played with gusto but questionable virtuosity. It was the gusto that won the hearts of the crowd. Besides, gusto was required to overcome the squeals of children who were darting in and out of the light, determined not to be "it."

The band was led by a stout young man who wore a bow tie and matching red suspenders. As the band labored through an unusual arrangement of the *Tennessee Waltz*, Ruth put her hand on top of Michael's and whispered, "I'm glad you came."

Michael glanced down at her hand on his. He looked back at her face and quietly said, "Me too."

Ruth kept her hand on his as the band launched into several more tunes. At one point, she turned his palm up and interlaced their fingers. The handholding was shielded from the rest of the Daniel clan by Ruth's body, but Michael stayed on edge, recalling that his predecessor had lost his job for being too interested in Ruth. In this case, however, it seemed that Ruth was interested in Michael. That, of course, might not insure that his job was in any less peril should their mutual attraction come to light.

As the band announced its final number, Brother Daniel handed everyone in the group, including Michael, several sheets of printed flyers touting the Good News Revival's schedule for Saturday and Sunday evenings. The flyers had blank spaces for times and dates which the girls had filled in with the appropriate information for their Seymour stop.

The group fanned out as the crowd was gathering up blankets and chairs and handed flyers to any and all who would take them.

As Michael was offering a flyer to a man accompanied by his wife and teenaged daughter, the man hissed, "I wouldn't come to that pervert's tent for all the tea in China," and he stuffed the flyer back into Michael's hands, turned and walked off.

Chapter Four
Brimstone and Fire

WHEN THEY ROLLED into Martinsville, just southwest of Indianapolis, it was the eve of Independence Day.

Martinsville was larger than their previous stops. It was the county seat of Morgan County, and the courthouse, an imposing red brick structure in an Italianate design, loomed in the center of downtown. Very few places in Indiana still had a pre-Civil War courthouse and Martinsville was one of them. It was likely the biggest building Michael had seen outside of his one visit to Louisville, where he had marveled at a seven-story building that reportedly had an elevator.

On the outskirts of town was a sign that read, "Welcome to Martinsville, Home of Purdue All-American, John Wooden." On the sign was a large illustration of a basketball player on the dribble to the basket. Michael certainly knew who Wooden was. Everyone who followed college basketball knew who he was.

Michael had played the game for the Calhoun High Cougars. He was considered one of the better players, starting every game of his sophomore through senior years. He wasn't the tallest but he came close. If Michael had had any college basketball dreams, those were squelched by lack of money and, besides, no college scouts came offering scholarships. Michael was good but likely not college good. Until he saw the sign, however, he had no idea where the Purdue all-star called home.

The stores and light poles downtown were draped with red, white, and blue bunting in honor of the holiday. The caravan continued through downtown and turned northwest near its western edge. They continued until they neared the White River. Petey had been Michael's navigator for this trip, although as long as Michael kept up with Bert's truck, Petey was just an annoying passenger.

A block or so short of the White River Bridge, they turned into a small white church's parking area. There was no paved lot, just a parched grass and dirt expanse that had been mashed down by vehicles. Directly beside where the two trucks would be parked was a thick line of Cypress trees. On the far side of trees was an impressively large house, its sides shingled, like pictures Michael had seen of houses in Maine and Massachusetts. When the trees were full grown they would block the view of the house from the little church.

There hadn't been a day in June when rained threatened an evening service. In fact, there had been no rainy days at all, and this part of central Indiana was drying out under a relentless summer sun. The daytime temperatures were topping ninety degrees, and Brother Daniel would sweat completely through a shirt with each service.

All of the grass around the Grace and Holiness Pentecostal Church was sere and honey brown. The grass around the big house next door was lush and green, and a water sprinkler was dousing a section of the yard, its round dispersal leaving a circle of glistening water droplets to evaporate in the sunlight. The large front porch, columned and covered, had three ceiling fans whirring. Michael had never seen ceiling fans anywhere, let alone outside. The front yard of the house sloped down to the White River, which was languid in its trip downstream.

"Judge Morgan built that house out here, three, four years ago. Nice place, being on the river and all," Bert commented as Michael took in the scene. "He still has his place in Indy where he had lived for years, until the missus died. He just couldn't give it up but he wanted to come back home. Morgan County is named for his kin who settled here in the middle of last century. I think that one of his daughters and her family live in the house in Indy."

"How come you know so much?" asked Michael.

Bert shrugged, "We became friends a couple of years ago when the house was spankin' new and our salvation troop moved in for a week here at the G and H Pentecostal Church. I've been looking forward to this stop since Tallahassee."

With that, Bert turned and began the process of unloading and setting up the family tents, Michael at his side.

Because imminent salvation couldn't compete with the Fourth of July, there was no plan to erect the main tent until Wednesday morning. This meant that Tuesday was truly to be a holiday unless Mother Daniel could think of busy work for the help.

That evening after dinner, Michael and Ruth pulled two chairs under the pole light to read their books when the twilight faded. Occasionally, Ruth would break the silence with, "Listen to this," and then read aloud a sentence or paragraph that she found particularly enchanting. Michael wanted to return the favor, but he didn't have the confidence that what he might select would be good enough.

Petey had whined and wheedled until Mother Daniel and Brother Daniel took Petey to look for a fireworks stand. They had just driven off when Ruth suggested a walk down to the river.

"Will that be alright?" Michael was hesitant in light of what had happened to his predecessor.

"Sure."

"Maybe we should ask Rebecca if she wants to come too."

"Becca does not want to come," Ruth got up and headed for the river, a route that would take them across the cool, green lawn of Judge Morgan's house.

Michael caught up and they walked past the side of the large house. On the porch, two girls were playing with dolls and a young woman, probably their mother, waved to Michael and Ruth from a rocking chair that was directly under one of the fans.

"Should be cooler down at the river," called the woman.

"Hope so," replied Ruth.

"Stop back for an iced tea," said the woman.

"Thanks, we might do that," said Ruth.

Once down at the river's edge they found a grassy spot just to the side of a weeping willow and sat down to watch as the twilight reflection changed the color of the water from mossy green to deep green to black. Two small turtles plopped into the water off of tree branch that had lodged near the bank.

"I'm coming down here tomorrow for a swim," said Michael. "I used to swim in the creek on our farm all the time. Well, just summertime."

"Why wait until tomorrow?" said Ruth. "Let's have a swim now."

"I don't think that's a good idea," said Michael. "We don't have bathing suits or anything."

"What?" You've never been swimming in your underwear," Ruth mocked his common sense.

"Well, sure, but just with the guys."

"I'll bet you guys went skinny dippin'," said Ruth.

Had there been more daylight left, Ruth would have seen a very flushed Michael.

"Well, dincha?"

"Yeh," Michael was feeling cornered.

"So, swimming in your underwear should be quite modest I should think," Ruth stood and unfastened here dungarees.

Before Michael could collect a reasonable protest, Ruth had removed her boots and socks, pulled off her dungarees and took a running leap, feet first, into the White River. She still had on her blue work shirt, which billowed up as it caught the air, revealing light colored underwear. Once she hit the water, the shirt quickly soaked through.

The White River, which meanders west southwest from Martinsville until it feeds into the Wabash along the Illinois border, is a gentle river, especially in summers as dry as 1933. The water tends toward green and is relatively clear unless a sudden thunderstorm muddies up its tributaries for a few hours. The current is usually docile in the flat land of the Midwest. The White is perfect for creating safe swimming holes. However, there was nothing very "safe" about the present situation.

Michael was nearly panicked. He wanted to join her but he knew that it probably wouldn't end well if it came to light that they had been swimming alone in their underwear.

"Come on, Ruth," he pleaded. "We can swim tomorrow."

"We can swim tonight and tomorrow too," Ruth was treading water and looking at him expectantly. "Peel off those overalls and come in."

"No." Michael stood up. "I'm going back."

"Wait, don't leave me here. I'll get out."

Ruth took a couple of breaststrokes to the bank and tried to heave herself up on the embankment.

"Here," she said, "Give me your hand so I can get out."

Michael grabbed a handful of weeping willow tendrils for support and reached his other hand to Ruth. He pulled her up; she was dripping White River water.

Ruth stood there for a moment, clinging to Michael's hand, her blue work shirt pasted against her body and covering her underwear. Her legs were exposed from the thighs down. She stood on her toes and kissed Michael on the mouth. He didn't recoil but didn't respond either. Ruth put her hand on the back of his neck and made the kiss more intimate, gliding her tongue along the inside of his upper lip. To this he responded. River water dripping from her hair ran down her nose and Michael could taste the White River as the drops breached his lips.

He pulled away.

"I think that we should get back," he said.

"Okay," Ruth turned and scooped up her dungarees and socks. She pulled on the pants and then sat down and tried to pull on the socks.

"It's too hard when my feet are wet," she said and reached for her boots, sliding them on without socks. She stood, leaving the boots unlaced. She stuffed the socks into her pockets and headed back up the Judge's lawn.

The woman on the porch saw them coming and called out, "Stopping for iced tea?"

"Another time," said Michael, "but thanks for the offer."

"Was it cooler by the water?" she responded. "Jim and I might walk down there after the girls are in bed."

"It was very pleasant," said Ruth. "I actually had a quick swim."

"Sounds lovely," the woman rose, collected her ice tea glass and waved briefly as they passed by the side of the house. "Have a grand holiday."

Michael and Ruth skirted the hedge and walked into the pale circle of light created by the single bare bulb near the family tents. Ruth's soaked work shirt accentuated her slim figure with its interesting curves. She ducked into her tent and Michael sat on one of the chairs under the light. He picked up his book but couldn't concentrate, staring blankly at the opened page. He wasn't exactly sure how he felt. There was a mix of thrill and dread. The thrill of infatuation and the dread of putting his job at risk.

Mother Daniel and Petey emerged from their tent. Petey, spying Michael, ran over to him holding a paper sack with several Roman candles poking out of the top.

"Look what I got, Mike," he said, plopping down in the other chair.

Petey unloaded the Roman candles, fished out half-a-dozen packets of one-inch firecrackers and half-a-dozen large round red cherry bombs. There was also a package of sparklers and several cork punks.

"These are for the girls," Petey said, indicating the sparklers. "I'm going to blast this other stuff all myself."

Mother Daniel stood behind Petey.

"Anything to report in our absence," she said.

"Not really," said Michael.

Rebecca came out of her tent and turned to go to the privy, which was set back from the rear of the church. She had a kerosene lantern in hand to help navigate the dark.

"Is Ruth already in bed?" said Mother Daniel.

"Not yet. She's drying her hair."

"Why is her hair wet? She just washed it Sunday," Mother Daniel turned slightly to look at Michael.

"She took a swim at the river," said Rebecca, "And she didn't even ask me to go along," Rebecca disappeared into the dark.

"Did you go along?" Mother Daniel asked Michael.

"Yes, Ma'am."

"Did you go for a swim with her?"

"No, Ma'am."

Mother Daniel stared at Michael for several seconds, her face impassive.

"Good night, Mr. Boone," she tapped Petey on the shoulder. "Gather up your fireworks and get ready for bed."

Tuesday morning the sound of voices woke Michael. The Daniel family was already sitting around on their campstools having breakfast. Michael made a visit to the privy. Bert had obviously been there already as the cigarette smoke lingered inside. This was not a bad thing, given the normal privy smell. He had a quick wash-up at the spigot, which popped up through ground near the tents. It was surrounded by pea gravel, confined by a small square perimeter of bricks.

"Sorry," said Michael, self-consciously gathering up toast, some bacon, and slices of peaches on his plate. "I must have overslept."

"It's a holiday, boy," said Brother Daniel. "We're patriots, not slave drivers. Isn't that right Sister Ruth?"

"We're just slave drivers on the non-holidays," she said.

Brother Daniel took a deep breath but held his tongue, in spite of his stepdaughter's mild impudence.

Michael looked around but Bert was nowhere in sight.

"Has Bert gone on an errand?" he asked.

"No," said Brother Daniel, "He's over at Judge Morgan's house. They're probably comparing their atheist's credentials and pokin' fun at the Lord."

"Harlow," Mother Daniel's voice had an obvious edge.

"Well, I'm just sayin'," said Brother Daniel. "The men seem to share similar opinions on the Lord's Word. Last year's conversation on the Judge's porch made that pretty clear. I'd just as soon not repeat that socializin'."

Breakfast dishes and cookware were being cleaned and stored when Bert appeared with Judge Morgan.

The judge, a man with blond/gray hair and matching mustache, was wearing tan slacks, a white shirt with the sleeves rolled up past his elbows, black suspenders, a red, white and blue bow tie, and tan and white dress shoes.

"Happy fourth," he thundered. Judge Morgan, after years of litigation and pronouncements from the bench, was not a man given to quiet speech.

Michael figured that the judge was in his sixties, maybe older. Even so, he was erect, fit, and an altogether imposing man in spite of his average height. He seemed bigger somehow.

"Bert and I have done some catching up already this morning, along with drinking several cups of Mattie's famous chicory coffee and downing some of her cinnamon buns. They can't be good for me because they taste too good. Mattie is bringing some over in a bit. Yours are still in the oven," the judge smiled a benefactor's smile at the entire group.

"Judge Morgan wants to invite us to his Fourth of July doins' later this afternoon," said Bert.

"That's exactly right," said the judge. "My daughter and her family are here from Indianapolis. Mattie, her daughter, and her granddaughter will be taking part and we have more wieners, potato salad, tomatoes, beans, watermelon, and sweets than we could possibly eat ourselves. You'll be doing me a favor to gobble some down."

"I'll believe we'll pass," said Brother Daniel. "We have much preparation before tomorrow night's service."

"Poppycock," said the judge, smiling more broadly, "It's the nation's birthday. Take some time to celebrate and have some fun."

"We would be delighted," said Mother Daniel, aiming her comment at her husband, who remained silent.

"Good, good," said the judge. "We'll get started with a swim for the adventurous about 4:00 this afternoon. We should be back from the parade by then. You'll want to see that. It starts at 1:30; runs south to north along Main. Then we'll have a swim, some food, and fireworks after dark."

With that, he nodded at the others, shook Bert's hand and strode off to his house.

"I've changed my mind," said Brother Daniel, "We need to put the main tent up today."

With that pronouncement, any thoughts of seeing the Martinsville Fourth of July Parade vanished.

"Harlow," Mother Daniel began to speak but he cut her off briskly.

"The tent goes up today, just like every other Tuesday, holiday or no."

Bert and Michael set about hauling down the heavy canvas and spreading it out on the ground that would soon become the scene of fire and brimstone warnings, stories of earthly shepherds doing "the Lord's work," fainting faithful and groping submersions. The tent-raising effort continued into the afternoon while the citizens of Martinsville stood on the Main Street sidewalk, waving little paper flags as the band passed by playing Sousa marches and high school fight songs. Several new Allis-Chalmers, rubber-tired tractors, pulled low, flat hay trailers along, each decorated by various civic clubs, one of which would get this year's grand prize for "originality and execution of a patriotic theme."

By 4:00 pm, the day had reached its heat potential. Bert emerged from his truck wearing a wool swimsuit of Navy blue, cinched up at the waist with a white cloth belt. He had one of the camp's skimpy towels draped over one arm.

"Come on Michael," he called, "The judge has a rope swing at the river. It's a hoot."

Michael stuck his head out of his tent.

"I don't have any swim trunks," he offered.

"I'll bet the judge has some extra," said Bert, "Or something that will work just as well. Come on, it'll be fun."

Michael hopped to the ground and they walked around the hedge to the back door of the house. Bert rapped on the screen door and a Negro woman appeared.

"Hey, Mattie," Bert said, "Do you suppose the judge has an extra set of swim trunks for my friend Michael?"

"Let me check, Mr. Bert," and she disappeared down a hallway.

Sure enough, the judge had some trunks that used to fit him before he got, as he claimed more than once, his "spare tire eating Mattie's home cooking." The trunks look almost exactly like Bert's, only the cloth belt was red.

Mattie motioned Michael inside.

"You can change in this hallway bathroom," she said turning to indicate a small bathroom with just a sink and toilet.

"Indoor bathroom," thought Michael, "This is really some house."

The rope swing was about twenty yards up river from where Ruth and Michael had been the previous night. It was attached very high on a sturdy tree branch and tied to another tree's trunk. Where it was tied there was a platform built beside the tree, about five feet off the ground with two-by-four inch lumber climbing steps nailed up on one side.

Bert was untying the rope when Judge Morgan and his entire family arrived. Bert already knew everyone and he introduced Michael to Jim Benefield, the judge's son-in-law, Miriam, the judge's daughter, Georgia, a seven-year-old granddaughter, Constance, her five-year-old sister and Louisa, Mattie's granddaughter. She appeared to be about Petey's age.

Jim was carrying two small, inflated inner tubes. He and his girls headed to the river and very quickly the two girls were bobbing around in the water, sitting in the tubes with their bottoms poking down into the water. The current slowly carried them downstream and Jim walked along the bank, keeping up with their progress.

"He'll haul 'em out when they get under the bridge. There are shallow ripples there," said the judge. "Have a go, Bert," he said as he turned back to the group at the rope swing.

With little need for encouragement, Bert climbed onto the platform, rope in hand and, with a whoop he swung high out over the water, released, and plunged awkwardly into a very placid river.

"No points for grace," the judge called out as Bert surfaced. He grabbed the swinging rope and handed it to Michael.

"Maybe the little girl would like to go first," said Michael, indicating Louisa. She stood there in a one-piece swimsuit with cotton legs that went half way down her skinny thighs.

"Excellent idea," beamed the judge. "Sprout, the fellow is giving up a turn so you can go. You remember how, I'm sure."

"Yes sir, Mr. George, I surely do."

She scrambled up the steps and onto the platform. The judge handed her the rope. She got a firm, two-handed grip, jumped up, back and to one side of the platform and swung out even higher than Bert had managed. When she released the rope she twisted mid-air and plunged headfirst and straight as an arrow into the translucent green water.

"Your turn, Michael," the judge said as he corralled the rope.

"I can't top that," said Michael as he mounted the platform.

"I'm sure you will do something creative," said the judge.

Michael's first attempt was a comical thrashing of legs and arms on his decent as he tried to get in without landing flat on the water somehow.

Miriam was next, her bathing suit a bit more revealing, with suit legs square cut higher than Michael had ever seen back home. Hers was a much more graceful feet-first entry into the White River than Michael's. She came to the surface all smiles, her bare shoulders sparkling with beads of water.

Judge Morgan, not one to be left out of the fun, sailed out next and managed a somewhat inelegant headfirst plunge.

He came up laughing. "I believe Louisa has won the initial competition."

The group was in the middle of their second round of airborne ballet when Mother Daniel, Ruth, Rebecca, and Petey arrived. All three of the Daniel girls had swimsuits very much like Miriam's. Mother Daniel's was black with white piping, and Ruth and Rebecca had on identical dark blue suits with light blue stripes around the bottom of the legs. The straps, crisscrossing in the back, were the same light blue.

Michael thought they all looked great, and likely stared a bit too long at Ruth.

Petey had on what appeared to be dungarees that had been cut off, mid-thigh.

"Ah, more beautiful women to take the plunge," said the judge, "and young Peter, of course. Step right up."

The girls held back, but Petey scrambled onto the platform. He made a passably graceful feet-first entry, but came up coughing and spewing water as he failed to pinch his nose on entry and the water slammed up into his sinuses.

"The boy sometimes forgets to engage his brain," Bert muttered to Michael.

Ruth and Rebecca were coaxed into having a go. The rotation continued but Mother Daniel demurred. She walked to the bank and jumped, exhibiting an expert's grasp of the forward dive. She surfaced and, with languid breaststrokes, made for the far bank.

After several swings each, the group broke into sunbathers, those who joined Mother Daniel on the little sunny stretch of sand across the river, and swimmers, a group that included Bert, Louisa, Miriam and Petey. The judge had pointed them to a shallower area, 50 or so yards downstream and then he got out, grabbed a towel and headed for the house.

"Keep your eyes on the children, Michael, just to be safe."

"Yes sir."

Very soon, Miriam joined the Daniel girls basking on the small beach. Bert went further downstream to check on Jim and the little girls, leaving Petey and Louisa to play together in the shallows. Petey, assessing the situation, immediately left Louisa behind and made quickly for the rope swing area. Getting out of the river was easier there by virtue of exposed rocks and some crude steps that someone had cut into the riverbank and laid with flat rocks.

"Getting tired already, Petey?" Michael handed him one of the sorry towels brought over from their camp.

"Nope," said Petey. "But I don't swim with niggers."

Michael was no stranger to this type of attitude. In Calhoun, Kentucky, there was no shortage of people who held the Negro in utmost contempt, and would say so publicly, regardless of the audience. Petey's racial vitriol, however, caught Michael off guard, especially because the little girl was so clearly very dear to Judge Morgan.

"That's not a nice way to speak of Louisa," Michael said. "She seems like a nice girl."

"You some kind of 'nigger lover'?" replied Petey.

"Compared to you, I guess I am. Dad says that everyone deserves respect until they prove they don't deserve it."

"My Dad thinks that niggers are apes; smell like it and act like it," said Petey.

"Seems like a bad attitude for a man of the Lord," said Michael.

"I'll let him know how you feel, nigger lover."

Michael got up and headed to the river. He dove in, doing what was very close to a belly flop. After paddling around for several minutes, he swam toward the sunbathers. Louisa had joined them already.

"Michael," said Rebecca as he walked up the sandbar and out of the water, "You need a tan. You are so white, you almost look blue."

"Becca, be nice," Mother Daniel admonished.

"Yeh, Becca," said Ruth, "Be nice for a change."

"Well, he does need a tan," Rebecca was a little pouty.

Self-consciously, Michael looked down at his belly and legs

for confirmation. It was only then that he realized that his wet wool bathing suit clung to every crevice, bulge, and protrusion of his mid-section. He froze, recalling Bert's "bank walker" observation. Without looking up at the women and girls, who he was sure were looking directly at him, he abruptly turned and waded back into the water.

"We didn't mean to run you off, Mr. Boone," Miriam's voice followed him into the river.

"It's okay," he hollered without turning around. "I need to change clothes before supper."

He exited at the rope swing steps and headed straight for the house, never turning around. His clothes had been neatly folded and were sitting on a chair in the hallway just outside the little bathroom. Once changed, he took the swimsuit out through the kitchen door and hung them over the railing of the porch.

Mattie and a young Negro woman were setting out food on a picnic table that had been covered by a red, white, and blue tablecloth. They both looked up when Michael came out the screen door.

"Mr. Michael," Mattie said, "This here's my onliest child, Isabella. She's Louisa's mama."

"Nice to meet you, Isabella," Michael called from the porch.

"And it's nice to meet you, Mr. Michael. How's the swim?"

"Lots of fun, and it sure cooled me," Michael stepped down from the porch.

"Izzy," said her mother, "Show Mr. Michael the blocks of ice and get him the pick. Since he's cooled down he can help ice down the churn and give it a few turns while we're awaitin' them others. You do know how to salt and turn an ice cream bucket don'tcha?" she said to Michael.

"Oh, yes Ma'am," and Michael followed Isabella to a tool shed hard against the Cypresses at the back of the yard. Just inside, on the dirt floor, were two wooden boxes. Each box had a square hundred-pound block of ice. Stuffed around and on the ice was wheat straw. A canvas tarp covered both boxes.

"Chip off some ice to pack around the cylinder," said Isabella. "Not too big. Smaller pieces work better. Colder."

She covered up the second box as Michael cleared away the straw on top of an ice block. He started chipping off hunks, which he caught with his other hand. If the hunk was too large, he placed it in the churn and poked it with the ice pick until it split into smaller pieces and settled further down into the bucket.

"I'll be back directly," said Isabella, "with the cream, sugar, and vanilla; salt's right beside you there."

Inside the tool shed, everything was orderly. There was a small workbench with hand tools hanging on pegs within easy reach. There were two garden hoses neatly coiled and hanging from hooks. A reel lawnmower was stowed just beneath the hoses. Several yard tools were hanging from similar hooks along the back wall, and a ten-foot wooden ladder was hung up the length of the wall opposite the workbench.

Presently, Isabella returned with heavy cream, sugar, and a small bottle of vanilla extract. Without using any measuring tools, she added the ingredients to the metal churn. She promised Michael that she would send additional "crankers" so he wouldn't have to wear himself down making the ice cream—but in the shade of the tool shed and with access to ice, Michael found the work easy going.

The entire river crew drifted back in clusters of twos and threes. Mother Daniel and Miriam, who Michael guessed were about the same age, walked up from the river together, deep in conversation. Miriam went in the house, and Mother Daniel wrapped one of the judge's towels around her waist. She took a handful of red grapes off of the picnic table and walked over to the shed.

"Here," she offered, "Have some nourishment, Mr. Boone."

Michael, cranking with his right hand and holding the churn in place with his left, looked at her and said, "I'd need another hand right now."

She reached down and put two grapes in front of Michael's mouth. He dutifully opened up and she popped them in.

"Very sweet," she said, "Someone must have grapevines near here, they're so fresh."

"I need to change," she said, "Tell the girls, when they come up, to get out of their wet swimsuits, too."

Michael had a momentary vision of Mother Daniel unwrapping the towel and peeling the suit down off of her legs. Her breasts, glimpsed briefly weeks before, were defined nicely by the wool swimsuit. In fact, the sides of her breasts were actually bare, given the close fit.

"Yes'm," Michael mumbled, trying, without success, to think of other things.

Later, when Jim was cranking the ice cream, Michael's imagination conducted the same visualization of Ruth shedding her suit as they stood together at the picnic table nibbling cheese and crackers. Ruth had prompted his reverie when she casually said, "Be right back. I've got to get out of this wet suit."

As late afternoon gave way to twilight, the judge grilled hot dogs on a stone grill fired with oak embers. He and Bert drank gin-laced lemonade and laughed frequently. Everyone seemed to be having a good time except Petey, who kept to himself. At one point, before dark, Petey went missing for a few minutes and Michael saw him return to the judge's yard, coming from the Daniel bivouac.

The judge's granddaughters and Louisa played tag and when they moved on to hide-and-go-seek, Rebecca and Ruth joined in, much to the delight of the young girls.

"Come on, Petey," said Rebecca, but Petey wasn't interested.

"How about you, Michael?" called Ruth. "Too big a boy for hide-and-seek?"

"I'm the northern Kentucky champion," he replied and rose from a campstool to join in.

The little girls got all giggly with his entry into the game.

Georgia was "It" first and the picnic table was selected as "free base." Whoever was discovered first was It. Failing discovery, whoever got to free base last was It.

"You have about thirty minutes," called Judge Morgan, "and then it's fireworks."

And so, with lots of squealing, laughing, and faked ineptitude on the part of Rebecca, Ruth, and Michael, the entertainment continued.

Before the judge dug into his stash of fireworks, everyone had ice cream. The consensus was that it was the best Elissa had ever conjured. She allowed as how "That got said every year but the recipe don't never change."

The judge asked Jim and Bert to help him with the fireworks, which mainly consisted of rockets attached to sticks. The sticks were pushed into the ground at an angle to insure that the rocket flew away from the house and the gathered celebrants. Once the fuse was lit with a pipe lighter, the rocket launched up to maybe fifty feet and exploded in a shower of colored sparks that rained down and mostly flickered out before reaching the ground.

Jim's primary job was to make sure that if any sparks caught anything on fire that it got stomped out immediately. The judge's yard, green and lush as it was, proved no fire hazard.

Bert drove a substantial wooden stake into the ground. A large nail near the top provided the axle for a pinwheel made of balsam wood, wire, and six or eight cylinders filled with combustible colored powder. The individual fuses from the cylinders came together in the center of the pinwheel, where they were twisted together. When the judge lit the fuses, they each burned rapidly to their rocket-shaped cylinders. At ignition, each cylinder spewed out colored flames and sparks send the pinwheel spinning in an impressive display of multi-colored energy. Everyone loved the pinwheels and the judge had purchased several. He thought that he had more of the rockets too, but had remembered wrong.

There were small clusters of one-inch firecrackers that Bert and judge helped the little girls light. The clusters jumped and popped across the yard to their delight.

Petey had retrieved his stash of fireworks. He, too, lit clusters of small firecrackers to add to the cacophony and fun. He lit his Cherry Bombs one at a time, which startled the group with their power and noise. The Benefield girls were frightened and ran to their mother for protection, covering their ears. Petey seemed delighted with their reaction.

Mother Daniel said, "Petey, let's not light any more of those right now. You can do them later."

Petey lit one more and threw it only a few feet away from the group. It went off in its intended menacing way.

"Enough," said Bert, his voice a no-nonsense timbre.

Petey retreated to his paper sack and took out the sparklers.

"Here," he said to Ruth, handing her the packet, "You guys can do the 'girl' stuff."

Ruth divvied the sparklers to Louisa, Georgia, Constance, and Rebecca.

Miriam said, "Jim, help the girls. Those things burn very hot."

Sparklers lit, there was a flurry of skywriting in the dark and much giggling.

Petey lit a Roman candle and fired the colored orbs of burning powder up and over a small tree. Rebecca asked to do one but Petey refused.

"You shoulda bought your own fireworks," he said.

"Actually, I bought the fireworks, Petey," said Mother Daniel, "Give your sister a Roman candle and one to Sister Ruth, too, if she wants one."

Ruth declined.

Roman candles lit, Rebecca and Petey crisscrossed their flight paths as Petey walked about twenty feet away. Suddenly, he turned and fired the two remaining shots at Rebecca. At that distance the burning powder was nearly spent but the sight of them coming at her rapidly caused her to shriek.

Petey laughed and said, "Too bad. You're out of ammo."

"Show's over," said Judge Morgan. "The safety rules have been breached."

This effectively ended the party. Mattie, Elissa, and Louisa, all of whom had shared the food and fireworks fun, began clearing the picnic.

"Girls, let's give Mattie some help," said Mother Daniel as she picked up an empty bowl and two glasses and headed to the kitchen. "Petey, you can help too."

Petey picked up his fireworks bag, depleted of Roman candles, and headed for the family compound.

"I've got to put these away first," he replied, disappearing around the Cypress hedge. He never came back, and a few minutes later the group heard the loud pop of several more Cherry Bombs and Brother Daniel and Petey laughing.

By 10:00 pm, everyone had retreated to his or her respective beds, and by eleven the lights in Judge Morgan's house had winked off.

Michael was preparing to turn off his lantern when he heard the familiar whoosh and crackle of a bursting rocket. He peered out the tent flap and saw Brother Daniel and Petey sticking another rocket into the ground. This one was lit and it arced over the Cypress hedge and burst into a shower of sparks. Two more were fired in a similar direction.

Michael hopped down and approached them.

"I didn't think that you had any of those rockets," he said to Petey.

"Uh, yeah, well the judge had a few extra," said Petey, smiling at his dad. "That was the last of them."

"Well, you shouldn't be aiming them over the hedge," said Michael.

"It's fine, Mr. Boone," said Brother Daniel, "Go on back to your truck."

As Michael walked back to his bedroll he heard the two of them murmuring and laughing. Lights out.

The dream was vivid. *Sister Ruth was kissing him, water ran down her nose. As he pulled away he realized that it was Mother Daniel. She had on Ruth's swimsuit and a man was yelling at them, but he couldn't see who it was. It sounded like Bert.* He yelled over and over until Michael realized he wasn't dreaming, and the voice was clearly Bert's.

"Fire! The house is on fire. Michael, get up. Get up!"

Michael stumbled out of his tent, pulling on his overalls. Without socks, his boots pulled on but not laced, he raced after Bert around the hedge.

The back of the shingled house was a torch sending sparks high into the night sky. The flames were curving up and around the eves where the wooden shingles were popping, one by one, into little individual fires, infecting their neighbors at a rapid pace.

Georgia and Constance were at the window above the kitchen. They were calling for "Mommy," then "Daddy," and then they just shrieked in terror.

Bert had gone to the far side of the house where the other second floor bedroom was located.

Michael looked around for a solution for getting to the two girls. His mind raced, nothing seemed to make sense. *Nothing to climb on. Got to climb on something. Got to get higher. Climb higher, climb . . . the ladder!*

Michael sprinted to the tool shed and lifted the heavy ladder to his shoulder and headed back across the lawn. Brother Daniel was there on his knees in the grass, hands clasped in front of his face and loudly, what? Praying? Beseeching? Condemning? Gloating?

"And the apostates shall burn in Satan's hell for their disbelief," he railed. "They will forever be cast out from God's presence and grace. He that mocks the Lord will suffer eternal damnation and be banished from Heaven, suffering a thousand painful deaths." On and on he railed as the noise and heat increased.

Michael set the ladder under the upstairs window. It reached almost to the sill.

The heat was unbearable. He felt as if his skin would catch fire any second. The shingles on the side of the house were oozing smoke as he climbed. He climbed on.

He reached the window but the two girls were no longer there.

Maybe they escaped through the door, he thought. *Maybe their dad saved them already.*

The smoke rushed out of the open window, burning his eyes and searing his throat with every breath. He turned his head to the side to get relief from the heat. He heard a small voice say, "Mommy."

"They're still in there," he said aloud above the roar.

He punched through the screen and ripped it entirely from the frame, tossing it behind to the ground. He basically dove into the smoke-blackened room. Flat on the floor, where the temperature noticeably cooled, he swung his arms out and forward, like Mother Daniel's breaststroke. His left hand touched a small hand. He seized it and pulled Constance toward the window. She made no sound and was limp. He took her under an arm and swung his leg out of the window to the first rung of the ladder.

"Drop her to me." It was Bert, standing directly below. Michael grabbed her hand and let her body swing free. The distance between the five-year old and Bert's reaching arms was only a couple of feet. "I've got her," said Bert. "Can you get the other one?" his voice was constricted by smoke and anxiety.

Michael could hear Brother Daniel in the background, continuing his monologue.

Not responding, Michael stepped back into the bedroom. Although no flames were visible in the room, the heat was literally breathtaking. He flattened to the floor and began his breaststroke search. He went to the left where he had found Constance, but made no contact. He moved further into the room, sweeping with both his arms and legs. His right arm bumped the bedpost. He edged away from that contact, flailing now, not sure that he could keep at it. He couldn't see the window; his sense of direction was gone. He turned to the right and his head banged into the wall. He crabbed back and then to the right again.

Maybe she got back onto the bed; probably not because it was hotter up there. He focused on the direction that the smoke seemed to rush. He couldn't actually see but he could feel the movement. He crawled in that direction. He felt that death was imminent; that his body would burst into flames.

Bump.

His arm hit forgiving flesh. He grabbed that direction, and clutched a handful what turned out to be Georgia's calf. He pulled her body toward where the window might be.

Above the roar he could hear Bert's voice, "Get out Michael; get out!"

The voice came through the window. The sound guided him there. He heard Bert, who had climbed the ladder say, "You have to quit looking or you'll die too."

"Here she is," choked Michael, as he lifted her, headfirst, over the sill. Bert grabbed her under the arms and pulled her outside. Her father was directly below and Bert eased her down into his arms. With Georgia in his arms, Jim ran away from the inferno.

Bert backed down the ladder as Michael's leg came through the window, searching for the first rung. He stepped on it and it broke completely through, the broken ends revealing the licking fire that had eaten the backside of the rung. His foot reached down to the next rung and it held. He pulled his other leg over the sill and sought that rung. There it was. He had just started his next step down when the entire ladder broke through the smoldering wall. Michael and the ladder crashed into the burning kitchen and banged abruptly on top of the Judge's new steel refrigerator. Outside, Bert grabbed the bottom of the ladder and gave it a mighty pull.

The ladder and Michael came free, dropped another four feet to the ground, where Bert pulled both the ladder and Michael twenty feet or more out into the yard.

Michael recalled hearing Mother Daniel's voice. "Get him into the car! Harlow, shut the hell up! Get him into the car!"

Before blacking out, Michael thought, *Why are they putting Brother Daniel in the car? Why is she telling him to shut up?*

Chapter Five
Indianapolis

MICHAEL'S STAY IN the Indianapolis hospital lasted nine days. Until his third day, he remembered almost nothing except for the pain and the light that never seemed to go out. He caught bits of conversation but hadn't the energy to figure out who it was.

During the day on Saturday, he started to get a handle on his situation.

He was in a hospital bed. There was another bed in the room, but it was empty. He had gauze bandages on both hands, thick enough to be boxing gloves. He also had a large bandage around his right forearm. He could move both legs and the left ankle hurt but it was nothing like the pain in his hands and arm. There were three different nurses who whisked in and out of the room. One of the nurses was very tall. She was the one who noticed that Michael was semi-alert and looking around.

"Well," she said, "it looks like our Eagle Scout has come to."

Michael worked his mind laboriously. *Fire. Children. Nurses. Hospital room. Tents. Ruth.*

"Where's Ruth?" he muttered.

"Who's Ruth?" said Tall Nurse.

"Are the little girls okay?"

"If you mean the little girls who you saved from the fire, they're fine; home already. Judge Morgan is down the hall with a broken leg. He asked me to let him know when you finally woke up. The pain medication knocks people out, and you've had very strong doses. Burns hurt like the dickens," and she began unwrapping his gauzed left hand.

"This one isn't too bad," she said, "We'll let it get some air today and wrap it lighter later on."

The back of his left hand and fingers were red and blistered, and some of the blisters had ruptured, leaking a clear fluid into the bandage. It hurt quite a bit when the nurse pulled the final gauze pads from the burns. Michael winced, but didn't cry out. The same was not true when she removed the bandages from his right hand and arm.

"I'm sorry," said the nurse, "The right side got burned badly. You'll have some scars on this side."

Michael could see that his hand and forearm were more than red and blistered. The burned areas looked like raw, slightly white meat, singed black on the edges and the gauze pads pulled painfully as the nurse slowly removed them.

She gently bathed the burned areas with a water and picric acid solution. She took some scissors and cut away most of the areas that had turned black. The bathing hurt but the cutting didn't. She soaked fresh gauze pads in the bathing solution, smeared them with Vaseline, and laid them across the burns, then re-wrapped the right hand and forearm. As she worked, Michael studied her. She was probably in her thirties, very pretty and didn't wear much makeup. Her hair was pulled back in a bun, very un-flashy but well-suited to her line of work. She made little humming noises as she worked as if there was a song in her head but she only hummed part of it

"We'll have to change these twice a day, Mr. Boone," she said. "We need to keep everything nice and moist for a while."

She then pulled the covers off of his left foot. He couldn't see it but when she lifted his foot he was aware of a throbbing pain.

"Bad sprain but not broken," she said. "I'll come back with an ice bag. Hungry?"

Michael had to ponder her question momentarily. "Thirsty," he finally replied.

"Well," said Tall Nurse, "I'll order you a beer, but you'll likely get milk. I'll send some potato soup too, in case your appetite suddenly returns," she gave him a wink and breezed out of the room.

A few minutes later, a young man came in with a glass of milk, a bowl of soup, and some saltines on a tray. His name-tag was hand-written: "William" it read, under the printed line, "Volunteer."

"Hi," he said, setting the tray on the high table beside his bed. "I'm going to raise your bed and help you with this food." With that, he reached down and cranked a handle and Michael's bed slowly brought him up to a sitting position.

Because of the wrappings, Michael couldn't grasp the glass or a soupspoon, so William fed him like a baby. Michael drank most of the milk, which triggered his hunger, and the young aide patiently spooned in the soup. It needed salt, but Michael wasn't in a position to be picky.

"You're a big hero, Reverend Boone," said William.

"What do you mean?" Michael craned his neck to catch a glimpse of the name badge again, "William?"

"Well," he said, "You saved those little girls from the fire down in Martinsville. Even the *Star* had a story about it, right on the front page. The headline said 'Young Minister Saves Toddlers'."

"I'm not a minister," said Michael.

"Well, that's what it said. And please, call me Billy not William. Nobody hardly ever calls me William, except my Aunt Mae and she only does that because she's a teacher and doesn't think that Billy is a proper name, though I really don't know why she thinks that but my Mom says that I should 'humor her' because of her being an old maid and all but she's really not that old and she's got a gentleman caller so she'll prolly get married although my Mom says that Mr. Leonard is just wanting to get into her knickers, but I've never seen her wear knickers, just dresses, the kind that old-lady school marms wear. Anyway, she calls me William. Everybody else calls me Billy. Yep, Billy Brite's the name, not William Brite. That just sounds stuck up."

In spite of his discomfort and situation, Michael had to smile at this enthusiastic and verbal volunteer. As the next week passed, Billy would become Michael's friend and confidant.

A fifteen-year-old high school sophomore, Billy was the son of a doctor, and he planned to be one himself. Volunteering at the hospital was just an early step in that process. His dream was to attend Indiana University, just like his dad, but first he had to make straight A's and, as he told Michael, "keep my nose clean."

Tall Nurse came back with a hot water bottle filled with ice. She showed Billy where to place it on Michael's ankle.

"Just ten or fifteen minutes," she instructed, "Then run some hot water in it and place it on the ankle for another ten. The next shift can repeat the process.

As twilight approached, Bert came strolling into the room. Michael's fogginess had steadily cleared during the day and he was feeling mentally okay but physically drained.

"The nurse's station called the church and let us know that you were awake and making some sense, so I thought I'd come see for myself," he said.

"Hey, Bert. Boy, I'm glad to see you," Michael struggled to get more upright.

"Take it easy, son," said Bert. "No reason to strain yourself for the likes of me."

"Tell me what happened, Bert. I don't remember much. Is everyone okay?"

"Mostly," said Bert, pulling the chair closer to the bed. "You got the worst of it, burn-wise. I lost my eyebrows and singed most of my lovely hair. That certainly smelled like hell. The judge's daughter sprained her ankle jumping from the bedroom window. I tried to break her fall, but sorta missed. Jim came down fine."

"But the little girls?" said Michael.

"A few tense moments, there, but both started coughing and crying within a minute or so after we got them away from the house. They had some smoke inhalation problems for a day or two, but Dr. Brite thinks that there was no permanent lung damage. So, he sent them home yesterday, according to that Amazon nurse down the hall." Bert pulled out his rolling papers and tobacco.

"Judge Morgan broke his damned leg, though," Bert added.

As if given a cue, a nurse rolled Judge Morgan into Michael's room. His lower left leg, in a plaster cast, was propped up with a metal contraption so that it stuck straight forward.

"Well," he said, "Two of my favorite fellows together again."

"Hey, Judge," said Bert, "How are you feeling?"

"Like a fool," he replied. "I'm wheelchair and bed-bound until the risk of swelling passes. It'll likely be another week but they're going to let me go home tomorrow."

"But, your home . . ." Michael trailed off.

"Ash heap," said the Judge. "The only thing standing is the chimney. The appliances in the kitchen melted down to bizarre blobs, at least that what Jim tells me. I haven't been back down there since Wednesday morning."

"But you said you were going home?" said Michael.

"Oh, that," said the Judge. "I meant that I'll be going to my old home, here in Indy. The kids and granddaughters live there now. The house in Martinsville was only a few years old, and I hadn't moved all of my stuff down there. Almost everything lost in the fire is replaceable." The Judge grew silent for a long moment after that statement. "I did lose a portrait of me and Jennie that she gave me on our twenty-fifth anniversary," he seemed to be thinking out loud as he looked up, probably imagining the portrait as he spoke.

Bert broke the uncomfortable silence.

"Are you planning to rebuild the house?" He scratched a match on the bottom of his chair and lit a smoke.

"You bet," said the Judge. "Only this time it'll be brick with some of those new asphalt shingles. They're supposed to be fire resistant."

"How did you break your leg, Judge?" Michael asked. "Did you have to jump out of a window?"

"Nothing so glamorous; I was trying to go up the front staircase to the bedrooms. Near the top my foot broke through, I toppled over backwards and my left shin caught in what was left of the stair and *pop*. I pulled myself free and bumped on my butt back down the stairs. I got up on my right leg and hopped out the front door like Long John Silver without his peg leg, down the steps and around to the side yard just as you were climbing in the window. Jim insisted that I move back from the fire and sit down. I had a ringside seat for the rescue. My heart was in my throat the whole time. Our family owes you more than could ever be repaid, young man."

"I didn't think very clearly or fast," said Michael. "It seemed like it took me forever to remember that ladder in the shed. I should have been quicker."

"Nonsense," Bert exhaled a steady stream of smoke, "I saw those little girls and my first reaction was to go the other side of the house, hoping that there would be another way upstairs. Not very logical when you think about it."

"Well," said Judge Morgan, "If you had both adopted the Brother Daniel strategy of asking the Lord to intervene, or whatever he was on his knees praying about, the outcome is unthinkable."

"The Lord helps them who help themselves has never been one of Brother Daniel's operating principles," said Bert. "He'd prefer to let others do the doin', the Lord included."

"The Lord especially," said Judge Morgan. Both men chuckled.

Bert said, "I believe that some of the Daniel clan are planning a visit tomorrow. Is there anything that you want them to bring?"

"That book of yours. The one I had been reading, uh, uh expectations something."

"Of course, *Great Expectations*," said Bert, "I should have thought of that myself."

"Great story," said the Judge. "I've read it twice but that was long ago. Has Bert got you interested in good literature?"

"Yes sir, I guess he has."

"So, does good literature fit into what you want to be in life," said the Judge, "Or is truck driving your dream job?"

"Hardly," Michael managed a wan smile. "I always hoped to go to college," said Michael, "But there wasn't the money, and my folks had to head out west to find work. Maybe, if things turn around, I can figure a way to work myself through some small school somewhere."

Bert asked, "So, what would you study if you did go to college? Make me proud by saying English literature."

"Sorry," said Michael, "But I always liked math and mechanical drawing best. If I ever go to college, I might become a math teacher or draftsman," said Michael.

"Or architect," said Judge Morgan, "or mechanical engineer."

"I guess." Michael thought he knew what architects did, but

he wasn't so sure what mechanical engineers did.

There were a few more minutes of discussion about educational matters. Bert and the Judge did most of the talking, and Michael strained to keep his attention focused on what they said instead of thinking about his discomfort. He learned that Judge Morgan had attended Vanderbilt College in Nashville, studied history, and then went to Indiana University for Law School. Bert revealed that he attended a college called Princeton. He was a Greek Studies major with a minor in English Literature, which gave him and the Judge a common topic of interest, books. Bert was studying for a Masters in Literature when he joined the Army and went to France. By then he had managed to secure a teacher's certificate in New Jersey. When he got that far into his educational background, Bert clammed up.

"Everybody out," said Tall Nurse. "We have bandages to change and then sleep to get. Has someone been smoking in here?"

"Guilty as observed, madam," said Bert.

"Well," she said, "It's allowed but I've never thought it was a good idea in my ward. Next time, please step out near the elevators."

"Elevators!" thought Michael, "Wow, his folks and Aunt Elizabeth would be impressed."

"I'll check in with you, tomorrow," said the Judge, pushing himself backward through the doorway.

"Here," said Bert getting up, "I'll treat you to a ride back to your room. Michael, I'll send the book with Ruth."

"Thanks," said Michael, a little relieved that he could lie back and close his eyes.

But first, the bandage ordeal had to be endured.

The next day, Mother Daniel, Ruth, and Rebecca came to visit in the early afternoon. The smell of freshly washed hair and hint of lavender reminded Michael that it was Sunday. All three of the Daniel ladies were wearing their best dresses, and had carefully brushed and styled their hair.

Ruth was first through the door.

"Michael," she said, "you look awful."

"Thanks," he replied.

"Oh, I didn't mean it that way; but with the bandages and

your hair all mussed, you just don't look right."

"I think he looks like a man who narrowly escaped death," said Mother Daniel. "From that point of view, I think that you look quite good Mr. Boone," she took a seat in the chair nearest his bed.

"Does it hurt?" said Rebecca, hoisting herself onto the empty bed.

"Of course it hurts," Ruth snapped at her sister.

"It's not so bad except when they change the bandages," said Michael. "They give me pain medicine and that helps but it makes me feel foggy."

"We called your aunt," said Mother Daniel, "I believe that I convinced her that you would be okay, else she was planning to drive here. She is contacting your folks."

"Thanks," said Michael, "I'd been fretting about that this morning."

"We're headed to Brick Chapel in the morning," said Ruth, "Do you think that you can meet us there?"

"I have no idea," said Michael. "Maybe the nurses can tell me when I'm likely to get out."

"Let's not worry about that right now," said Mother Daniel. "The main concern is for you to be well on the mend before you come back to work. I spoke with Brother Daniel this morning, and he agreed that I could pay you half-wages during your time in the hospital."

"He should get full pay," said Ruth, "after what he did to save those girls."

"Perhaps," said Mother Daniel, "but let's accept what is possible."

Billy Brite appeared at the door.

"Oops, sorry," he said, "I didn't know you had company." Billy had a pitcher of ice water, and he was making his rounds of the rooms filling up water glasses. Michael was going through several glasses a day because of fluid loss.

"Come in, Billy," said Michael, "You can meet my employer and her daughters."

Billy set the pitcher down and solemnly shook hands with each visitor as Michael did the introductions—Mother Daniel, Ruth, and then Rebecca.

"Billy is going to be a doctor," said Michael, "Just like his father, Dr. Brite. He's the doctor who is looking after me."

Billy turned to Mother Daniel, "Does your revival church have other ministers besides Michael?"

As Mother Daniel and the girls exchanged looks, Michael said, "I keep telling you, Billy, I'm not a minister."

"Well, that's what it said in the *Indianapolis Star,* and they should know what they're talking about, being a big newspaper and all with professional reporters and tons of advertising from all the big stores in town like Vonnegut's Hardware and Duesenberg Motors on Washington where my Dad gets his cars which are real nice but hardly anybody can afford them anymore and they mostly buy cheaper Fords and Chevys or Studebakers which look kinda funny to me but some people like 'em but not my Dad; he said that if they stop making Duesenbergs that he would probably switch to a Packard which almost looks like a Lincoln to me but Lincolns are made by Ford so I guess they are just a fancied-up Ford if you think about it."

"I'm afraid that Mr. Boone is correct," said Mother Daniel. "We only have one minister in our revival group, my husband, Brother Daniel." She gave a broad smile to Michael and the girls.

"Oh, okay," said Billy. "But somebody needs to tell the *Star* that they got it wrong. Here's more water, Michael. Nurse Adams says that you need to keep drinking."

With that, Billy said a polite and brief "goodbye," lingering a bit longer when shaking Rebecca's hand. "I hope to see you all again."

"Maybe so," said Mother Daniel.

His visitors shared their stories about the night of the fire, and how they had raced Michael up to Indianapolis in the big sedan, Mother Daniel at the wheel, Rebecca in the passenger seat and Ruth in the back with Michael's head in her lap. Michael remembered nothing. James Benefield was speeding along ahead of them in his car with, Miriam, Judge Morgan, and both girls. The cars were headed for Methodist Hospital in downtown Indianapolis where a beacon atop the building, installed just that year, guided the sick and injured to care and comfort.

Rebecca observed, "You moaned and groaned a lot during the ride."

"Can we get anything for you while we're here, Mr. Boone?" asked Mother Daniel

"Nothing I can think of," said Michael. "Did Bert tell you to bring me *Great Expectations*?"

"We haven't seen Mr. Gilbert since he left yesterday afternoon," said Mother Daniel. "I expect he'll show up in time to make the drive to Brick Chapel tomorrow. Whether he will be in condition to drive is another matter. A city of this size has many distractions for a man of Mr. Gilbert's appetites."

"Maybe the hospital has a copy," said Ruth. "I'll go ask."

"That's okay," said Michael. "I'll get Billy to check."

"We'll stop by Judge Morgan's room as we leave," said Mother Daniel. "I'll let him know about our travel plans for the next few weeks. We'll be in Linden week after next and then Elwood after that. Perhaps the Judge can arrange some transportation for you."

"I'll just hitchhike," said Michael.

"I'll inform the Judge in any case," said Mother Daniel.

His visitors all rose to leave and each one came to the bedside and gave him a peck. Mother Daniel's cheek kiss was a little moister than he expected, but not so much that anyone but Michael would notice. Ruth placed her left hand on his hair as she brushed her lips across the side of his mouth. Rebecca didn't seem too keen on the whole idea but dutifully planted a modest kiss on his forehead. Then they were gone, but the sweet lavender smell lingered a few minutes.

Indeed, Methodist Hospital had a small library, and *Great Expectations* was included. For the next few days, duties permitting, Billy read the book aloud to Michael. He even rigged up a reading stand for the bandaged patient. Michael came up with a way to turn the pages with his left hand as the bandages became increasingly less cumbersome. Before Dr. Brite was willing to release him, Michael had finished the book. Billy was so taken with the parts he read to Michael that he kept the book and started from the beginning.

"It's just like being in England," said Billy, "only different, probably."

"Probably," Michael had replied.

Tuesday evening, Billy came in and pulled a chair close to

Michael, who was sitting in the armchair. He was writing a letter to his folks.

"Sorry to interrupt," said Billy.

"What's up?" said Michael. "Questions about Miss Havisham?"

"No, no. I've got a problem at school," he looked down at the floor as his ears turned crimson. "There's this girl, Sarah, she's really, really pretty and she sits right next to me in algebra, which is sorta like math but not exactly like math 'cause it uses all kinds of letters and symbols and stuff besides numbers which then turn into numbers when you figure out the answer and..."

Michael interrupted, "I know about algebra, Billy. What's the problem with the girl? Try to keep it short."

"Yeah, yeah, okay, I know."

Billy squirmed in the chair, "Well, like I said, she's really pretty and she's really smart and really popular and she smells good and she smiles at me and then I get a boner. If I have a boner when Miss Holladay asks me if I can solve the equation on the board, I have to say 'no' because I can't go up there with a boner, even if I know the answer, which I always do. I'm afraid that Miss Holladay is going to give me lower marks and I need to make straight A's to get into med school and this boner thing could ruin it."

Michael couldn't help himself, he laughed.

"Hey, it's not funny," said Billy. "I don't want this boner problem to ruin my life."

"Well," said Michael, "This is not the last time that a 'boner problem' will interfere with your plans. I don't have a great solution for you but I've had my own experiences and here's what I did: I wore my jock strap to class almost every day for three years. It can be uncomfortable, but when the boner shows up, and it is totally out of your control when that happens, the jock strap contains a good bit of the problem."

"I don't play sports," said Billy. "I don't have a jock strap."

"If you're old enough to have visible 'boner' problems, you're old enough to buy two or three jocks at the pharmacy."

"I'll be embarrassed," said Billy. "What if the cashier is a girl?"

"Take it to the pharmacist."

"That's a great idea. He's got a cash register there and everything."

"Piece-o-cake," said Michael. "It's like an algebra problem. If boner equals no trips to the blackboard then B equals NT. And, if jock strap equals trips to the blackboard then JS equals T, and if trips to the blackboard equals an 'A' grade, then T equals 'A' and JS equals 'T' and 'A'."

"I knew you could help," said Billy. "It's not the kind of thing that I could discuss with my parents, y'know."

"Certainly not," Michael said.

"Thanks, Michael, you're swell." With that, Billy got up and headed for the door. "Oh, I think that my Dad may let you out of here in a couple of days 'cause I heard him talking to Nurse Adams."

Michael thought about that news for a few minutes and wondered how he would get to Brick Chapel and back to work. He finished writing the letter and put the latest news of his release into it, even if it was only a rumor spread by his loquacious young friend. He addressed the letter to the PO Box in Portersville, California. The letter wouldn't reach his family until October, when it was finally forwarded to Healdsburg in Sonoma County. The family had run out of farm work options in the Central Valley and moved to California wine country, itself struggling with the results of prohibition.

On Wednesday afternoon, the entire Benefield family came to visit. Miriam rolled Judge Morgan into the room as well. Georgia and Constance weren't that interested in the visit, and squirmed and fussed until Miriam shushed them. Jim commented on how 'good' Michael seemed to be doing, and then made an uncomfortable attempt to express his gratitude to Michael. He was struggling with his emotions, not wanting to get all blubbery in front of everyone. Miriam inserted herself to salvage Jim's dignity, but her thanks were accompanied by tears and throat-choking sobs as she expressed the family's feelings for what Michael had done.

Michael flushed with embarrassment, not feeling at all worthy of such praise.

The little girls looked at their Mother and Constance, sensing something was wrong, began to cry as well.

Miriam sat in the chair and pulled the little girl on her lap and assured her that everything was "just fine and Mommy was okay."

Constance grew quiet and stuck a tiny thumb in her mouth.

Judge Morgan broke the brief silence.

"They're taking great care of me at home," he said, nodding toward Miriam and the girls.

He had been released on Monday, once the threat of his broken leg swelling inside the cast had gone away.

"Jim even fashioned a 'scratcher' from a coat hanger so I can get to an infernal itch on my calf. And, the food is better and I can finally get a full night's sleep."

"Do you know when Dr. Brite will let you go?" said Jim.

"Maybe tomorrow, but that's not from official sources," said Michael.

"Well," said Jim, "Whenever it is, I'll drive you to catch up with your caravan."

"Oh, I can hitch to wherever."

"We wouldn't think of letting you do that," said Miriam.

"Thank Mr. Boone, girls, for getting you out of the fire," she added.

Georgia whispered a quiet "thank you" but Constance just looked at him and sucked her thumb.

"Close enough," said the Judge.

The family offered final goodbyes and left Michael to his latest book, *The Jumping Off Place*, fresh from the hospital library.

The next morning early, Dr. Brite made Michael's release that afternoon official.

"You are healing nicely," said the doctor, "And there isn't anything we can do for you here that you can't do at home. But, I want to see you in a week."

Michael explained the challenges of that requirement, given that his home was his truck, moving every week.

"I'll look into it," said Dr. Brite, he turned and left the room.

A few minutes later he returned.

"You'll be staying at our house for a week," he said. "Billy has an extra bed in his room and you're welcome to it. If your recovery is such, perhaps we can make it less than a week."

Michael was dumbstruck for a few seconds and by the time he could say thank you, Dr. Brite was gone.

After lunch, Billy came to the room with a bundle of clothes: dungarees, two shirts, two pair each of socks, boxer shorts and undershirts, plus a pair of work boots. "Where's my own stuff?" Michael asked.

"Either burned up or cut up here at the Emergency Room," said Billy.

"Where did these come from?"

"It's a church hospital," said Billy, "We get clothing donations all the time. Some's awful but some's pretty good. Nurse Adams estimated your sizes and picked out stuff she thought you would need. She had your old boots and got the size from them and then threw them away. The soles were mostly melted."

"Get dressed," said Billy, "Mom's picking us up in half an hour and you have to check out."

Sporting some of his new used clothes, Michael, with a laundry bag holding the rest, accompanied Nurse Adams and Billy to the hospital's business office. They took the elevator to the first floor. It was his first elevator ride and he felt a twinge of panic as the first door slid shut. Nurse Adams pulled the folding metal door shut and he felt the bottom gently drop out.

It wasn't until they reached the business office door that Michael was gripped with the anxiety of realizing that hospitals weren't free and that he had no money.

"I . . . I don't have any money," he stammered to Nurse Adams.

"Oh, oh," she said, "We'll have to set you on fire all over again for non-payment."

Billy laughed.

"Your care has been paid for," said the chubby lady behind the desk. "Here are your discharge papers Mr. Boone, sign here, here, and here."

Although confused, Michael signed himself out of Methodist Hospital on July 13, 1933, three days after his nineteenth birthday. He wouldn't spend time in a hospital again until August of 1942 and again, burns would be the reason.

Chapter Six
Sticky Situations

    MICHAEL'S STAY IN Dr. Brite's home was more like a vacation than a painful recovery. Lenore Brite had been a nurse before marrying. In addition to being a gracious hostess, she was able to tend to his burn wounds expertly. There was another bed in Billy's room because, at the age of ten, Billy's twin brother, Wesley, had died of rheumatic fever. Michael pondered the fact that having a doctor as your father did not guarantee that disease would not strike you down. The pain of that loss, only five years removed, was evidenced in Dr. Brite's circumspection and his wife's silence when Billy broached the topic at dinner that first evening.

    The Brite's house was comfortable but not grand. Michael decided that he could get very used to having indoor plumbing and meals served on china with a full complement of utensils. He was confused at having two forks, however, one smaller and one larger, and Mrs. Brite eased his embarrassment with a brief explanation about salad forks and a self-denigrating story about the first time she encountered two forks at a wedding dinner and tried to give the smaller one to the waiter when he came around to fill the water glasses.

    The Brite's house was full of books: novels, medical tomes, books of wondrous photography, cookbooks, puzzle books, nature books, histories, biographies, and more. Michael found that he could lose himself for the better part of a day just thumbing through the nature and photo books alone. The low level of activity was good for his healing process. He would find, however, when he returned to the physical work of driver and stagehand, the days of hospitalization and recovery had taken a toll on his stamina.

It wasn't until July 19, just over two weeks since the fire, that Dr. Brite was satisfied that Michael could return to work without fear of infection. By that time the revival troupe had vacated Brick Chapel and was in Linden, bringing the good news to the local faithful.

So, on Thursday afternoon, Jim Benefield and Judge Morgan picked Michael up at the Brite residence and headed for Linden, which was northwest of Indianapolis about forty-five miles. Once there, Jim asked a service station attendant for directions to the Calgary Bible Church. In a town the size of Linden, nothing was more than a few blocks away, and they soon drove into the small parking area next to the tents.

Bert was working under the hood of Michael's truck, and came up smiling broadly at their arrival.

"Ah, the reserve troop has arrived," he said. "Dealing with this bunch without a good right-hand man has been wearying."

"I'm afraid that your 'right-hand man' will be using his left most of the time, at least for a while," said Michael, raising his bandaged arm.

"Hey, Bert," said Judge Morgan, greeting his friend, "Dr. Brite said that the healing is going better than expected. He's entrusting you and the Daniel clan to see to the complete recovery. He sent some instruction," handing Bert a typewritten page.

"Best give these to Mother Daniel," said Bert.

The men's conversation brought Rebecca and Ruth out of their tent.

"It's Michael!" Ruth cried, running to him and throwing her arms around his neck. She hugged him enthusiastically.

Michael flushed, "Easy," he said, pulling his bandaged arm out of well-meaning harm's way.

"Oh, oh, sorry," she said, and immediately unlatched.

"Mr. Boone," said Mother Daniel, emerging from her tent, "Very good to see you looking so much improved. We've missed you."

She came over to the group and gave both the Judge and Jim affectionate hugs. She took the Judge's arm as he balanced on his crutches.

"I'm so sorry about your beautiful house. It must be awful to lose everything."

"Thank you, Annie," said Judge Morgan. "Lucky for me, most of my records and prized possessions were still in storage in the attic in Indy. Books I can replace, along with furniture and such. Mattie is helping me plan for the re-build and what we'll need to make the new place livable."

"And your leg?" said Bert.

"It throbs some, but aspirin and elevation usually do the trick. Miriam and the girls are pampering me something awful."

Brother Daniel emerged from the tent and raised his chin in acknowledgment of the arrival of the visitors, but he slipped back in without joining the group.

"Must be working on a new sermon," said Bert. "He likes to freshen up the standard material to keep from repeating himself." Bert winked at Michael.

"Brother Daniel isn't the socializing type," said Mother Daniel, "I'm sorry."

"Not to worry," said Jim, "We can't hang around. We promised Miriam that we'd stop by the Northside farmer's market for fresh tomatoes before dinner."

"Well," said the Judge, "We'll see you next July. I'm not sure if the new house will be completed by then, but the river isn't going anywhere, so we can have some fun, right Michael?"

"Yes sir."

Judge Morgan hobbled a step or two and put Michael in a bear-hug.

"I owe you more than can be expressed," he whispered directly into Michael's ear.

When the Judge let him go, Jim grabbed Michael in another heartfelt hug.

"You will always be welcome in our home, and you will always be in our hearts," Jim's eyes brimmed as he stepped back.

"Please stay in touch."

"Okay," said Judge Morgan, "back to civilization."

With that, handshakes and hugs were completed and the two men drove off, the Judge waving from the window.

Ruth had edged closer to Michael and clasped his left hand but said nothing. Mother Daniel eyed the familiar touch but she too remained silent.

"Okay," said Bert, "Back to the replacement water pump."

"I'll help as soon as I put this duffel in my truck," Michael said.

* * *

The chemistry among the group was different than it had been before July 4th. Brother Daniel, though still the ostensible leader of the group, had somehow been marginalized. Michael sensed a different attitude from the group toward himself. Petey didn't spout any smart aleck remarks to Michael, and he refused to ride with Michael on the travel days. Ruth volunteered to be Michael's navigator. Mother Daniel usually named Rebecca for that duty, but not always. Once, traveling between Brookville and Vevay, Mother Daniel opted to be Michael's navigator. Only Bert seemed to relate to Michael just as he had before the fire. In fact, Bert had been particularly upbeat since Michael's brush with disaster and subsequent recovery. As it turned out, his positive mood had little to do with Michael's condition. Late Saturday afternoon, a sport chevy coupe pulled into the parking lot, Tall Nurse at the wheel.

"Hello, Michael," she called from her window.

He straightened up and worked his memory for her name.

"It's me, Linda Adams from Methodist Hospital."

"Oh, sure, right," said Michael. "You came all this way to check on me?"

"Well," she said, "That would be one of the reasons. Is Bert about?

"I am indeed 'about' and ready to not be 'about'," said Bert as he hopped from the truck bed to ground. He was wearing a pair of slightly rumpled khaki pants and a white shirt. His hair was slicked back and he had on a pair of tan shoes.

He slid into the passenger side of the car.

"Tell Mother Daniel that I'll be here in time for travel day. She'll dock me half a day's pay for Sunday afternoon, but there's not much to do then, so I figured you can handle it," Bert gave Michael a wide grin. "We're off for fun and trouble in Crawfordsville."

With that, Tall Nurse blew Michael a kiss through the windshield and spun her tires on the gravel getting out of the parking lot.

When Mother Daniel asked about Bert during the evening meal, Michael relayed the message that Bert was going down to Crawfordsville with a friend and would be back for travel day. Mother Daniel said that he would miss his half-day Sunday pay.

"He said that he'd risk it," Michael said, trying to sound like something Bert would have said.

Brother Daniel's baptismal groping was particularly noticeable that night. The line of faithful to be dunked, wearing their see-through garments, included four post-pubescent girls, two of whom were prematurely buxom. Brother Daniel took his time with them, grabbing handfuls of firm breast in an effort to "steady" the girl's entrance and exit from the water. He had a knack for turning the girl's torsos in a way that blocked from the congregation's view of his manipulation. If you happened to be behind him, however, as Mother Daniel and both her daughters were, his bit of trickery didn't hide the nature of his slight-of-hand, especially on those young sinners whose breasts were not so slight.

After the last of the faithful had cleared the parking lot, Michael heard raised voices coming from the larger family tent. Mother Daniel was berating her husband for his shameful behavior during the baptism and he, defending himself weakly, kept to his story of "simply caring for the safety of the sinners who God has put in my care."

"Sinners, my ass," she raged. "Those girls aren't old enough to know about sin, certainly not your kind of sin; but if you had the chance you would sure like to show 'em," Mother Daniel threw back the tent flap and walked quickly out of the light, past the trucks and down the walk that led to the church's front door. She disappeared around the corner. Brother Daniel peered out of the tent but did not follow.

A few minutes later, Rebecca and Ruth came to Michael's truck. "Can we come in?" Ruth asked.

"Sure."

Both girls climbed onto the flatbed and under the overhead tarp. Michael had just lit the lantern. "Sorry that you had to hear all that," Ruth said.

"Yeah, sorry," said Rebecca.

"It's okay," said Michael. "I remember my folks arguing some, especially about money."

"Did they ever argue because your dad was a child molester?" said Rebecca.

"Well, no." There was a stretch of silence.

Michael finally said, "Maybe it's like Brother Daniel said; you know, safety and all."

"He's a liar and a pervert." Ruth spit the words out as if they tasted awful.

"We just keep doing this salvation crap because all our money is in this damned show," said Rebecca. "He's the one who can preach and keeps people coming back and putting money in the plate, otherwise we'd be back in Tallahassee with our friends."

"What'd you think we should do, Michael?" Ruth edged closer.

"Well, I, uh, the thing is . . . I can't give you any advice," Michael felt the color rising in his face. "Maybe you should talk with Bert."

"We've already done that," said Ruth. "Last summer he advised Mom to pack up the car, take us and head back to Florida. But, here we are again. Still, if it wasn't for Bert, that pervert would be trying to get my panties off every time Mom leaves us alone," Ruth's voice quavered.

"And he still tries to feel my tits when he gets a chance," said Rebecca.

"Brother Daniel raped you?" Michael looked at Ruth. He was incredulous, "And your mother didn't do anything?"

"She doesn't know," Ruth said, her voice catching. "Besides, I didn't say he raped me, I said he 'tried' to. I've only told Rebecca and now you. Bert thinks that Brother Daniel was just groping me, like he's done with Rebecca and the girls he baptizes. Bert told him to 'watch himself' or he'd find himself in trouble with the law; Bert said he would see to it."

The three sat in silence for several minutes. Ruth composed herself after quietly sobbing a few times.

"Maybe we ought to shoot the bastard," Rebecca finally offered.

"You shouldn't say that," said Michael.

"Yeah," said Ruth, "That's a terrible idea, Becca, but it makes me smile. Besides, you don't have a gun."

"Brother Daniel has one," said Rebecca.

"Let's not talk about shooting anyone," said Michael. "There has to be a better way."

"Let us know when you think of one," said Rebecca.

"What's the pow-wow in here," said Mother Daniel as she pulled back the tent flap. "I could hear your voices when I came around the corner of the church."

"We were talking about your argument with Brother Daniel," said Ruth, showing genuine courage given the latest turn in their conversation.

"Let's not air our problems with Mr. Boone. He has plenty of his own worries, I'm sure."

Mother Daniel gave them a wide smile. "Come on ladies, we'll have a girl's slumber party."

With that, she turned and headed for their tent. "Come now," she called.

Sunday morning, Michael slept in until the cars started filling the church parking lot for the regular Sunday service. Brother Daniel, in his ill-fitting black suit, attended the service as usual so that he could encourage attendance at the final revival service that evening. None of the other Daniel clan made an appearance.

After the sparsely attended evening service, Ruth and Rebecca helped fold and stack the chairs in preparation for travel day. Their work was nearly complete when the Chevy coupe turned into the lot. Bert was at the wheel. He skidded to a stop and then leaned over and shared a long kiss with Tall Nurse. They both got out and she walked around and got in the driver's seat. He leaned into the window and gave her another smooch.

As she started to pull out of the lot, Bert called out, "See you next week."

Mother Daniel, still counting money at the card table, didn't look up but said loudly, "You won't be paid for today Mr. Gilbert."

"Money truly well-spent," he replied. "I'll help with the rest of the chairs, ladies. It's pro bono."

Michael didn't know what that meant exactly, but assumed it had something to do with the Sunday pay issue.

Later, when the work was complete, Bert and Michael sat at the back of Bert's truck. Bert rolled a smoke.

"Michael," he said, "It's women like Linda who make life worth living. She's smart, funny, has a great car, a good job and perky tits. Man-o-man!" He blew out a slim stream of grey smoke.

"Keep your eyes open, Mr. Boone, we may find you a girl like that before the summer is over. Maybe Linda has a friend about your age."

"Don't bother."

"Suit yourself, but that was one great weekend. Crawfordsville is a college town and there was plenty of illegal beer and carrying-on. Linda knew all the best gin joints because that's where she went to school."

"Sounds great, Bert, but I need to ask you something," said Michael.

"Shoot."

Michael briefed Bert on his conversation with Ruth and Rebecca, leaving out the part about Brother Daniel trying to have sex with his stepdaughter, but zeroing in on their disgust and fear of the man's taste for young girls. The latest Saturday baptism ceremony was offered as more proof of his predilections. He replayed the main points of the loud argument that followed and even mentioned Rebecca's comment about 'shooting the bastard.'

"Brother Daniel is, as far as I know, an unsuccessful and frustrated pedophile," Bert said. "One of these days, though, he is going to go too far and end up in the pokey. He's got Mother Daniel in financial bondage or she likely would have left him already. The whole family relies on the money he attracts to the collection plate. It's not a good situation, but it hasn't been desperate enough for her to bolt. I've had strong words with him about Ruthie and Becca regarding his fondness for fondling. At least he's not trying to bugger little boys, yet," Bert stamped out the glowing cigarette butt he'd tossed on the ground.

"He's your classic Bible-thumper hypocrite," continued Bert. "Preaches the dreadful wages of sin to the bumpkins but doesn't fear hell himself."

"I hate to ask this, Bert, but what's a pedophile?"

Bert looked at Michael and shock his head slowly. "Michael, my work to turn you into a cosmopolitan has fallen short. A pedophile is an adult who gets his or her sexual stimulus from children. It seems that this aberration mostly occurs in males."

"I guess I could have figured that out, huh?"

"It's okay," said Bert. "It never hurts to be absolutely certain when dealing with pedophilia, bestiality, or necromancy."

"I'm not even going to ask," said Michael, now shaking his head.

"These other sexual deviations will be covered in subsequent lectures and there will be a quiz," Bert hopped down from the truck bed. "Off to the outhouse in preparation for the sleep I didn't get while Linda was in bed with me; man-o-man."

"You already said that."

"It bears repeating," said Bert, not turning around as he headed into the dark.

Travel day found Sister Rebecca as Michael's navigator on the drive to Elwood. Their conversation was sparse and never touched on the topic of Brother Daniel. Rebecca did say that she could hardly wait until they were back in Tallahassee in mid-November, when she could be back in regular school with her friends. Michael noted that school started in September not November.

"Mom's worked out a deal with our schools," she said. "We show up late in the fall and leave early each spring so that we can help with the revival. Besides, Bert has us ahead of our classmates on the core subjects."

Ruth would graduate in absentia next May, and Rebecca would become a rising senior at the same time.

"No caps and gowns for Brother Daniel's girls," she said, her voice edgy with distain. "No cheerleading, no class offices, and no homecoming bonfires."

Michael thought back to school experience and how odd it would have been to miss big chunks of time at the beginning and end of each year, when some of the most memorable events occurred. He gained a new admiration for what Ruth and Rebecca endured because they were integral parts of the family business. He supposed that as time went on, Petey would feel the sacrifice as well when his duties, of which he had few now, became more central to the salvation effort.

Elwood, Indiana, was another small Midwest town of no great distinction—pleasant, quiet, and mostly free of distractions. The Mt. Holyoke Friendliness Church was their host for the week. The revival and family tents were anchored on the asphalt parking lot, so there would likely not be many "divers" moved by the spirit to thrash around in ecstasy, risking skinned elbows and knees.

On Wednesday morning, which happened to be Ruth's eighteenth birthday, two black and white police cars pulled into the church lot. An overweight officer heaved himself from one of the cars and two younger, trimmer officers popped out of the other. The portly cop was clearly in charge.

He walked over to Bert who was re-knotting a frayed tie-down strap.

"I'm looking for one Harlow Eugene Daniel," he said without introduction. "Are you him?"

"Not only am I not him, neither am I he," Bert said, remaining seated on a folding chair, tie-down strap across his lap.

The officer, aware that his grammar was being mocked but not sure why, placed his fists on his wide hips and glared at Bert.

"Look, wise guy, is Harlow Eugene Daniel around here or not? I'm told that he runs this sideshow."

"Try that tent over there," Bert indicated the larger family tent and went back to his work.

As the officer moved toward the tent, Mother Daniel emerged, wearing her work clothes and a most charming smile.

"Good morning officer, how can we help you this lovely day?"

"I need to talk with Harlow Eugene Daniel."

"I believe that he has just gone to the church building to use the facilities. He should be back in a minute or two. Can I offer you gentlemen some coffee?" her smile caused his demeanor to soften, and he accepted her offer. Mother Daniel motioned the pot to the two young policemen, but they waved her off and leaned against their car.

"What on earth could be your business with my husband?" Mother Daniel poured coffee into the mug he held in his pudgy hand.

"That's something I can only discuss with Mr. Daniel," he narrowed his eyes over the rim of the mug and slurped the hot coffee loudly.

Michael noted that the policemen reminded him of the Germans he had seen in the newsreel back in Jasper, except, here in Elwood, the uniforms were blue.

"How long will you be staying in Elwood?" said the officer.

"We leave for Portland next Monday," said Mother Daniel.

"Well," he said, "Those plans might have to change."

Brother Daniel came out the side door of the church and walked to where the policeman and Mother Daniel were standing near the family tent. As he approached, Mother Daniel said, "Harlow, this gentleman needs to talk with you."

Brother Daniel extended his hand but the officer did not respond. Instead he tersely said, "Are you Harlow Eugene Daniel?"

"That's correct, sir and please call me Brother Daniel. We're all brothers in this world aren't we?"

"Depends," said the officer. "I'm Sheriff Potts and those two," pointing to the two officers leaning on their car, "are my deputies."

"Gentlemen," said Brother Daniel, nodding to the policemen.

"I need to ask you some questions," said the Sheriff. "Get in my car where we can have some privacy."

Brother Daniel got into the black and white sedan, and the Sheriff plopped into the driver's seat and shut the door. The two young officers continued to lean against the front fenders of their car and take in a scene that now also included all three of the Daniel's children.

"Miss," one of them said to Sister Ruth, "Suppose you could bring me some of that there coffee?"

"Don't mind if I do as well," said the other one. They exchanged smirking glances. Ruth looked at Mother Daniel who nodded an almost imperceptible 'yes.' Ruth took the pot and Mother Daniel brought two mugs. Both officers mostly ignored Mother Daniel, but made it clear with their leering that they considered Ruth worth closer inspection.

Once the coffee was poured, Mother Daniel instructed her children to return to their tents and their schoolwork.

Michael overheard one officer say to the other, "I've always had a thing for schoolgirls," and they laughed.

The conversation inside the squad car went on for twenty minutes, maybe longer. Finally, the doors opened and Brother Daniel and Sheriff Potts emerged from either side.

Sheriff Potts looked across the hood of the car. "I may need to talk with you again, Mr. Daniel, after I converse with the department in Linden. I'm told that you will be here until Monday. Make sure that you don't leave before then."

"Not to worry," said Brother Daniel, "We have the Lord's work to do here in Elwood right through the weekend."

"Yeah, well make sure that your work is done in a decent manner," the sheriff said, punctuating his statement by getting in the car and slamming the door. The two patrol cars left the lot as Brother Daniel stood there waving as if saying farewell to visiting relatives.

"Big misunderstanding back in Linden," Brother Daniel said loudly as he turned to face Mother Daniel. "It'll get straightened out."

"And if it doesn't?" she replied.

"It will, it will," he walked past her and disappeared into their tent.

She looked at Bert and then Michael and shook her head. She poured herself a mug of coffee and walked off to sit at a sorry-looking picnic table moldering under a beautiful elm.

The remainder of the week went without incident but there was a sense of anxiety regarding the possible reappearance of Sheriff Potts. The Saturday night baptism did not present Brother Daniel with any tempting targets, although Michael guessed that he wouldn't have been very grabby even if all of the faithful had been ripe teenage girls. The argument with Mother Daniel last week and the visit by the sheriff certainly had put Brother Daniel in a defensive mood. His sermons were less bombastic than usual. Even his fire and brimstone sermon on Thursday was lukewarm.

"Well, that effort won't scare the shit of the children and old ladies," Bert commented after the sermon.

On Friday afternoon, Tall Nurse's Chevy coupe zipped into the parking lot and she and Bert made another quick departure. This time, however, Michael knew that she was due to show up because Bert had confided that they planned to spend the weekend at her place back in Indy. Apparently, Bert had also told Mother Daniel and they had agreed on the amount of pay that he would forego in order to "indulge my sinful ways," as he expressed it.

After the regular church service on Sunday, while Brother Daniel was still working the congregation for that evening's attendance, Sheriff Potts pulled into the lot. Michael and Ruth were sitting at the dilapidated picnic table reading and with the sheriff's arrival, they exchanged looks that could be translated as, *Uh, oh.*

The sheriff waited in the car until Brother Daniel was walking back to the revival area from the church. Then, he pried himself out of the patrol car and leaning on the top of the door called to Brother Daniel, "C'mere bud."

The sheriff did virtually all of the talking while Brother Daniel sagged a bit and repeatedly rubbed his temples. The sheriff ended the conversation, after wedging himself behind the wheel, no small effort, by calling out from window as he pulled away, "And make sure you do!"

After that evening's revival service, Michael and the two girls were stacking chairs when Ruth told them what she knew about the Sheriff Potts encounter. Her story was based on what she had learned from Mother Daniel, which meant that it might not be totally accurate.

A family in Linden complained to their police chief that Brother Daniel had traumatized their sixteen-year-old daughter during the baptism ceremony by "repeatedly squeezing her breast." The chief contacted the minister at the Calgary Bible Church and found out where we were headed after Linden. He called Sheriff Potts about arresting Brother Daniel. During the week, the family changed their mind; so, no charges.

"Damn," Rebecca slammed a chair onto a stack.

"Well said," Ruth replied.

Michael kept stacking and said nothing, but his mind was working over the situation, which was more troubling than salacious. He often dreamed of cupping a firm breast himself, but he wanted to do it with a willing partner, not some scared victim.

About 10:30, the Chevy coupe pulled into the lot, Tall Nurse at the wheel. Bert was slumped against the passenger side door, his head on his forearm, which was resting on the open window. She got out and came around to the passenger side and roused Bert to an upright position. Pulling the door open, she put a hand on his right shoulder, making sure that he didn't tumble out.

Michael had been reading under the light pole. He walked over to the car as Linda was determining how to wrestle Bert out of the seat and into his truck.

"I can help," Michael said to her as he stepped around.

"Much appreciated."

"What happened?" asked Michael.

"Did you know that he's a mean drunk?" Linda asked.

"Sorta," said Michael. "He took a swing at me once when he was stewed."

Bert didn't look so good. His right eye was swollen shut. There was a bruise on his left cheekbone. A trickle of dried blood was sneaking out of his hairline above his left eye, his khaki pants were ripped open at the knee, and his right hand and fingers were puffed and skinned at the knuckles.

Between the two of them, Michael and Linda got Bert to his truck, Bert making pain-induced grunts with nearly every step. At the truck, they propped his back against the rear bed, Michael got up in the truck and, as Linda pushed, Michael pulled Bert onto the bedroll, his hands under Bert's shoulders. Michael tucked a blanket around his moaning friend and hopped to the ground.

"He drank too much and argued politics with a guy at a speakeasy. The guy was dumb as dirt and Bert made sarcastic remarks about the guy's bone-headed ideas and bad grammar, mean-spirited things. The regulars at the bar were laughing at the guy. When the idiot made an off-color remark about me, Bert smashed him in the face and the guy ended up on the floor. His buddies got him on his feet and hauled him outside. All three were waiting in the street, jumped Bert and were giving it to him pretty good until my screaming and kicking put an end to it."

"Thanks for stepping in," said Michael.

"Well, when Bert has slept off the alcohol, tell him I'm sorry and to look me up when he solves his drinking problem," Linda said, as she headed for her car.

She turned as she neared the driver's door, "Oh, and how is the right arm coming along?"

Michael unbuttoned his shirtsleeve and pulled it up, revealing the red scar tissue.

"It doesn't feel too bad now but it is very sensitive to sunlight," said Michael. "Otherwise, I can do all the things I need to do around here."

"Good, good," she replied. "The sunlight sting will likely be with you for quite awhile. Those scars are like a baby's skin; very sensitive." She leaned over and pecked Michael on the cheek. "Work on Bert to moderate his drinking. He's got my number when he's ready."

"Yes, Ma'am."

Michael stood there while the Chevy's taillights disappeared into the Indiana night.

The drive to Portland, Indiana, was a straight shot east on Highway 28 to Albany and then a northeast jog on Highway 67. Bert did his work Monday morning, but talked very little and he was clearly sore from the beating he had taken. He moved slowly and deliberately. Michael told him what Linda had said, and Bert acknowledged the information by nodding but said nothing.

Their host in Portland was His Light and Word Bible Church, located on S. Boundary Pike, southeast of downtown. While Michael and Bert were setting up the tents on the grassy expanse behind the little clapboard church, Michael told Bert about the visit from Sheriff Potts in Elwood, and what Ruth had related about Mother Daniel's version.

"Dumb son-of-a-bitch is going to end up dead or in jail. I'm surprised some angry father hasn't shot him already," Bert said while he rolled a smoke. "The law probably has him spooked for now, but he'll backslide when his testosterone builds up and Mother Daniel won't provide her wifely duties."

Michael just then realized that the late Sunday night spiritual sessions between Mother and Brother Daniel hadn't been occurring lately—or if they had, they were damned quiet sessions.

Brother Daniel regained some of his bombast with the Thursday evening fire and brimstone sermon in Portland. He pointed to *Thessalonians 4:16* and hammered away on the event of the Rapture when believers, both dead and alive, would "join Jesus in the sky," while non-believers would be left behind on Earth to suffer seven years of "tribulation." According to Brother Daniel, the tribulations would include those mentioned in *Thessalonians*—siege, war, famine and pain—but also "rape, boils, plagues of locust, dust storms, lightning and massive earthquakes that will swallow entire sinful towns like Portland."

"I think Brother Daniel has read too much about the Jews in Egypt and the story of Job," remarked Bert as he and Michael looked on from the bed of Michael's truck.

In any case, many of the faithful left the worship tent that night vowing to stop their sinful ways in order to be in the group who were qualified to rendezvous with Jesus in the clouds when Rapture time came around. It could be any minute, according to Brother Daniel.

At breakfast Friday morning, Bert, his left eye still partially closed from the swelling, asked Brother Daniel if he could clarify something for him about the Rapture.

"Mr. Gilbert, I'm surprised that you have an interest in such matters. Perhaps your recent weekend experience has caused you to reflect on your own relationship with God."

"That could be it," said Bert, "But I think it's probably more of a practical matter."

"And that would be?" said Brother Daniel.

"Well," said Bert, "When the faithful rise up to meet Jesus in the sky, will they float up slowly and majestically, giving the rest of us a chance to look up under dresses and such or will they fire up like Fourth of July rockets, perhaps shedding a shoe or other loose pieces of clothing in the process?"

Michael had just taken a drink of fruit juice and his reaction to Bert's question was to shoot juice through his nose and to begin choking on the rest, which was the perfect cover for his mirth.

"Mr. Gilbert, your mocking question illustrates why you are to be left behind," said Brother Daniel as he rose up to return to his tent.

"No, really," said Bert to the retreating figure, "Will everyone have to be outside when it happens or will those inside thump up against the ceiling until they can work their way over to a window or open door?"

Brother Daniel disappeared into his tent.

Michael looked around the table. Mother Daniel and Ruth both had a hand over their mouth, and a tear was working its way down Mother Daniel's cheek. Ruth's eyes were squeezed shut. Rebecca had put her head down on her hands, which were resting on the table and her shoulders bobbed up and down. Petey his face, a mask of bewilderment, just looked from one person to the next.

"These are just practical questions," said Bert as he stood to clear away his dishes. "It doesn't mean that I question the theology. Brother Daniel is perhaps too sensitive; back to work, Michael."

* * *

The on-going drought was briefly interrupted while the revival was in Union City. On Wednesday of that week the sky darkened about four in the muggy afternoon. The bottom of the massive thunderhead to the southwest looked like an upside down green and purple egg carton. Bert observed that such a cloud formation indicated "wind and ice." What southerly breeze there was died to calm and the smell of rain preceded a rise in the wind coming from the southwest. The thunder started in long, cloud-to-cloud rumbles sounding like potatoes rolling down a metal roof. The regular sound of birds, insects, or barking dogs simply stopped.

Michael and Bert untied the cords holding the rolled sides of the revival tent and let the sides drop to the ground. They quickly secured the flaps to the ground with wooden stakes. As the work progressed the wind gained force and one side of the tent bowed in and the opposite side puffed out. Once the flaps were all secure, the tent regained its primary shape but it buckled and bucked as the wind buffeted the entire encampment.

"Come on," yelled Bert over the wind. "Button up our truck flaps and I'll check on the family tents. This storm could have strong winds or worse."

Michael was just securing Bert's truck when pea-sized hail started to pepper the area. He started to climb into his truck when Bert yelled from over near the stone Church of the Redeemer. "Get inside here," he waved from the church's back door. Michael saw that the others were already taking shelter there. In the seconds that it took Michael to tie his rear flap shut, the hail became grape-sized, and then instantaneously, golf ball-sized. The ice rocks pounded at his head and he covered it with his hands but that simply exposed his hands to the pounding. He ran toward the church and Bert reached out and pulled him inside.

The noise was overwhelming as the hail and wind combined to make normal communication impossible. Bert motioned everyone over near the stairwell that led to the choir loft, although there weren't many stairs and it wasn't much of a loft. The seven of them hunkered along the stairwell. Ruth pressed herself against Michael and he could feel the give of her breast against his arm.

The pounding of the hail suddenly stopped, but the wind seemed to press down angrily on the entire scene, and Michael's ears popped from a change in air pressure. There were startling flashes of light coming through the fake stained-glass windows on the west side of the sanctuary and the immediate thunderclaps were deafening cracks and crashes, not rumbles. The storm was on them.

The window nearest the back door, where they had come in, suddenly exploded as one of their tent poles, propelled by the wind, came through like a long, heavy javelin.

"Jesus Christ," yelled Brother Daniel as he covered his head with both arms and burrowed behind Mother Daniel, who was sheltering Petey with her body. Rain and wind blasted through the broken window. The rain was nearly horizontal and the far wall and all the pews in between got soaked.

Gradually there was an abatement of the onslaught, then, within a few minutes, a dramatic silence followed by a roll of thunder to the east. Bert got up and went out the door. Michael followed.

To the west, a ribbon of blue sky stretched across the horizon. The clouds just above them were not green and purple but grey and beginning to lighten. They walked around the little church, crunching through the hail littering the ground. They looked to the northeast, where the sky was still bruised and threatening but moving away with flashes of cloud to ground lightning, making menacing exclamation points during the storm's track northeast.

"Ohio is in for a beating," said Bert.

When they came back around the church, the Daniel clan was walking around the ruin that was their home. The revival tent was folded to the ground except for one corner, which was leaning perilously. The largest family tent was completely flat except for the lumps and bumps that were cots, camp chairs and such underneath. Ruth and Rebecca's tent was folded in on one corner but in some sort of cosmic joke, both Bert and Michael's truck tents were standing proud.

The whole affair had lasted less than thirty minutes.

Bert took charge and directed efforts to get the largest family tent back to a standing position. Everyone pitched in, some more helpful than others. By six pm the family tent was up, although much of the inside was wet and in disarray. Next, Bert and Michael re-set the girl's tent. Most of their belongings were still dry.

"Let's get the revival tent up for tonight's service," said Brother Daniel.

Bert looked at Brother Daniel with a mixture of distain and disgust.

"Perhaps you could get the Lord to perform a miracle," he said. "Otherwise it isn't going to happen."

"Mr. Gilbert, your job is to erect the main tent so that I can bring the Lord's Word to the local sinners," said Brother Daniel.

"On a good day we can't get this tent up in less than two hours, and it's already six o'clock. It's pummeled, wet and heavy. I haven't the time or the inclination to wrestle it into place this evening. Besides, after a storm like that, the faithful will have better things to do tonight. You and Mother Daniel are welcome to use my truck for your lodging tonight. I'll bunk with Michael." With that, Bert turned and walked to his truck to retrieve his personal items.

"You'll do as you're ordered," said Brother Daniel.

Bert stopped and turned slowly and said in a firm quiet voice, "I obey orders that make sense and with which I can comply. Orders from idiots don't qualify."

There was silence as the two men glared at each other, a silence of tension, given that the distant thunder still rumbled.

"One day," said Brother Daniel, "Someone is going to silence your incompetent mouth."

"I believe the term is 'intemperate'," replied Bert

At that uncomfortable moment, The Reverend Mr. Beasley and three church members wheeled into the parking area in the Reverend's aging Reo. All four men emerged from the car slowly, gapping at the shattered church window and then the flattened revival tent.

"Praise God," said the Reverend, surveying the group, "Everyone seems to be okay"

"Thanks to your sturdy house of God," said Brother Daniel. "I shepherded the entire group in for their safety. My men can help you secure the broken window."

Michael exchanged looks with Bert.

"No need," said Reverend Beasley. "I brought three deacons to address any damage to the building. We can board up the window ourselves, thank you. Besides, it looks like you still have plenty to do to be ready for tomorrow's service."

"We could hold tonight's service in your sanctuary," said Brother Daniel, pondering the lost revenue of a cancelled evening.

"I strongly doubt that more than a handful will even show up tonight," said Reverend Beasley. "All of Union City is a mess, and so too the sanctuary, I presume. Besides, there's no electricity. We'll plan on tomorrow."

With that, he and the deacons headed for the church storeroom to gather the materials needed to cover the gaping window.

"I'll share Ruth and Rebecca's tent this evening," said Mother Daniel. "Brother Daniel and Petey will sleep in your truck, Bert. Thank you. Now, let's figure out how to prepare a quick meal before we lose the daylight."

Before things returned to near normal and everyone regained their proper quarters it was Saturday. None too soon for Michael, as Bert was a restless and often noisy sleeper.

August in Indiana was a succession of hot days and warm evenings made tolerable when the breeze was light and steady. Most nights, everyone slept with their tent sides rolled partially up to allow the breeze through. After lights were off, Michael could hear the rustle of the canvas being hoisted up with a tug on the rigged pulleys. He usually left his tent sides up all of the time, except for the side that faced the compound. Even after lights out he left it down; partly because he was modest and partly to discourage himself from watching any of the Daniel's women up and about in their underwear or pajamas—more often than not garments that were one and the same.

The down sides of sleeping in an open tent included insects and the moisture that collected on everything by morning. Everyone seemed resigned to a few insects buzzing around and the heat of the days resolved the overnight moisture problem.

In spite of Brother Daniel's flaws—and he was once again fondling girls during baptisms in those August weeks—Michael admired his skills as a preacher. And, even though the sermons were canned, he was convincing as a man who was just discovering his message as he got inspiration from God. On his best nights, the words and phrases began to establish a rhythm, a syncopation, which he often reinforced with "Amens" and "Praise the Lords" at the end of a stanza.

The congregation would be pulled into the rhythm and the movement in the tent settled into a recognizable call and response of verbal and body language. Calls of "Praise Jesus" and "Amen" in response to Brother Daniel's staccato delivery were accompanied by faces turned toward heaven, arms waving like stalks of wheat in a breeze and closed eyes on rapturous faces. The women, in particular, were given to these theatrics, although the occasional husband would join in. Most men, however, simply rocked side to side and nodded their assent to the message. Clearly, there were genuine emotions being stirred. Brother Daniel worked his message cleverly around the breaks, where rousing hymns were sung, followed by more call and response. When the emotional level in the tent was at its highest, Brother Daniel called for the offering. On the nights when Brother Daniel was really cooking, and there was a diver or two, the collection plate was always fuller.

The remainder of August included stops in Greens Fork and Brookville. The first week of September they were in Osgood. The second week of September they made their last Indiana stop, on the banks of the Ohio River in a town called Vevay. It was here that the aforementioned mayonnaise jar made its first appearance.

Vevay, a river town of almost 3,000, was established by Swiss immigrants in 1802. The settlers were determined to grow grapes and turn the area into an American wine region. It was, in fact, the site of the first commercial winery in the country.

"The thing I like about Vevay is the local hooch is first rate," said Bert. "The locals make a good, if somewhat sweet, wine—and great dark beers—in spite of Prohibition. Compared to most small towns, it's pretty easy to find a place to buy. I've gotten plenty drunk on that beer last couple of years."

Michael and Bert were setting up the larger of the family tents in a grassy area near the gravel parking lot of the Light and Faith Baptist Church.

"And did that activity cause any problems?" asked Michael, knowing that Bert and too much alcohol was often a recipe for trouble.

"That's all history, nosy," he gave Michael a grin.

Wednesday, after the evening service was complete and the troupe was preparing for a pleasant sleeping night, thanks to the cool breeze coming off the nearby river, a single black-and-white police car pulled slowly into the parking lot. Two uniformed policemen got out, and walked toward the light pole near the family tents.

Ruth looked up from where she was stacking hymnals and called out, "Brother Daniel, you better come out here."

Moments later, Brother Daniel came out of his tent. He had taken off his sweat-soaked shirt and his suspenders hung loosely from his waist. His ratty undershirt was wet except on the sides and he looked tired.

"Harlow Daniel?" said one of the officers and Brother Daniel acknowledged that he was.

"We've an arrest warrant for you for lewd and lascivious behavior," said the officer, holding up a sheaf of papers. "This was issued by Judge Clark up in Brookville. Get a shirt on and come with us."

"There must be some mistake," Brother Daniel said as he looked first at one officer and then the other.

"Probably not," said the one without the warrant. "If there is, Judge Clark will set it straight. Let's go."

With Brother Daniel holding one of his white shirts in one hand, the police put him in the back seat and closed the door.

"Can we post bail?" asked Mother Daniel.

"That's up to the judge. Mr. Daniel will get a preliminary hearing in the morning. That's when bail gets set...or not," said the officer with the warrant. "You'll have to come up to Brookville tomorrow to find out."

The squad car did a u-turn in the empty parking lot and drove away. Harlow Eugene Daniel had turned in his seat and was looking at his family. They watched his face grow small, and his blank expression never changed.

"Nothing to do tonight," said Mother Daniel to no one in particular. "Mr. Gilbert, tomorrow you take the Lincoln to Brookville and find out the particulars. I'll get with the Faith and Light people and cancel services for tomorrow and Friday. Now, let's finish up and get to bed."

"Is Daddy going to prison?" asked Petey, his voice tremulous.

"Just a night or two in jail, sweetie," said Mother Daniel, "Nothing to worry about."

"How serious?" Michael asked Bert as they walked back to their trucks.

"Don't know, exactly," he replied. "'Lewd and lascivious' sounds better than 'child molestation' but for all I know the law sees them the same. Either way, it can't be good for the revival business."

"You'll be Mother Daniel's First Mate tomorrow," said Bert. "Better brush up on command protocol. We're living through interesting times, boy. Get some sleep."

Bert left before 8:00 am for the seventy-mile drive to Brookville. Without the laboring trucks and trailer in tow, the Lincoln would be in Brookville around ten thirty that morning. With no scheduled service that night or Friday—Mother Daniel explained to the local preacher that Brother Daniel had been called back to Brookville to pray over the wife of the pastor who had hosted the revival there. The poor woman, she said, had suffered a stroke, and the locals in Brookville thought so highly of Brother Daniel's connection to the Lord that they had sent word down with two policemen with whom Brother Daniel returned to minister to the ailing woman and likely wouldn't be back until Saturday.

With no service to prepare for, Michael, Ruth, and Rebecca had the leisure time to spend the afternoon walking along Main Street and visiting the Wine Museum, which, thanks to Prohibition, had no wine. After lunch, Petey grabbed his father's fishing gear and headed down to the river.

Late that afternoon, Bert called the Faith and Light Baptist Church. Pastor Leroy came out and got Mother Daniel. She was only in the church office three or four minutes.

When she came out she went straight to her tent. Ruth and Rebecca put the evening meal together. Mother Daniel came out and joined them.

"Brother Daniel and Bert won't be back tonight. The judge postponed the hearing until tomorrow morning. Whether we have any more services here in Vevay is unclear. We'll have to be patient."

"Let's pray for Daddy," said Petey.

"Daddy can pray for himself," snapped Mother Daniel. She took two deep breaths, "Sorry, Petey, you're right. Why don't you pray for Daddy?"

Petey did his very best Brother Daniel impression, asking the Lord to "Free his father from the shackles of his bondage, as Moses had freed his people from the Pharaoh and to return to minister to the fallen and the sinners."

Michael glanced up at Ruth and she rolled her eyes dramatically.

Only three or four cars of the faithful showed up for the cancelled service, and Mother Daniel explained the reason for the change of schedule to each group. People nodded, looked serious, patted her hand, which she rested on their window, and offered best wishes. "Poor dear," they said of the pastor's stricken wife. "We'll pray for her."

By nine thirty the light had completely faded from the western horizon. Michael and Ruth sat under the bare bulb reading, Ruth's toes occasionally rubbing Michael's bare leg above his droopy socks. Rebecca and Petey were playing slap jack in the girl's tent, and Mother Daniel was pacing, walking out into the dark, coming back, pacing some more but never sitting down or retreating to the tent.

"You are awfully fidgety," said Ruth. "Can I get you some iced tea or lemonade?"

"What? No, no, I'm just restless that's all."

"Brother Daniel will be fine," offered Michael. "Bert's on the case."

"Harlow's got nothing to do with it," she said, dropping the 'Brother Daniel' pretext.

"Oh," said Michael, "I just assumed…"

"Stop assuming, Mr. Boone. It will take you down the wrong road many times."

With that, Mother Daniel took to her tent and prepared for bed. Within the hour, everyone else headed for bed as well.

Michael burned the lantern in his truck until after 11:00 so that he could finish a chapter. When he turned it off, the night was starlit but moonless, and all the lights of the compound were off. The starlight of rural Indiana made the Milky Way a truly amazing bright brush stroke across the sky. Michael was soon asleep.

"Mr. Boone, Mr. Boone." The whispered name struggled to break through to Michael's conscious mind.

"Mr. Boone, wake up," Mother Daniel tugged at his foot.

"Wha . . . what is it, what's the matter?" Michael propped himself up on one elbow, rubbed his eyes, and briefly shook his head clear. He could see Mother Daniel standing at the back bed of the truck.

"Nothing's the matter," she whispered. "Keep your voice down. Let's not wake anyone."

"Yes Ma'am," he croaked quietly.

"I need your assistance, Mr. Boone." Mother Daniel crawled up onto the bedroll.

Even in the dim starlight, Michael could see that she was wearing a pajama top, but that her legs were bare. In her right hand was a small glass jar with a worn familiar label, "Blue Plate Mayonnaise."

"I can't sleep," she whispered "My skin is so dry that it itches. It's been keeping me up. I can't reach my back to rub this in," she held up the mayonnaise jar. "I need for you to moisturize my back."

Michael had sat upright as Mother Daniel had climbed aboard his bedroom. He scooched back and propped himself against the truck cab, tucking his right foot against the inside of his left thigh, his left leg straight out.

"Can't Ruth or Rebecca do this?" he whispered.

"The children need their sleep," she replied, and her answer made his heart kick a small lump up into his throat.

Mother Daniel crawled into the space directly in front of him, turned around and sat cross-legged, her butt pressed against his right foot and shin. She handed him the jar.

"Just scoop out a teaspoon or so and use both hands to work it into all those places on my back that I can't reach."

Michael twisted the lid off and the scent of lavender floated in the night air.

"Is this mayonnaise?" he whispered, a hint of doubt in his voice.

"Of course not, silly. It's moisturizer. I make it myself."

With that, she raised her hands to her shoulders and with a gathering motion, pulled the pajama top up around her neck, exposing her bare back. Michael could see the sides of her breasts, the imagined remainder hidden by her body.

"*Oh no.*" he thought, as an erection announced its initial stirrings.

He scooped out some moisturizer, rubbed his hands together and began rubbing the slick concoction across Mother Daniel's shoulders.

"All the way out to the sides, please," she whispered, "Down my sides, too. That feels lovely."

Her skin, indeed dry, absorbed the cream quickly and she suggested that he be liberal in its application.

"*Mmmmmm,*" Mother Daniel offered implicit approval of the process.

As he spread the moisturizer along the sides of her back and down toward her waist, the tips of his fingers felt the soft bulge of her breasts on both sides and his sexual arousal was at full sail, straining against the fabric of his undershorts. He shifted slightly and the damn thing broke free, the bare end of his penis rubbing along the inside of his own left thigh.

"Do my front, too," she said, her voice husky and low. With

that, she pulled the pajama top completely off, stretched her legs to the front and leaned back against Michael's chest.

Michael's breathing was shallow and rapid. His mind would have raced but it was stuck in a lust-induced neutral. All he could think to do was to comply with demands. He wasn't sure what he was doing, but Mother Daniel seemed certain.

Now that she was up against him, he could look over her shoulder and down her front. First stop, her breasts. He had seen them briefly once before. This time, however, he was shocked at their proximity and availability. Below the breasts was the pooch of her belly. Not fat, really, just a faint reminder that three babies had occupied the space over time. She wore light-colored underpants, loose around the legs and almost high enough to cover her navel, but not quite.

Michael dipped into more of the lavender-scented cream and began massaging it into her belly, the weight of her breasts pressed against the top of his thumbs as he rubbed.

"The breasts, too," was her quiet demand. Her right hand was at the top of her crotch. He could see her first and second fingers pressed lightly at that small space, working rhythmically against the thin cotton cloth.

Michael inhaled deeply, scooped more moisturizer and cupped his slick hands over both breasts and marveled at their feel, their modest but noticeable weight, and the way they recovered their shape as he rubbed and kneaded the cream into them. Mother Daniel's right hand quickened at their task. "Squeeze the nipples, Michael." She pressed back against his body.

He took both nipples, larger now than when he had first looked down, and squeezed lightly, a fear of injury holding him back.

"Harder," she demanded. She began to rock slightly side to side and a low hum came from her throat.

It was at about this juncture in the proceedings that Michael's orgasm announced that it was beyond the point of recall, and somewhere below the layer of his carnal desire was a giant ball of mortification. At the same time, but not enough of a distraction to postpone the inevitable, his right leg, below the knee, was fully asleep from lack of circulation. The pins and needles of discomfort registering modestly as the orgasm throbbed to completion.

"Harder," her whispered demand seemed panicked.

As Michael tried to measure how much harder he dared squeeze what seemed to him rather delicate tissue, applying mounting pressure, hoping not to go too far, Mother Daniel tensed, her rocking stopped, her breathing stopped and she pushed back hard against his chest. Suddenly and vigorously, she began to buck.

Her vocalizations were guttural and low "mmmms" and "ooooohs," finally punctuated with a distinct "Oh, God" as she slumped, seemingly lifeless, against him.

He pulled his fingers from her nipples.

"Please, no, Michael, don't stop yet. Just brush them lightly with your palms."

Michael registered what gave her pleasure—squeezing, light brushing, and the touch of her own fingers. All of this was new, and likely wouldn't have occurred to him if left to his own imagination and instruction.

Presently, Mother Daniel sat up, turned slightly, and reached her left hand behind her and found his erection.

"Oh, my," she whispered. Her hand also felt the sticky issue of his orgasm. It covered the inside of his upper left thigh.

"I guess you don't need my help this time," she whispered, and she leaned forward retrieving her pajama top.

"Yes, Ma'am," he mumbled.

"Yes, you don't need my help or yes, you do need my help?"

"No, Ma'am, I mean yes, Ma'am, I don't need your help," Michael's brain functions were decidedly jumbled at this point.

"Perhaps another time," she whispered as she pulled the pajama top on and crawled toward the back of the truck. "Goodnight, Mr. Boone and thank you for your cooperation. It was quite wonderful."

"Yes, Ma'am. Oh, don't forget your mayonnaise."

She reached in and took the jar from his hand.

"It's not mayonnaise, remember?" she gave him a slight smile.

As Michael worked hard at drifting back to sleep he kept mulling the fact that his life had become much more complicated.

Chapter Seven
Panhandle Bound

A FRIDAY CALL from Bert indicated that the earliest he and Brother Daniel would be returning to Vevay was Saturday. The judge had listened to both sides. A local attorney, also the town's part-time DA, presented the accuser's complaint. Brother Daniel, using his oratory skills, made his own case, thus saving the expense of an attorney.

Bert told Mother Daniel that the "lewd and lascivious" charge came down to a "he said, she said" argument, and that Brother Daniel had been eloquent in positioning himself as a devout, well-intentioned, but perhaps clumsy servant of the Lord. He expressed amazement that anything he had done while baptizing this "innocent lamb of God" could be construed as inappropriate. He had turned and faced the accusing family and apologized, tears of remorse welling dramatically in his eyes. Bert said that it was performance "bravura."

The judge would issue a decision on Saturday morning regarding whether to schedule a trial. Bert agreed to call back as soon as the judge made his announcement.

Given this opportunity, Mother Daniel visited Michael again that night. This time, his continuing instruction on the how to please a woman included actual copulation, and in three different positions at that. Being his initiation to intercourse, the first position was significant for his rather embarrassingly premature finale, which Mother Daniel ignored. At nineteen, Michael's recovery time before a second and, eventually, a third orgasm, was minimal.

By the time Mother Daniel was teaching Michael the wonders of the woman astride position, those lovely breast within easy pinching range, her own arousal was made evident. She bore down on his pubic bone, creating the pressure and friction required for her own pleasure and eventual shuddering finish. This final activity was more than a little uncomfortable for Michael but circumstances being what they were, he made no complaint.

The multi-part lesson conducted in near silence except for the unique noises associated with wet, well-lubricated entries and exits, and the occasional slap of bare skin against bare skin. Kissing was not allowed by Mother Daniel.

As she was leaving, she turned and whispered, "Mr. Boone, you need to trim your toenails."

"Yes Ma'am."

After her quiet departure, Michael abruptly fell asleep, exhausted.

As had been the case during the day on Friday, Mother Daniel's interaction with Michael on Saturday morning was no different than it had been for the entire summer: businesslike. Michael tried to catch her eye for some indication that their relationship was changed, but she gave no such sign. No sly smiles, no secret touches, no winks, no nothing. The seeming lack of any emotional connection caused Michael to feel ashamed of what had occurred. Realistically, however, he hadn't had much say in the matter, and the carnal pleasure was a powerful counter-balance. He was afraid that it would happen again, and afraid that it wouldn't.

Brother Daniel's late-morning phone call confirmed that he and Bert were headed for Vevay. The judge determined that without other verification, the charge wasn't sustainable. He warned Brother Daniel that the Good News Revival wouldn't be welcome in Brookville again. Promising not to schedule that particular town in the future, Brother Daniel made a hasty exit from the courthouse, Bert trailing behind. Given their departure time, he estimated that they would be in Vevay by late afternoon, and to notify the local church members that there would be a baptism ceremony that evening.

*　*　*

The remaining travel schedule would have the troupe back in Tallahassee before the end of October so that Ruth, Rebecca, and Petey could join their respective classes by the first part of November. They had left school at the end of March early that year, missing all of April and May. This was the schedule that Mother Daniel had arranged with school officials, with the promise that the children would be tutored by a qualified educator during their travels. Mother Daniel had no intention of letting her children suffer from a lack of education, even hoping that college would not be out of their reach.

As Michael was able to piece together, Winslow Gilbert was certainly qualified. He had graduated from Princeton in 1915 with a Bachelor's degree in Greek Studies and a minor in English literature. He was the scion of a prominent Philadelphia family and was expected to carry that prominence forward as was his older sister. She was married off soon after her debutant ball to a very successful Wall Street banker. Her husband predicted the 1929 crash and put his portfolio into precious metals in 1928. By 1933 he was scooping up certain stocks for pennies on the dollar and anticipating huge returns when the economy recovered. His in-laws, the Philadelphia Gilberts, lost the bulk of their money in the crash and eventually relied on their son-in-law to help them maintain a modicum of pride in their living standards.

Back in 1917, Bert left his nearly completed graduate studies for the patriotic stampede to join the military. He qualified for a Reserve Army commission and headed to Europe as second lieutenant in the Signal Corps. By the time he was mustered out of the Army as a major in 1920, he had seen the actual horror of the War to End All Wars from a very close and searing vantage point. Among men such as Bert, who witnessed the leadership stupidity, veniality, hubris, and pride that resulted in the carnage, "war stories" were seldom told, because to tell them was to relive the nightmare. These men had nightmares enough.

Bert tried to finish his graduate studies on his return to Princeton but he couldn't study. He was spooked by the calm; he would suddenly yell out and duck under a table in a quiet library when the vision of a disemboweled corpse appeared in his mind or cower behind a light pole or mailbox when noises were loud and unexpected. He found that alcohol, never difficult to obtain, although illegal, was a salve that dulled the mental anguish. He took a high school teaching job in Philadelphia but only managed three semesters before the drinking did him in. His brother-in-law got him a job in a private school in New York City. Things started well but the combination of too much liquor and an affair with the headmaster's neglected wife blunted his career as an educator after only eighteen months.

Sometime late in 1924, Bert took a train to Key West where he soon had a menial job working for a deep-sea fishing captain. They took wealthy clients into the Gulf to catch trophy fish. Bert, given his background and general smarts, soon became the captain's stand-in for those trips when the captain was "indisposed" due to his own relationship with bathtub gin.

In the fall of 1927, Ernest Hemingway and his new wife, Pauline, chartered the boat for marlin fishing. That day, Bert was at the helm. He was aware of Hemingway's work and was soon discussing literature with his client as they trolled through the warm, blue water. A marlin was caught, beautiful but small, so after photos were taken, released. Some kingfish stole bait from the large marlin hooks and they had a good laugh reeling in the bare barbs, nibbled clean by the silver bandits. They shared several strong drinks made with rum that Ernest had secreted in from Cuba. A friendship was born.

For several months, Bert took the Hemingways fishing or acted as first mate when the captain was feeling fit. The Hemingways asked Bert to their rented home, where they drank late into the nights and talked writing, politics, fishing, war, and booze. Pauline loved Key West, unlike Elizabeth, Hemingway's first wife. But in January of '28, Ernest and Pauline headed to Paris so that he could meet his publishing obligations, give readings, and stoke book sales.

With the Hemingways gone to Europe, Bert spent more time drinking alone and to excess. Late one afternoon, in no shape to be skippering the forty-six-foot *Miss Conduct,* Bert ran the boat into a concrete piling at the opening to the marina. The jolt threw a nine-year-old boy overboard and grievously damaged the trawler. The boy was quickly hauled out of the water by his father and Bert's First Mate, CJ, but the ordeal cost Bert the job, and he became persona non grata in the small Key West community. Until then, Bert was known as Winslow. Upon leaving Key West he shed his given name and adopted "Bert," in an effort to distance himself from his tawdry post-war life.

After a series of brief odd jobs in Fort Meyers and Sarasota, Bert answered an unusual-sounding "Driver/Tutor" want ad in the Tampa paper and subsequently joined Brother Daniel's Good News Revival in Tallahassee. He signed on just as the troupe was preparing to head north for their annual swing through Georgia, Tennessee, Kentucky, and Indiana. Since the spring of '28, he had been a skilled tutor, effective stagehand, reliable driver, and a thorn in Brother Daniel's spiritual side.

Michael learned these details, not from Bert, but in scraps and pieces from Mother Daniel, Ruth, Judge Morgan, James Benefield, and even Brother Daniel. Michael's more robust understanding of Bert's back-story wasn't fully complete for many years.

* * *

With a scheduled Tallahassee school start date of November 2 for Ruth, Rebecca, and Petey, the caravan had only six more weeks of bringing good news to the faithful. This meant that there would only be two stops each in Kentucky, Tennessee, and Georgia. The downside of this schedule were the long drives between towns. This situation put a real burden on Bert and Michael to have the gear packed and ready to go for early morning departures, followed by stints at the wheel of twelve to twenty hours of bone-jarring travel, including frequent stops for tire repair, over-heating, and miscellaneous mechanical challenges.

Bert explained that the reason for concentrating on Indiana during the summer was that the competition among the traveling "God shows" was much reduced north of the Mason Dixon line. The Bible Belt Buckle of the Deep South was crawling with such troupes. In addition, spending more time in small northern towns meant that Brother Daniel faced less possibility, remote as it might be, that he would encounter any Negroes attending services or, God forbid, requesting baptism. But in Lawrenceburg, Kentucky, Brother Daniel's fear came to pass.

The revival had set up in the side yard of the Sardis Baptist Church. The routine had been normal in prepping for the Wednesday evening service. About 6:30 the faithful started to populate the tent. Ruth and Rebecca directed early arrivals to the front. Fifteen minutes before the 7:00 service was to begin, a family of Negroes entered. The group included wiry man in overalls, his wife, a head taller than her husband and some pounds heavier, a teen-aged boy, also in overalls, and twin girls, probably ten-years old, their hair sticking nearly straight out to the side of their heads in two carefully crafted sets of pigtails.

Ruth and Rebecca exchanged glances, but made no attempt to bring them forward. As the tent neared capacity, the family got up and stood at the back, making the seats available to the late-arriving white folk.

When Brother Daniel and the host pastor and his wife emerged from the family tent and stepped onto the stage, Brother Daniel scanned the congregation to determine the monetary value of the assembled. He came to an abrupt stop when seeing the Negro family, causing Pastor Spinder, who was checking the crowd for familiar faces, to plow into Brother Daniel from behind and, in a chain-reaction, his wife to respond to the collision by falling backward onto the ground from the stairs with a very audible "My Lord!"

There was a scurry of activity as Mother Daniel and Ruth, descending from her piano bench on the riser, helped the poor woman to her feet, pulling down and smoothing her flower-print dress and inquiring as to her general condition.

"I'm fine, just fine, thank you. Good Lord, Harry!" she looked up at her startled husband, "Let me know when you are going jump backward for no apparent reason."

"I'm so sorry dear," he replied. "Brother Daniel, uh, he, uh."

"I lost my footing, Mrs. Spinder," Brother Daniel came to the pastor's rescue. "I hope that the fall caused no harm; my apologies."

"Oh, lawsy, I'm fine. Fit as can be. Let's start the service. These good folks," she waved her hand toward the gathered, "Came to hear your words, not watch me bumble around." Polite laughter skittered through the crowd.

Pastor Spinder offered the opening prayer, which was, by Michaels's estimation, one of the better, less rote prayers that he had heard throughout the summer. His voice was of the same deep timbre as Brother Daniel's, a gift for those who choose the ministry and his message seemed somehow more literate and well-considered than most. Plus, it didn't drone on.

From his perch on the truck, Michael observed that Brother Daniel didn't reverently bow his head during the prayer, but stared, his jaw firmly clenched, at the Negroes.

When the pastor returned to his seat after introducing Brother Daniel, the two exchanged sotto-voice comments, and Brother Daniel eventually nodded his head slightly. Pastor Spinder took his seat and beamed a pastoral smile worthy of the Pope.

The remainder of the evening proceeded in much the way every Wednesday night "shepherd service" tended to, with this exception; the Negroes could flat-out sing, and in harmony. They didn't seem to need hymnals; the words were all familiar. Even the twins could belt out the songs and often created interesting soprano runs while their mother would lend a lustrous alto voice to the hymn. The teenage boy had a strong tenor and his father, lacking the ability to go very low was, at best, a high baritone. Nevertheless, when the singing started, the rear of the tent provided an extraordinary sound.

Ruth, not often given to overt reactions from her place at the piano, couldn't seem to stop beaming when the music she initiated, usually a subdued mixture of monotones and hesitant delivery, seemed to literally lift the spirit of the service with its exuberance. Even Michael, alone on the back of his truck, found himself singing along with those familiar hymns that he learned at the Second Coming Pentecostal Church in Calhoun. The only person in the tent who didn't seem elevated by the energy of the music was Brother Daniel. His usually enthusiastic music direction was subdued to the point of non-existence.

Thursday morning breakfast found Brother Daniel unusually quiet. The initial conversation was small talk about the nice weather and comments on the food, which had been supplemented with homemade canned fruit, compliments of the ladies of the Sardis Baptist Church.

"By golly, that music sure sounded great last night, Ruth. You really had the locals belting it out," Bert said as he approached the table, arriving later than the rest.

Before he could consider his role in the conversation, Michael responded, "Ruth did a great job alright but it was that Negro family who made the difference."

"Those impudent niggers had some nerve showing up here. They have their own damned church," Brother Daniel was nearly shouting.

"No doubt, Jesus would have said much the same thing had any black folks showed up at the Sermon on the Mount," said Bert calmly.

"What do you know of Jesus?" Brother Daniel was now in full shout fury. "Those niggers, the mark of Cain on their skin, aren't fit to worship with real Christians. They only joined the human race through intermarriage with the world's first and worst sinner. They are little more than beasts of the field."

"Well," said Bert, "Those 'beasts' sure could sing God's praises better than most."

"Yeah, dad," offered Petey, "Those niggers really sounded good."

"Shut up, boy," Brother Daniel turned his wrath on Petey. "Learn your Bible. Niggers were never meant to be anything more than slaves."

"Actually," Bert interrupted, "The Bible says nothing of the sort."

"*It is* in the Bible, Mr. Gilbert, and I won't stand for any more of your smart-assed remarks. Get to work."

"I can explain it to you," said Bert, "But I can't understand it for you."

"Get to work, you bastard," Brother Daniel seethed.

Bert shrugged his shoulders, gathered his utensils and left the table. Brother Daniel remained seated and the rest remained silent for a few seconds. Finally, Petey broke the quiet.

"I'm going to fish that pond over there," he indicated the one-acre pond that was part of the Sardis Baptist Church grounds.

"Pastor Spinder says there are crappy and catfish.

With the tension slightly cracked, everyone, except Brother Daniel, followed Bert's example, and breakfast was over. Brother Daniel remained fixed to his seat. When Michael walked back from the church's privy several minutes later, Brother Daniel was still there, staring straight ahead, arms on the table, fists clenched.

Bert later explained to Michael that the Wilkins family was known and accepted around Lawrenceburg. As the only Negro family in town, their uniqueness dampened down most of the overt racism that might have occurred had they been just one family in a community of Negroes there. However, there were no others, and that fact likely worked in their favor in most ways.

Michael also learned while riding with Mother Daniel that the wiry father, Jesse Wilkins, was the grandson of a former slave who had walked north to Kentucky in 1869 from just south of Chattanooga in rural north Georgia. Using government assistance provided by Reconstruction, the man managed to buy twenty acres of farmland just outside Lawrenceburg. Three generations had farmed that land for over sixty-four years.

Besides the crop revenue, Jesse also shod horses in his smithy shop, and people from all over the county came for his services. He was known for a very fair price and meticulous work. His wife raised chickens and sold eggs to the local grocery or to anyone who came to the farm wanting the big brown eggs.

The Wilkins children attended the local public schools as had their father, and aunts before them. The inclusion of Wilkins children in the grammar and high school of Lawrenceburg had become so entrenched in local memory that any thought that it might be another way rarely surfaced, except among outsiders.

Every Sunday, the family drove to Lexington, twenty miles east and attended the First African Baptist Church. The church, founded by slaves in 1790, was located at the corner of Short and Deweese Streets since 1832. Its choir was renowned in north-central Kentucky, and often sang for festivals, fairs, and holiday celebrations throughout the area. The Wilkins parents and their son were members of the adult choir, and the twins sang in the children's chorale.

Jesse met his wife, Beatrice, in Sunday school at the First African Baptist Church, and that summer their boy, Walter, had a crush on one of the young altos in the choir. For several generations, the church was fertile ground for budding relationships among the Negroes in the Lexington area. It is no wonder that Sunday church activities were a day-long affair for a family who spent the remainder of the week somewhat isolated on the fringe of Lawrenceburg.

The family seemed comfortable attending a revival at the Sardis Baptist Church. They knew Pastor Spinder and members of his congregation well. Michael noted that the family acknowledged several other attendees with nods of recognition and smiles. Ruth later told Michael that the First African Baptist Church choir had come over from Lexington and sung in Lawrenceburg several times over the years and the Wilkins family got much credit from the locals for making these enjoyable entertainments possible. But the fact that they graciously surrendered their back-row seats in the revival tent to white folks was a reminder that for all of the goodwill they enjoyed in this small community, they knew their place.

The Saturday baptism would take place in the pond where Petey had angled for fish earlier in the week. Over the years, members of the church had covered the shallow bottom of one corner of the pond with sand, gravel and river stones for this very purpose. There would be no squishy mud bottom for the baptizers or baptizees to negotiate.

When the Saturday congregation began to arrive, among them was the Wilkins family. This time, they were dressed in their Sunday best. Dark suits for Jesse and Walter, a smart, belted dress for Beatrice, and matching white dresses for the twins. The girls had their hair pulled straight up and bundled in a neat top-knot, secured by a small yellow bow. Once again, they took up residence at the rear of the tent.

Even though Brother Daniel spotted them early on, he remained stoic.

The service began, prayers were offered, scripture was read, and music was sung. Again, with the Wilkins singing, it sounded far superior. Again, however, Brother Daniel offered only the barest of direction.

The baptism ceremony was set for early in the service, prior to the sermon and collection of tithes and offerings. When

Brother Daniel launched into the invitation to be baptized as a sign of commitment to "Jesus our Lord and Savior," six attendees made their way forward, including the Wilkins twins. As the girls walked toward the front of the tent, Brother Daniel went pale, his eyes widening. Besides the twins, the group included one teenage boy, a nine-year-old boy, and a stout, middle-aged woman and her husband.

Brother Daniel stepped down off of the platform. He bent down, hands on knees and spoke quietly to the twins. As he straightened up, the twins turned and walked back to their family. As the Wilkins family left the tent, Brother Daniel stepped back on the platform and addressed the crowd. "I'm sure you will agree, it is best that those little girls be baptized by their own kind. To immerse them in the same water as these devoted white folks would not sit right with the Lord."

The congregation began to buzz. A man's voice called from the rear, "The Lord don't mind what color them little girls are!" The man got his family to their feet, and they headed to the exit at the rear.

A woman in the front row stood and approach the baptism group, "Come, boys, there will be no ceremony for you tonight." With that, she and the teenage boy and the nine-year-old left out the side of tent, leaving the wife and husband standing at the foot of the platform.

While a few in the tent remained seated, there was a ragged exodus of couples and families while Brother Daniel stammered and pleaded for them to stay. When the movement subsided, about two thirds of the crowd were either walking home or cranking the family car in the parking area.

Sister Ruth ushered the wife and husband into the family tent to prepare for their dunking in the pond. While they did that, Brother Daniel paced the platform and quoted from the Old Testament about Cain and his "mongrel" wife.

"Those Negroes must understand that trying to mix with God's people is against what the Bible teaches," he thundered.

"Amen," said a pinched-faced woman in the second row. "Yes sir, Brother Daniel," said a man by her side; he sported a large port wine stain across his forehead and right cheek. "The niggers have their own church in Lexington. Let 'em get in the water with the other darkies."

When the baptizees emerged from the family tent, the remaining worshippers followed them and Brother Daniel to the pond. Once the ceremony was finished, a few more people peeled off, not returning to the revival tent. Brother Daniel's sermon was offered to but a handful of the faithful, and what that handful offered Brother Daniel in terms of their tithes was pitiful indeed.

With the service over, Brother Daniel simply slumped on the piano bench. Michael and Bert began straightening the chairs, and Mother Daniel sat at her counting table staring at the meager take.

"Well, Harlow," she said, "I think that worked out well."

Michael looked at Bert, who seemed to be biting his lower lip to keep from laughing, and they exchanged a quick glance and went back to the task at hand.

The Sunday evening service was unusually sparse, once again reflected in the offering plate. Pastor Spinder approached Mother Daniel as she counted and secured the money.

"Mother Daniel," he said, "Likely best that you folks don't come back here next year. The folks around Lawrenceburg are mostly fond of the Wilkins family, and word of their humiliation will spread well beyond the Saturday attendees."

"I'm very sorry, Pastor. My husband's views regarding Negroes are not shared by all in our group. Please relate that to the Wilkins family for me. I will miss not coming here, but I understand."

Pastor Spinder patted her on the shoulder, "God bless you dear." He turned and left.

* * *

The Monday drive to Somerset, Kentucky, was difficult not because of the distance; it was the geography and mechanical issues that cropped up along the way. The mountains and hills were beautiful, but the road was never straight for long and the average speed dropped down to less than twenty miles an hour. When they finally arrived in Stanford it was late afternoon, and they were only half way to their destination.

Mother Daniel and Rebecca went to a small grocery across from the service station where Bert was repairing a tire and

Michael was re-securing the tie-down straps on both trucks. They came back with bread, some canned meat, over-ripe fruit, and a gallon of milk. It wasn't a hearty meal but it would have to do.

They headed for Somerset, hoping to get there before it got too dark. Ruth swapped places with Rebecca at the last minute and joined Michael as navigator.

They rode in silence for quite some time.

"Michael," Ruth broke the quiet, "Do you like me?"

Michael quickly glanced over his right shoulder to determine if Ruth were kidding him or what.

"Well, sure," he said, "Who wouldn't."

"No," she said, "Not 'like' as in 'yeah, you're Okay' but 'like' as in 'I want to always be with you'."

Michael grinned broadly, his eyes on the road.

"Are you proposing to me," he said.

"You're making fun of me," she stared straight ahead and pooched out her lower lip.

"I'm sorry," said Michael, "I didn't mean to be rude or anything. Sure I like you. I like you a lot."

"You've never tried to kiss me or take me walking alone. I've always had to be forward with you, you know, holding your hand or taking you swimming at night."

"Hey," said Michael, "Bert told me about the guy who lost his job because he was being to forward with you. I need this job."

"Mother Daniel only fired Jimmy because I asked her to. If I had liked him, he would still be with us. I didn't want him to lose his job, but he wouldn't stop pestering me. But I like you, Michael. I want you to pester me."

Ruth moved to the middle of the bench seat, put her right hand on Michael's left cheek, turned his head and kissed him firmly and somewhat wetly. He cut his eyes hard left to see the road but didn't resist her.

Ruth pulled back. "I think that you could be a better kisser. You kiss like you are kissing a relative. Loosen up your lips. Don't mash 'em closed. Keep your mouth open some."

Michael knew what she meant. He wasn't totally inexperienced in the kissing department. In Calhoun he had had a girlfriend for awhile and they spent some time groping, fumbling, and kissing when they had some privacy.

"Try me again," he said.

This time, there was passion in the connection and by the time Ruth pulled back, her breathing was heavier and her heart raced; Michael's too.

"Wow," he said.

Ruth came back for more, but Michael turned his head away.

"Whoa, this is dangerous. Not that I don't like it, but it's very distracting."

"Promise you'll kiss me again when you're not driving," said Ruth, putting her head on his shoulder.

"Sure."

"No, promise."

"I promise," said Michael.

As the twilight closed in on the caravan, Ruth put her head on Michael's right thigh and seemed to doze. His mind, however, was in turmoil. The relationship that Mother Daniel had started might not be over. If it wasn't, he wrestled with the notion of whether he could or would refuse her advances. He also knew that Ruth was like no other girl he had known in Calhoun. She was worldly, smart, self-assured, a true musician, and very attractive. He had dreamed of her several times during the summer but had kept his distance, feeling that his job depended on it. Now, she was maneuvering him into relationship that he found appealing but fraught with problems. He continued to twist the various scenarios in his mind, never finding one that turned out well. He was still in this reverie when Ruth sat up as the caravan slowed upon entering Somerset.

"The church is straight ahead," Ruth said, the dim lights from the gauges barely revealing her face. "It's on the south side of town."

Just three or four minutes later, Michael followed Bert's truck into the gravel parking area next to the Narrow Way Bible Church.

Tuesday afternoon, Reverend Smiley, Narrow Way's portly minister, walked out of his house next door to the little church and came searching for Brother Daniel. He had just had a telephone call from the pastor of the Wind Valley Bible Church in Oneida, Tennessee, where the revival was scheduled to set up camp next week. It seemed that the city fathers of Oneida had just passed an ordinance requiring that all traveling entertainment troupes needed a permit to erect temporary structures. The new ordinance was targeting carnivals and patent medicine purveyors, but revival troupes had not been excluded—an oversight, or maybe not. The permit fee was a prohibitive seventy-five dollars, so the Wind Valley Bible Church was pulling the plug on next week's revival.

Brother Daniel, not one to let a fallow week ruin the cash flow, decided that Mother Daniel should take the Lincoln and drive down into Tennessee and find another church to host the group. And the sooner the better, so that the local information network could promote their arrival.

"Annie," he said, "It don't matter which town or which church, so long as it ain't too much drive and it's on the way to Cleveland."

Cleveland, Tennessee, was scheduled two weeks hence.

"Harlow," she said, "That could take a lot of travel and expense. It might not be worth it."

"Just a couple of days, Annie. Travel cheap; sleep in the car if need be." Brother Daniel was adamant.

"Well," she responded, "I can't do this alone. I could be hours behind the wheel."

"Sister Ruth can go with you."

"Who would play the piano for the services?" she replied.

"Okay," he said, "Sister Rebecca can go."

"Harlow, she can't drive. Besides, how would it look to have a woman and her young daughter driving around the countryside like gypsies, all by their lonesome?"

Brother Daniel seemed to ponder the problem. Before he could find a solution, Mother Daniel offered one.

"Mr. Gilbert has nothing much to do, once the tents are up— he can go and share the driving."

"Like hell," said Brother Daniel. "You'll not go traipsing around the boondocks with him; talk about inappropriate. Take the boy."

"What possible good can Petey do in this situation?"

"Well of course not Petey," said Brother Daniel. "I'm talking about young Mr. Boone. He's barely older than Ruth. He could be your son. You might even position it that way if you need to."

"This idea is sounding more and more ridiculous," said Mother Daniel. "Let's just take next week off and have a little rest."

"So, we're just supposed to feed and pay the hired help for a week without any income? I don't think so," color rose in Brother Daniel's face. "The quicker you get on the road, the better."

"Mr. Boone," Brother Daniel called to Michael who was unloading chairs, "We have an assignment for you."

Early Wednesday morning, with Michael at the wheel and Mother Daniel studying a Tennessee road map, the Lincoln headed south in search of revenue.

Mother Daniel had targeted Harriman, Tennessee, about 100 miles south of Somerset. That destination was chosen because there were two other towns, Kingston and Rockwood, in the same general area, and all three towns appeared to have the population needed to hold a well-attended revival for several nights in a row. If Harriman wasn't receptive, they could move on to either of the other two.

As they drove, Mother Daniel told Michael what she knew about the Wilkins family and their unique relationship with the town of Lawrenceburg. As Michael knew, Kentucky was a place where Negroes were considered lesser humans by most white citizens and usually treated as such. His father had encouraged Michael not to be one of those people.

Michael and Mother Daniel didn't have much more conversation as they drove along in the powerful Lincoln. Neither said anything about their sexual relationship. Michael certainly wasn't going to broach the topic, although it was nearly always on his mind.

Michael drove into Harriman shortly after 2:00. In the center of town was American Temperance University, originally the headquarters of the East Tennessee Land Company, which had founded the town in the oxbow bend of the Emory River after the Civil War. The Norman Turrets at the four corners of the three-story university building looked oddly out of place and time.

Mother Daniel spied a small café still open for lunch across Roane Street and they went in.

"I'll have a fried egg sandwich," Mother Daniel told the waitress who also appeared to be the cashier. "May I get some bacon and tomato on it as well? And, sweet tea if you have it."

The waitress wasn't writing anything down. "You want mayo on the sandwich?"

"Why, yes," said Mother Daniel as she caught Michael's eye and smiled. "Mayonnaise would be wonderful."

Michael's cheeks flushed and he quickly looked down at the menu.

"Can I get this 'lunch special'?" Michael asked the waitress, pointing to a hand-written note attached to a well-fingered menu.

"You may have whatever you want, Michael," said Mother Daniel, dropping the formality of Mr. Boone.

When the waitress went to the kitchen with their order, Mother Daniel explained to Michael that the waitress or perhaps the handful of patrons who lingered over lunch would be good sources of church names in the community. She wasn't looking for the largest churches, easy to spot in the main part of town, but rather the smaller, more fundamentalist congregations, usually tucked away on the fringes of such communities.

Mother Daniel also noted that Harriman, a town with the American Temperance University in the heart of its business district, was likely pretty fundamentalist on the conservative Christian scale. She allowed that locating an appropriate church would probably not be difficult.

Her intuition proved correct. The waitress, Hazel, was also the owner of the café and a lifetime resident of Harriman. Not a church-lady herself, Hazel offered the names and locations of several local small congregations. Mother Daniel wrote them down on the back of a green order ticket that Hazel ripped from her order pad. She also suggested that if the travelers needed a room for the night that the Imperial Hotel near the railway depot was "Where the railroad people stayed." If The Imperial, with only ten rooms, was full, she suggested, "Miss Potts on Crescent has a roomin' house that is comfy and cheap."

Mother Daniel paid the bill, thanked Hazel for her help, and directed Michael back to the driver's seat as they set off to strike a revival deal.

Their first stop was a storefront building on Clinton Street. Christ the Redeemer Church did not look promising. There was no place nearby to set up the tents, and the parking situation would be a problem. The space in the building indicated that the congregation was likely no more than twenty-five or thirty people.

"Let's not bother with this one," said Mother Daniel.

From there they drove southwest on Roane Street, across the Emory River bridge, and turned right on Riggs Chapel Road, which ran hard by the river as it made its sweeping curve westward. Perhaps half a mile on the left was the Lighthouse Gospel Church, which was more promising. It was a stand-alone clapboard church on a couple of acres of land. However, there was no evidence that anyone was around. Michael tried the side door while Mother Daniel tried the front. Both were locked. Michael found another door in the back but it too was locked.

The white painted wooden sign out front included the preacher's name, Reverend Billie John Wagner. Mother Daniel wrote it down, and they headed for the Abundant Life Ministry Church, which was the back the way they had come on Riggs Chapel, but on the far side of Roane.

Abundant Life also looked promising, given its location, well off of the road and blocks from the town's center. There was an old Ford sedan parked by a side door of the brick building. Mother Daniel instructed Michael to stay in the car and she went up and opened the unlocked door and disappeared inside. He could hear her voice, faintly, calling out, "Hello." Perhaps ten minutes later she came out of the church and a very thin woman stood in the door behind her. The woman called out, "I hope that we can work something out Mrs. Daniel," and spotting Michael in the car, waved. Without turning around, Mother Daniel waved her hand in friendly acknowledgement and climbed into the car.

"She's the volunteer bookkeeper," said Mother Daniel. "I talked with the minister by phone. He's a car mechanic somewhere back in town, and says he needs to talk with his 'elders' before committing to us. Let's move on."

They went back across the bridge and down Roane Street where the Princess Theater's façade dominated the otherwise drab storefronts. A few doors down from the Princess was the Imperial Hotel, a solid-looking two-story brick building, its signage somewhat weathered. They were headed for the Calvary Miracle Church out on Webster Road. Spotting a pay phone beside a filling station, Mother Daniel had Michael pull over.

"Let's see if we can find Billie John Wagner before it gets too late."

Mother Daniel thumbed through the skinny phone directory until she got to the W's. She found Billie J. Wagner, slipped a nickel into the slot, got an operator and read her the five-digit number. A woman answered the phone.

"Is this the residence of Pastor Billie John Wagner?" Mother Daniel asked.

"Surely is, dear. Just a minute, he's in the chicken yard."

Once Pastor Billie and Mother Daniel were connected, the conversation lasted several minutes. Finally she hung up and returned to the car.

"That man missed his calling," she said. "He should have been a loan shark."

"I don't understand, Ma'am," said Michael.

"He was willing to host us if we split the take with him fifty-fifty. I offered him 25 percent, which is higher than usual, but he laughed it off. Said we'd be lucky to find a host round here on short notice. We'll see."

They found the Calvary Miracle Church where a half-dozen scruffy-looking cars and trucks were parked. It was nearing five o'clock, and this being Wednesday, the choir was rehearsing for the evening service. Once again, Mother Daniel left Michael in the car and went in the church's front entrance. She didn't come out for almost an hour.

The choir director had led her back to Reverend Herman's tiny office where Mother Daniel made her pitch for the spiritual uplift and additional funds that Brother Daniel's Good News Revival could bring to this corner of Tennessee. All the while, the eleven-person choir was mewling out hymns in the small sanctuary. Michael could hear the muffled songs, and noted that the choir was going to need a whole lot more practice than they had time for before the evening service.

Reverend Herman had many questions about Brother Daniel's interpretation of the scriptures, views on dancing, alcohol consumption, smoking, and the nature of the five sermons that would be offered during the week. When Mother Daniel mentioned the Wednesday service, which always focused on the local pastor as the personal shepherd to his congregation, Reverend Herman was sold.

"Stay for this evening's service," he had told her, "And you can make a personal plea to the congregation. You are a very convincing young lady."

Mother Daniel agreed but explained that she would first have to secure a room for night, and then come back for the 7:00 service.

"I'd try Miss Potts's roomin' house on Crescent," Reverend Herman had offered.

Mother Daniel returned to the car.

"Let's go back to town and find out if Miss Potts has room for us. It's somewhere along Crescent. It crosses Roane; can't be that hard to spot." As they drove, Mother Daniel gave Michael most of the details of her conversation with Reverend Herman.

"When I told him how wonderful his choir sounded, it likely sealed the deal," she said.

Michael wondered what percent of the "take" Mother Daniel had offered, but it was none of his business.

Miss Potts's rooming house was a faded Victorian gingerbread wonder of columns, scallops, turrets, and a wrap-around porch—chock-a-block with crumbling wicker furniture—and a stained glass panel in the front door. Two guests were sitting on the porch having a smoke. One of those guests was a tall, severe-looking woman who used an ivory cigarette holder to maximum sophisticated affect by holding it from the underside.

As Mother Daniel and Michael approached the house, nodded greetings were exchanged, but no words.

Just inside the door on a small table was a small service bell. Next to the bell was a neatly printed note: "Ring and let me know you are here." Mother Daniel rang the bell.

From down the narrow hall came a woman's cheerful voice, "Be right there." Miss Potts was nothing like the mental picture that Michael had formed of her back in the café. Instead of matronly and middle aged, Miss Potts was young, slender, fashionably dressed and quite attractive.

"Miss Potts?" Mother Daniel's voice reflected the same doubt that was crossing Michael's mind.

"In the flesh. Are you looking for a room?" the woman's smile was so engaging that Michael couldn't stop staring.

"Yes we are. My son and I need lodging for two nights," said Mother Daniel.

This statement yanked Michael out of his reverie.

"Two rooms or will you share?" said Miss Potts.

"We'll share," said Mother Daniel, "We're on a bit of a tight budget."

"These days, who isn't?" The question required no answer. "For sharing, all I have right now is a room with a trundle. The bed is a double and the trundle pulls out to a single," Miss Potts said.

"As you can see," said Mother Daniel. "My oldest is also my tallest. He'll probably insist on the double so he can sleep diagonally. We'll work it out."

"I'm sure you will. It's twenty two dollars a night and that includes breakfast and supper for both of you. You will share the upstairs bath with Mrs. Henlein in room three, and Mr. Danforth in room five; lovely people, both. Will you be having supper this evening?"

Mother Daniel explained her commitment to attend the Calvary Miracle Church service. She offered that Michael, however, could stay for supper. And so, after taking their modest luggage to Room Four, Mother Daniel drove back to the Calvary Miracle Church, and left Michael to join strangers around the long dining table.

Besides Mrs. Henlein, the cigarette-holder woman, and Mr. Danforth, a school supply salesman from Knoxville, both of whom they had seen on the porch, the other three guests included a man from Nashville, who worked for the electric company, and two middle-aged brothers who were in Harriman to settle their father's estate.

The meal was served by Miss Potts and an older woman whose graying hair was a swirling, soaring pile held together with costume jewelry clips and pins. They brought in platters and bowls of chicken thighs, cream corn, baked potatoes, pickled beets, and squares of corn bread. There were two pitchers of iced tea, and on a side table, a coffee pot kept hot with a small flame underneath.

This was a meal like Michael hadn't seen since leaving Calhoun and Aunt Elizabeth's home cooking. Once the table was set, Miss Potts offered a brief blessing from where she stood near the kitchen door. Then, the guests began passing the platters and bowls, left to right, around the table. Michael paid attention to the portions that others were taking so that he wouldn't embarrass himself for seeming a glutton.

"Take all you need, Mr. Daniel," Miss Potts said as she watched her guests fill their plates, and noticed that Michael was taking smallish portions.

Of course, Michael, not realizing that she was talking to him, made no reply. The Electric company man, sitting across from Daniel said, "Son, I think Miss Potts wants you to eat more of her victuals."

Michael looked up at the man and then realized that he, Michael Boone, was "Mr. Daniel," and that he could be in danger of revealing their mother-son cover.

"Oh, sorry," he blurted out, addressing Miss Potts, "I wasn't listening. I guess I was too busy thinking about all this wonderful food. I'm sure I'll have seconds."

"Well," she replied, "There's plenty, so don't be shy."

There was polite conversation around the table including queries into how much longer the brothers would be in Harriman working out their father's estate issues.

"Two days more, probably," offered one of the brothers.

"We just have to arrange the auction with the attorney. We won't be here for that but we need to sign the contract," said the other.

"So," said cigarette-holder lady, "Young Mr. Daniel, what brings you and your mother to Harriman?"

This time, Michael knew that the comment was directed at him. He explained that Brother Daniel's Good News Revival was up in Somerset, Kentucky, and that he a Mother Daniel were booking the troupe to appear in Harriman next week at the Calvary Miracle Congregation Church.

"Your father's a preacher then," said Mr. Danforth.

"No," said Michael, "My dad is a farmer."

"I'm confused," said the electric company man. "I figured that Brother Daniel would be your father, given that you are here with your mother, or is Brother Daniel her father?"

Michael looked across the table and felt himself flush. He hesitated and then began slowly, trying to think ahead of what to say.

"Um, well, Brother Daniel isn't my real dad. He's my, uh, stepdad. He, uh, married my mother after my dad went to Oregon."

"So, your real last name isn't Daniel, I assume," said the cigarette-holder lady. "Or did the preacher adopt you?"

"Uh, no Ma'am, my last name is Boone," said Michael. "I just use the name Daniel."

Michael was learning, in the heat of the moment, that lying convincingly was an art, one at which he wasn't very good. The web of deceit could truly become tangled.

Michael grabbed a coffee cup, got up and headed for the side table coffee pot, hoping to change the topic of conversation away from himself.

"May I get coffee for anyone else?"

"Capital idea, lad," said Mr. Danforth.

With that, the conversation changed directions to include predictions of weather, rumors regarding federal public work projects that might come to Tennessee, and some good-natured speculation that the electric company man might not be telling all he knew about those proposed programs. He just smiled and shrugged.

After peach cobbler dessert, everyone but Michael went to the front porch for more conversation and, for Mrs. Henlein and Mr. Danforth, a smoke. Michael, anxious about having to explain his life by telling more lies, went up to his room and pulled out the trundle bed. He took the opportunity to have a proper bath, and then sat in the overstuff chair near the window, where there was a table lamp, and read from the book he had brought along. Around 9:30 he turned out the light and shoehorned himself into the trundle. Knowing that Mother Daniel would be coming in and preparing for bed sometime soon, Michael couldn't sleep. His expectation of what would happen caused his breath to become shallow and his penis to rise. He lay there on his side, staring across the wooden floor thinking about the feel and smell of her. Her skin, smooth and then damp as their efforts became more ardent; her breasts, with their modest weight and firming nipples, and the musky smell of lavender and sex.

A large wooden table clock atop the chest-of-drawers ticked loudly and seemed to slow. He heard someone in the hallway and then the bathroom door close. Water ran. He could hear Mr. Danforth gargling then the distinct sound of urination into the toilet, followed by a flush. Time was definitely slowing.

Several minutes later, Mrs. Henlein used the bath to prepare for bed. She made many of the same sounds as Mr. Danforth, except Michael couldn't hear her peeing. Maybe she doesn't pee, he thought. He could smell her cigarette smoke, and Michael imagined her standing at the mirror practicing her elegant under-hand hold on the ivory holder. She ran a bath, and it was at least twenty minutes before he heard the bath door open and her room door close. The minutes ticked by.

Finally, the room door quietly opened and Mother Daniel slipped in. The only noise was the creaking of the floor as she tiptoed across the room to where her suitcase was sitting. She put it on the bed. Michael heard the two snap latches pop open and the rustling sound of Mother Daniel gathering things. She left the room and the bath door closed softly. The water ran briefly. Eventually, the toilet flushed and she came down the hall and padded into the room on bare feet. Michael could see her feet from his vantage point until she passed the foot of the bed.

There was additional rustling as she put the suitcase on the floor and draped her clothes across the chair where Michael had sat reading. The box springs squeaked as she put her weight on the bed and she lay back.

"Oh, God," she whispered into the darkness, "a real bed."

Michael wanted to answer with something clever but couldn't think of anything. He was nearly holding his breath so as not to reveal his state of anxiety.

"Good night, Michael," she said just above a whisper.

Michael did not respond. Within minutes of saying goodnight, Mother Daniel was asleep, her breathing steady and relaxed. He lay there awake for at least another hour, calming himself. Maybe his fear that their coupling would never happen again was true. That would be a good thing, he thought to himself, wouldn't it?

The next morning, Michael awoke early and he very quietly slipped into his dungarees and checkered shirt and, carrying his shoes and socks, slipped into the hallway. He stopped at the bathroom and peed against the porcelain side of the bowl to keep his activity as noiseless as possible.

In the dining room, the woman with the high hair was setting the table for breakfast. She offered Michael some coffee and he took it to the front porch where he put on his socks and shoes. The morning was pleasantly cool, and dew covered the little bit of front lawn between the house and the sidewalk. He could see where a squirrel had left a trail from one tree to another across the grass, soaking up the dew with its body. The coffee was a bit weak and the coffee cups daintier and more fragile than what he had ever used before.

Breakfast was served between 6:30 and 8:00. As the guests arrived at the dining room, Miss Potts would have the high hair lady prepare the breakfast. Michael was the first one to eat. Mother Daniel was the last. After he ate and to avoid idle conversation where he might slip up again, Michael took a walk down to Roane Street and looked into the shop windows. He wandered back to Miss Potts's rooming house just before 8:00.

He went up to the room and put his dirty underwear and socks into his canvas duffle. He went to the bathroom, brushed his teeth and ran wet fingers through his hair. Using a comb on his tangle of reddish-brown hair was impossible. When he went back to the room, Mother Daniel was sitting at the vanity brushing her hair. She looked at him in the reflection of the mirror.

"Good morning, Mr. Boone. Did you sleep well in the trundle?"

"Yes Ma'am. It's very comfortable compared to the bedroll in the truck," Michael replied.

"Good, because we have lots of work to do today," she said.

"I told them that Brother Daniel is my step-father," Michael blurted out.

"Told who?" Mother Daniel turned on the vanity chair and look at him.

"The folks at dinner last night," he said.

"Why did you do that?"

"Well," he said, "I told them that my dad was a farmer before I could stop myself. So then, I had to explain why Brother Daniel isn't my father."

"Did you explain anything else that I need know?" Mother Daniel had turned back to the mirror.

"I don't think so," Michael slumped into the chair.

"Okay," said Mother Daniel. "I divorced your father years ago because he was a drunk and found you a better father in Brother Daniel, a man of the cloth."

"My dad isn't a drunk."

"Your dad was never my husband, either. But that's the story and we're both sticking to it. Understand?"

"Yes Ma'am."

They met Reverend Herman at the church at nine-thirty. Mother Daniel had brought fifty flyers promoting Brother Daniel's Good News Revival. Each one had to be filled in with the correct dates, times, and location. Between the three of them, all of the flyers were ready to be displayed by eleven.

Reverend Herman took about ten of the flyers. His job was to approach those churches in town that might deign to post a flyer on their bulletin board. Mother Daniel and Michael headed to Roane Street where they split up and canvassed each retail location, hoping to place a flyer in as many storefront windows as possible. This took longer than Michael had anticipated because not all of the stores had someone on-hand who could make such a decision, or that someone was busy "back in the office." Mostly, Michael felt the sting of rejection and a time or two, outright hostility. When he and Mother Daniel met back at the car, he still had fourteen of his original twenty flyers. She had been a bit more successful, but still had placed only ten.

Michael apologized for not having done better.

"Don't be silly," said Mother Daniel. "We've put flyers up in sixteen businesses in this little town. That's better than I thought we would do. We can tack up the rest on light and telephone poles at the stop signs around town."

They went back to the café where they had eaten yesterday and Hazel greeted them by pointing to their flyer, already in her front window, thanks to Mother Daniel. She motioned them to take the front booth and came over with two waters and some silverware.

"Whatcha havin' today?"

"Michael, why don't we both try Hazel's Thursday Special? I like Salisbury steak, collards and fried potatoes, don't you?" asked Mother Daniel.

"Yes Ma'am."

"Two specials comin' up," Hazel turned and headed for the kitchen.

Michael looked at Mother Daniel once Hazel was out of earshot and said, "What's Salisbury steak?"

"You'll see."

After lunch, they drove back to the Calvary Miracle Church. Reverend Herman was in his small office. He hadn't had much luck posting the fliers at other churches. Most of them didn't want their congregants attending a revival on a Wednesday night, thus missing their own service, and they didn't want to see diminished amounts in their offering plates Sunday because people had offered money to the Lord via Brother Daniel earlier in the week.

"We certainly understand, Reverend Herman. It is not unexpected. Michael and I will tack up the remaining flyers around town this afternoon. We will head back to Somerset after breakfast in the morning. Our group will be here at the church Monday afternoon," said Mother Daniel.

"I hope we can generate good attendance," said Reverend Herman. "We sure could use a morale boost around here, and Lord knows our church needs extra revenue."

"We always do our best," said Mother Daniel.

Goodbyes were said, Michael climbed behind the wheel, and they were off to post flyers wherever Mother Daniel determined that they would get the most readership. By the time they were out of flyers it was nearly 6:00, and dinner at Miss Potts's was at 7:00.

When they arrived back at the boarding house, Michael retrieved his book and took it to the far end of the wide front porch. Mother Daniel went to the room to "freshen up." Neither took the opportunity to visit with the other guests until they gathered at the dinner table. As it turned out, no one asked more questions of Mother Daniel or Michael about his lineage. While there was polite inquiry about their day's effort to generate interest in Brother Daniel's Good News Revival, and a question or two about Mother Daniel's other children, nothing required Michael to lie.

After dinner, Mother Daniel and Michael were invited to play a new version of The Landlord's Game, a board game that had recently been renamed Monopoly. The other players included Miss Potts, Mrs. Henlein, Mr. Danforth, and the electric company man, Michael had trouble recalling his name. What Michael noted about the man was his odd haircut. Whoever cut the man's hair hadn't seemed to notice that it was very lopsided or even tried to even it up. Every time Michael looked at him it seemed that the man was always tilting to one side.

With six players, the game was fun but slow, and by 11:00, with most of the money and property in the possession of the electric company man, the other active players yielded. Michael had been the first to go bankrupt, followed by Mrs. Henlein. Both stuck around to watch the others struggle to avoid their fate. With catty remarks about "the big utilities taking over the world," the guests said their goodnights and headed for bed or the front porch for a final smoke.

"You and your son have the bathroom first, while Mr. Danforth and I retire for a smoke on the porch," said Mrs. Henlein to Mother Daniel.

"Thank you, that's very kind," said Mother Daniel.

Michael and Mother Daniel went to the room where she instructed him to do his bathroom business first. He didn't take long, and when she left the room upon his return, she turned out the light, leaving the only illumination a distant and dim street lamp that barely penetrated through the thin curtains pulled across the bay windows.

Michael peeled down to his underwear and tucked himself into the trundle. He could hear the bath water run, and then the soft splashes of Mother Daniel having a proper bath herself.

Given last night's experience, Michael had little sense of anticipation, but the thought of sharing the room with her still caused a twinge of anxiety. He closed his eyes and tried to think back through the plot of the book he was reading, *Jumping Off Place* by Marian Hurd McNeely.

Mother Daniel came into the room quietly and padded barefoot across the floor. There was the rustle of clothes being draped over the chair and things being put in or taken out of the suitcase. Then the bed springs gave a soft groan as she pulled back the covers and slipped between the cool sheets. She rolled to her left, reached her arm down and touched Michael's hair. Startled, he jerked slightly.

"Still awake?" she said.

"Yes Ma'am."

"Come up here," she said as she raised the covers on his side of the bed, as if horizontally opening the flap of one of their tents.

He unwound from the cramped trundle, got onto his knees and crawled into the welcoming semi-darkness. He could see enough. She wore nothing but a hint of lavender.

Chapter Eight
Love, Letter

IN THE FOLLOWING four weeks, Brother Daniel's Good News Revival made its way south through Tennessee and Georgia. The Harriman stop did not produce much money, mostly because their presence was promoted on such short notice. After Harriman there was Cleveland, Tennessee, then Greenville, Georgia, and finally, Camilla, forty miles north of the Georgia-Florida state line. Tallahassee is only eighteen miles south of that line. Ruth and Rebecca were excited to be getting close to home and friends.

During the two weeks following Mother Daniel and Michael's trip together to Harriman, Michael found himself craving private time with Mother Daniel. His mood, more morose than was his nature, piqued Bert's attention. While they were in Greenville, a small town southwest of Atlanta, Bert started probing Michael about his subdued demeanor.

On Thursday night, when fire and the brimstone were being dished out in heaping quantities to the faithful and fearful, Bert motioned Michael over to his truck.

"Let's have a walk, it's too loud to concentrate around here," said Bert

They walked down the gravel drive of the Victory Life Mission

Church toward the blacktop road.

"You want to talk about what's bothering you?" Bert struck a match with his thumbnail and lit a cigarette.

"Nothin's bothering me," said Michael.

"That's damned hard to believe. Ever since you got back from Harriman on that trip with Mother Daniel, you've been hangdog and quiet. Even Ruth asked me what your problem was," Bert blew smoke from his nostrils.

"Really, I'm fine; maybe homesick some," said Michael, staring into the distance.

"Kinda late in the season to just now be getting lonesome for your aunt and cousins. Seems like that would have happened back in the summer," Bert had stopped walking and was looking at Michael's eyes.

Avoiding direct eye contact, Michael blinked several times and looked at the ground.

"Let me tell you something," said Bert. "In '31, up in Indiana, Mother Daniel made herself available to me. She found an excuse to get me alone and made it clear that she wanted me to be her lover. She is an attractive woman and I was sorely tempted. However, I had lost a good teaching job in New York for dipping my wick in the same pot from whence my paycheck came, if you understand the tortured metaphor. So, I refused her advances and she has held it against me some, but I didn't get fired or shot by an irate husband. I'm thinking that maybe something of similar nature might have happened to you on that Harriman trip."

"Maybe," said Michael, still staring at his sorry shoes.

"Okay, Michael, I'll stop giving you the third degree. But I will give you some advice. If you are screwing the boss lady, you're on dangerous ground."

"It wasn't my idea," Michael almost swallowed the words.

Bert let a few seconds pass before he said, "That doesn't surprise me, but it won't change the heartbreak or blame if someone, besides me, catches on. Watch yourself, Michael."

Michael nodded but said nothing.

Bert was right, Michael thought as they walked back toward the lights of the revival tent. He needed to refuse any further advances by Mother Daniel, even if it cost him the job. He didn't know when she might arrange another sex education class, but he felt sure that she would find a way, perhaps even a risky visit to his truck one night. Michael had a brief vision of Brother Daniel standing at the bed of the truck, pistol in hand, aiming to shoot the lovers.

Determined to do the right thing, Michael's mood brightened and he made an effort to spend more of his leisure time reading with and talking to Ruth as they made their way back to Florida. Ruth seemed pleased with the renewed attention, and managed to be his navigator on the trip from Greenville to Camilla. As Michael drove, Ruth read aloud from one of her new novels.

She had bought three more books when they were in Cleveland, Tennessee, where there was a small stationary store that sold school supplies. It also had a small inventory of novels and non-fiction books. With Bert's advice, Ruth bought two Joseph Conrad books, *The Rescue* and *Payment Deferred,* and a recently released book by William Faulkner, *The Sound and the Fury*. Bert borrowed the Faulkner book right away, anxious to see what the writer had done within the format of a novel.

Ruth had chosen *The Rescue* so that she and Michael could share the experience during the tedious road trip. The story is an adventure and love story set at sea in the Far East. Ruth had a knack for reading aloud, and changing her voice very slightly as the different characters spoke. Soon, Michael was able to follow who was saying what without the normal narrative identifiers.

When Ruth finished the first chapter, she closed the book and asked Michael, "What do you think? Is she a 'good' or is she a *great* writer?"

Michael, his eyes on the road said, "I don't know. Good, I suppose."

"Why not great? There must be some reason."

"You sound like Miss Darnell, my English teacher, back in Calhoun," Michael said, grinning at his own comment.

"I think she's great," replied Ruth.

"Maybe," said Michael. "If people are still reading her book fifty years from now, then I would say she qualifies as great."

"I'll bet Hemingway's books will still be popular fifty years on," said Ruth. "What do you think?"

"Come on Ruthie, let's see what happens next; read the next chapter."

"Keep your shirt on, buster," she replied. Then, she looked at him slyly and said, "But, you don't always have to keep your shirt on."

He stole a glance. With the hint of a smile, she cocked her head slightly to the side and shrugged her shoulders. With that, she opened the book and began Chapter Two.

It was a long haul from Greenville to Camilla, and there were several stops for gasoline, restroom breaks, snacks, and three flat tires. Michael's loathing of the air pump only increased. By the time the caravan reached the Mount Gilead Redeemer Church in Camilla, it was well past dark.

"Let's just get the big family tent up tonight," said Brother Daniel. "The girls can put their cots in there for one night."

No one argued, so Michael and Bert, with some help from the rest, erected the family shelter and populated it with the necessary bedding. They used the headlamps of the trucks and the Lincoln to illuminate the process. By the time the task was complete, everyone quietly sought sleep. Everyone was deep-muscle tired.

Their late evening arrival meant that Tuesday would be a more hectic day of work for everyone—except for Brother Daniel, who kept to his tent "working on the week's messages to the fallen."

Across the field from the church was Camilla's High School. The Eagles has a gymnasium with shower facilities, and over the years, Mother Daniel had arranged with Pastor Glazner, who also taught Mechanical Drawing at the school, for the Daniel troupe to use the showers after the track team had vacated, late in the afternoon. Tuesday's arduous work schedule put Michael into a showering frame of mind by the time Mother Daniel and the girls were setting up for supper.

He asked Mother Daniel for a towel, bundled up some fresh clothes and trudged across the open field. Bert hollered after him, "Hey, bank walker, save some hot water for me. I'm coming over after supper."

Michael gave him a wave without turning around.

The boy's shower room had hooks on the wall and long benches bolted to the floor but no lockers. Michael hung up his clean clothes and pulled off his grimy work clothes. There were three metal tanks sitting about nine feet overhead and against the wall, supported by a sturdy wooden frame. Each tank had small pipe projecting from the bottom to which was screwed a round head that looked like the end of a flower watering bucket, with little holes all over the surface. On each pipe was a knob that, when opened, allowed the water in the tank to drizzle down. Each tank had its own small gas heater that had to be lit by hand to warm the water. Michael had no matches, so the temperature of the shower was tepid but not unpleasant. If there had been hot water earlier, the track team had used most of it.

Scrubbed clean with the school's industrial-grade soap, Michael did his best to dry with the thin towel. He avoided his tangle of hair at first, knowing that it would simply soak the towel and make further drying fruitless. He used what was left of the dry part of the towel on his hair and then used his fingers to arrange his hair in some sort of orderly fashion, a task that never satisfied a young man who always wanted straight hair. He wrapped the thin, damp towel around his waist and continued to pick at his unruly mop of hair.

"Better put your shirt on, buster," Ruth's voice startled him and he turned around. "Supper's almost ready."

Michael clutched at the towel, insuring that it wouldn't slip off.

"Uh, sure," he said, "I'll be right there."

Ruth walked over to the row of hooks and took down his shorts and undershirt. She came to Michael, holding his underwear to her chest.

"Will you need any help getting dressed?" she said, her voice low and flirty.

"No, no, but, uh, thanks."

She took his right hand and placed the underwear in his grip. He looked down at his skivvies and then back into her eyes. Ruth raised herself on tip toes, put her left hand on the back of his neck and pulled him close for a kiss like the one that they had shared in the truck several days ago. He felt the bulge of her breast against his bare chest.

There was no escaping the fact that his ardor was beginning to show through the towel. He felt it press slowly against her as she held the embrace for more than just a few seconds. He knew that she could feel it.

Ruth pulled away, took a quick glance at the rising projection, turned and walked to the door. Without turning around she said, "We need to talk about things, Michael."

Ruth's comment concentrated Michael's mind. It wasn't a pleasant anticipation but neither was it dreadful. Anxiety was more the feeling, like waiting for test results when you were unsure of your answers even though you had studied. How bad could it be? Not that bad, surely; very, very bad, maybe. He had to endure a few days of not knowing. Many thoughts crowded each other aside. Maybe Ruth suspected his relationship with her mother? Or, perhaps, she was planning to bolt, and wanted Michael to go with her, stealing the truck and heading for California to find his parents and siblings. Oh, wait, could it be that Rebecca or Ruth had stolen Brother Daniel's pistol and were plotting his demise? His thoughts became jumbled and none of them seemed like good things.

Sunday morning, both Mother Daniel and Father Daniel attended services at the Mount Gilead Redeemer Church. Petey and Rebecca went as well, all of them supplied with flyers to hand out to the congregation. Ruth had begged off, citing a "terrible headache."

Michael was sitting in the shade of the truck, trying to read Faulkner, whose style was difficult. Bert had recommended it, but warned that the author was brilliant but complex.

Ruth came around to Michael's side of the truck.

"Let's go for a walk, Michael. We need to talk."

Michael got up, dusted off his butt and followed her away from the compound and towards a small copse of trees where the church members had put a picnic area with a fire pit and three tables in the shade.

They walked in silence. When they got to the trees, Ruth sat down on top of one of the tables, her feet on the bench seat. Michael sat beside her.

"I want a different life," she finally said, "And I want you to help me."

Michael said nothing.

"They'll pull me out of school next March to start next summer's swing but I don't want to go back on the road. I want to stay home and graduate with the rest of my class in May. Brother

Daniel wouldn't stand for that," she said. "So, I plan to sneak out of Tallahassee by the end of March and stay away until they're too far away to come back and get me. Mother will be angry but she'll understand."

Michael was just shaking his head while she talked.

"We can take the bus to Jacksonville, stay there a week and then come back to Tallahassee. I'll only miss a week of school, and we can stay in the house."

"We?" said Michael, turning to stare at her.

"I can't do this on my own, it would be too dangerous."

"Your plan has several problems, Ruth. First, I would lose my job and they would probably send the cops looking for us. Second, your neighbors would know we were back living in the house, track down your mom, and she would jump in the Lincoln and come back to Tallahassee to shoot me and wring your neck while she was about it. No thanks," said Michael.

They sat there in silence for several minutes. Ruth seemed to be concentrating.

Finally she said, "You're probably right. But I'm serious, Michael, I won't go back on the road in March. If my plan has problems, let's come up with another.

"Let me think about it," said Michael. "There ought to be a way that doesn't involve breaking the law, running away, sacrificing my job, and risking death at the hands of an angry parent." Michael's thoughts included the complicating factor of his history with Ruth's mother. Running off with her daughter seemed like a particularly bad idea, although the thought of he and Ruth on the lam together had a certain appeal.

"Well," she said, "We have the winter to come up with something."

"Why are you assuming that I will play a role in any solution?" said Michael.

"Because you love me."

"I do?"

"Sure you do," she smiled, "You just haven't figured that out yet."

Ruth leaned over and pecked Michael's cheek. Michael slowly shook his head and failed to suppress a smile.

Although Tallahassee was the capitol of Florida, the population was less than 11,000 in 1933, and most residents lived within a mile or two of the capital building downtown. It was a small town that impersonated a city when the politicians were there. The place that the Daniel clan called home was at the northeast outskirts of town, on Highway 90, which zigzagged east from there until it ran into the Atlantic Ocean at Jacksonville Beach.

The sturdy stone house that Mother Daniel owned was on five acres of land and sat well back of the blacktop highway. In previous winters, Bert and some local contractors had built a permanent out-building some fifty yards behind the house. The wooden structure included storage space for the revival tent and other equipment, and a workshop where Bert could mend things, paint, work on the vehicles or whatever needed to be done to prepare for the next travel season. The building also included a sleeping room with twin beds, a shower and toilet room, a small kitchen area with a running-water sink, a propane stove and oven, and an electric refrigerator. It was, as Bert referred to it, a bunkhouse with two trucks in the corral instead of horses.

When the caravan pulled into the property on October 27, it was just after noon. Bert directed Michael to drive his truck to the bunkhouse and backed it up to the big metal door at the far end.

While Bert and Michael were attending to equipment stowage, Brother Daniel unlocked a metal switch-box attached to a light pole near the highway, and as he threw the large double-pronged switch, electricity surged through the house and outbuilding. Ruth went to a silver propane tank behind the house. She had a special tool and used it to open the valve that sent gas into the house. She came to the bunkhouse and repeated the process on a smaller silver tank outside the rear door. Brother Daniel fetched a three-foot iron T-bar and opened two separate water valves, one for the house and one for the outbuilding.

Although Michael was used to electric power in a house, the propane gas appliances and running water were luxuries to him.

He and Bert worked until 7:00 pm and then gave the shower its winter debut. The water sputtered, stopped, started, and great bursts of air, trapped in the line, exploded out every few seconds until a steady flow of rusty water circled the drain. Gradually the water cleared and warmed. The propane water heater had done its work since being lit early in the afternoon.

"Be my guest, roommate, and have the inaugural bath," said Bert. "I'll go up to the plantation house and collect us some supper. There are some of the famously cheap Daniel's towels in that cupboard by the sink."

Michael shed his clothes and stepped under the warm water and let it run down through his hair, across his face, down his neck, and soak his weary body.

By the time he was putting on some of his semi-clean clothes—washing clothes on the road had been a very haphazard affair and not always fully successful—Bert returned from the house with large wooden tray full of food including roast chicken, creamed corn, mustard greens with bacon, and a tossed green salad. He pulled two plates out of a cabinet by the sink and silverware from a drawer in the table that was both workbench and dining table.

"Michael, grab a couple of glasses from that shelf by the ice box and run us some cold water from the sink," said Bert.

"Mother Daniel and Rebecca made a grocery run this afternoon and we're eating like kings tonight," he said, pulling up a wooden chair to the table. "And," he continued, "we'll dig in without the interruption of the famous Brother Daniel dialogue with his maker. On the other hand, you can say your own grace if it suits you."

"It's okay," said Michael, "I believe that the Lord knows that I am grateful."

When they had finished, Michael took it upon himself to clean up and put the dishes and utensils away. Bert headed to take a shower. Just as Michael was finishing up his chores, Ruth appeared at the screen door.

"Are you the lady of the house?" she teased through the screen. She was holding two small plates, each one loaded with a generous slice of chocolate cake.

"I certainly am if that cake is for my family," said Michael.

He stepped over and opened the screen and Ruth brushed past. She smelled of good soap and lavender. For a moment, the scent evoked the memory of Mother Daniel's naked body, beckoning him to join her in the rooming house bed. He gave his head a quick shake to clear his mind.

"I thought that you and Bert should get your dessert delivered in person," she smiled at Michael and he again realized that her pale blue eyes, pecan shell-colored hair and athletic body were the mirror image of her mother, minus the eighteen or nineteen-year difference in age.

"Hey Bert," called Michael, "dessert has been delivered by a beautiful princess."

From the sleeping room Bert yelled back, "Just let me get decent so as not to embarrass her highness."

Ruth asked if everything was working in the bunkhouse, and if he and Bert needed anything.

Michael asked if he would have time to go a grocery store in the next day or two to get some things to stock the little icebox. He really wanted to have some milk and fresh fruit on hand.

"It's a refrigerator, Michael, not an icebox."

"Oh, yeah, okay, refrigerator," he acknowledged her teasing.

"Just tell mother what you want and she will get it," said Ruth. "She's going to town again tomorrow for more groceries and the mail."

The troupe had received general delivery mail twice during the summer, once in Brick Chapel in mid-July and once in Brookville, the last week of August. Mother Daniel had arranged for these mail deliveries before the group had left Florida last spring.

Michael didn't get his mail from Brick Chapel until he rejoined the group in Linden after leaving Indianapolis. There were two letters from Aunt Elizabeth, including a fat envelope stuffed with two letters from his mother.

Michael learned several key things from these missives, not the least of which was that Baby Nell had contracted scarlet fever last April and nearly died, but was now fully recovered, as recounted in his mother's second letter. Further, his father's skill as a farmer had made such a good impression on a fellow who was in the Central Valley buying grapes for his grape juice facility in Sonoma County, that he offered Mr. Boone a full-time job as the farm's agronomist. Over the Fourth of July holiday, the whole family moved into a two-bedroom house on the grounds of the Orchard Fresh Grape Juice Farm. As soon as Prohibition was lifted, as it looked like it surely would be, the whole operation would go back to making wine, just as it had before the nation's foolish Constitutional attempt to legislate the public's consumption of alcohol. Ironically, while this good fortune was upon his family, they had no idea that Michael was recovering from severe burns after his heroic action in Martinsville.

Matthew, Michael's little brother, was proving to be quite the accomplished guitar player after one of the immigrants from Oklahoma gave him the instrument in return from some of Matthew's help baby-sitting his three motherless children. The poor man's wife had succumbed to typhoid fever during the trip to California. Matthew was also showing promise as a baseball standout among the migrant boys his age and was a devout Brooklyn Dodger fan. Michael's mother mentioned that Matthew kept a picture of his big brother beside his cot and often asked his parents to tell him things about Michael that he might remember. Matthew, she said, looked very much like Michael with beautiful tousled red-brown hair just like their Irish grandma.

Michael had sent several letters to his parents and Aunt Elizabeth, all addressed to Aunt Elizabeth's farm, but he never mentioned the Fourth of July fire, his actions, or the resulting injuries. He decided that there was no need to create worry. Besides, he was fine now.

"Want a moonlit tour of the Daniel's plantation?" Ruth's question brought Michael back from his reverie.

"Uh, well," he said, looking at Bert, "I don't know just now."

"Take a walk with the princess," said Bert. "But watch your manners and keep an eye peeled for the King and Queen."

"Yeah, sure," said Michael, speaking to both of them.

Ruth and Michael walked along the fence line that separated the property from a small cattle farm that surrounded the Daniel's property.

"That's the Kelly's land," said Ruth indicating the neighbor's pasture. "They raise beef cattle, and if the wind is in the wrong direction, it really stinks."

"We have some cows back home," said Michael, "but they're dairy cows. I guess Aunt Elizabeth is milking them now. It was my job before."

"A dairy cow killed my father," said Ruth.

"I know," said Michael, "Rebecca told me. I'm sorry."

"It was a long time ago. I barely remember him. He had pale blue eyes just like mother and he used to push me around in a wheelbarrow."

"He sounds like a nice man."

"I guess."

Ruth took Michael's hand and they cut back across the property to the bunkhouse, coming up from behind where the trucks were parked under a roof extending from the structure. Ruth stopped at the back of Michael's truck. She turned and faced him.

"You said that you would kiss me again, remember? Well, here's your chance."

Michael's hesitation was brief. He took her face in his hands and initiated a rather long and very wet kiss. There were tongues involved, as well as changes in breathing. Ruth put her arms around his back and pulled them firmly together. There was clearly desire in her actions. He was aware of the press of her hips and her breasts and his own ardor kicked in.

This time, Michael was the more aggressive as desire flooded clearer thoughts from his head. He slipped his left hand under Ruth's blouse and discovered that Mother Daniel wasn't the only one to go without a bra from time to time. Using his recently gained knowledge of things breast related, he cupped his hand under her right breast and, using his thumb, lightly brushed the nipple back and forth. Almost immediately, it stiffened and Ruth began a faint humming.

Michael pulled back and softly asked if she wanted to get up on the truck bed where his bedroll was still spread.

Ruth hesitated and then whispered in his ear, "Not tonight, it's not a good time."

Michael pulled his hand away and took a short step back.

"You don't have to stop what you were doing," she said.

"Yes, yes I do," he replied. "It will get to be too much. I'm sorry, I really am."

"Too much is what I want, Michael," said Ruth, "Just not this particular night; maybe in three or four days."

She stepped forward and re-engaged their embrace.

"You do love me, you know," she said.

Michael wasn't sure he could disagree. Lust and love, however, are often mistaken for one another, a lesson that Michael had yet to learn.

***

The next morning after breakfast, Michael and Bert set about changing all the fluids in both trucks. Michael was halfway under Bert's truck trying to loosen the drain plug when he heard Mother Daniel's voice.

"Mr. Gilbert, Mr. Boone," she called, "I'm going to the grocery. What can I get for you?"

Michael looked out and saw her feet next to his own.

Bert, who was putting new oil in Michael's truck, wiped his hands on the oily rag that did little to clean off the grime, stood up and turned around.

"Well, Ma'am," he offered. "I could use some good strong Cuban coffee, a fifth of Kentucky bourbon, a box of chocolate truffles, a can or two of goose pate and some of that special French bread, you know, the kind with crispy crust and the warm soft inside," he beamed at his own quick wit.

"I'm sure those items won't be a problem, Mr. Gilbert," she responded. "If they don't have exactly what you want, I'll find suitable substitutes as usual. And for you, Mr. Boone?"

Michael, still on his back under the engine called back, "I'd like some fresh fruit of any kind, Ma'am, and if I could have some milk and creamer in the ice box that would be great."

"Refrigerator," she replied.

"Yes, Ma'am," he said, "refrigerator."

"We get our milk and cream from our neighbor," she said. "I'll have one of the girls bring a large pitcher of milk. Let it sit in the refrigerator overnight, and skim the cream off in the morning. I'll see what decent fruit they have at the store. Do you have any letters to mail, gentlemen? I'll be stopping by the Post Office."

Bert had a letter ready to mail to Tall Nurse even though she had not responded to the other two he had sent from the road.

Mother Daniel was walking away when Michael called out, "Ma'am, if they have enough, I'd like some of that goose patey too."

Neither man could see if she was smiling but she was nodding her head slightly as if enjoying the exchange and said, "I see that you have developed Mr. Gilbert's more refined taste in food and humor."

Bert came over to where Michael was prone, bent over and looked under the truck, his face almost upside down. "Good one, Michael." His upside down smile was grotesque.

Just a few minutes later, Rebecca came to the bunkhouse with a pitcher of milk. She let herself in the front door and put it in the refrigerator.

She called back toward where they were working on the trucks, "Milk's in the ice box," and she headed back to the house.

"Refrigerator," Michael called out.

It would be another generation and more before people stopped saying "icebox" on a regular basis. Years later, Michael's grown children would needle him about using such old-fashioned terms, including calling their hi-fi system "the Victrola," and the Sears washing machine "the wash tub." Michael would laugh it off and told them that old habits are hard to break.

After lunch, which Ruth had brought down to the bunkhouse, Bert and Michael sat in the shade while Bert rolled a smoke.

"I'm planning to hitch up to Indy next week. I need to set things straight with Linda."

"What about work?" Michael asked.

"Not that much needs doing right now, and Brother Daniel will be happy to have me off of the payroll for a few days, believe me. You can handle any chores."

"You really have a thing for that Nurse, huh?" said Michael.

"I suppose I do. I don't want my affinity for alcohol to mess up what could be an important relationship. At least I need to try."

As the afternoon wound down, Mother Daniel came to the bunkhouse with supplies and mail. Instead of Cuban coffee she brought Eight O' Clock Coffee, in place of bourbon she had a six-pack of RC Cola, no truffles but there were four milk-chocolate bars, no goose pate but two small cans of deviled ham and in place of the French bread, a loaf of unsliced white bread from the local bakery.

She handed Michael four pieces of mail, three from Aunt Elizabeth's address, two of which were bulky with other letters inside, and a large manila envelope with a return address for Vanderbilt University in Nashville, Tennessee. Michael didn't know anyone in Tennessee.

His curiosity piqued, he opened the big envelope first. Inside there were three printed booklets, "Vanderbilt, a University of Tradition", "Schedule of Classes, Winter Semester 1934" and "Vanderbilt Housing and Board Plans."

Covering those documents was a letter.

"Dear Mr. Boone,"

"We are pleased to welcome you to the freshman class scheduled to matriculate in the spring of 1937. Given that you will not begin your studies here until January of 1934, the university will insure that, through taking summer school class in 1934 and 1935, you will be able to graduate with your class in 1937.

Your enrollment here is the result of an application and high school documentation arranged to be sent to our Admissions Office by one of our most distinguished alumni, Judge George Morgan, Jr., of Martinsville, Indiana. His letter of recommendation for you was very compelling.

Judge Morgan and his family have arranged through the Bursar's Office to pay for all books, tuition, board, and incidentals as needed.

New freshman orientation for the winter semester will begin on Tuesday, January 12, 1934 at 10:00 am in Room 100 of Kirkland Hall. You should plan to send back your request for classes for no fewer than 15 hours of course credits, focusing on those classes required for freshmen. The request form is in the back of the "Schedule of Classes" booklet. Upon arrival, please report to the Bursar's office in Kirkland Hall for dorm room assignment and issuance of an ID card to be used in the bookstore and cafeteria. Classes will begin on Monday, January 18.

Please refer to the general brochure for instructions on appropriate personal items to bring including clothing, linens, toiletries, etc.

Once again, we are delighted to welcome you to Vanderbilt University and look forward to the contributions you will make as a unique student and scholar."

Johnathan L. Lambert, PhD., Dean of Admissions.

Michael was confused. Was this some sort of prank? If so, who would be behind it? Judge Morgan was mentioned, but certainly he wouldn't toy with Michael in this fashion, would he? Judge Morgan's family was also mentioned, but James Benefield and his wife hadn't seemed the practical-joker types.

Bert sat in the shade, a letter open in his lap, but he wasn't reading it. He was smiling, staring into empty space.

"Hey, Bert, what do you make of this?"

Michael's comment snapped Bert back into the moment.

"Make of what," he said.

Michael walked over to where Bert was sitting and handed him the documents and letter. Bert read the letter and as he did, he started shaking his head slightly and his smile transformed into a broad grin.

"Boy," he said, "You just hit the jackpot."

"This is some sort of joke, right?"

"No, it's no joke. The Morgan clan is repaying an un-payable debt with the most valuable thing that they can give you. Wow!"

Bert stood up and gave Michael a bear hug. When he pulled away, Michael could see that his eyes had welled.

"Judge Morgan is some kind of man, that's for sure," Bert said and grabbed Michael again.

This time, when he let Michael go he said, "This is a Red Letter Day, Michael. You find out that you're going to college and I found out that Linda wants to see me again," he waved his letter at Michael. "Red Letter Day, indeed."

Michael returned to the shade to open the other mail. There was a letter from his mother in one of the bulkier envelopes, and a letter from G. Morgan, Martinsville, Indiana in the other. Michael had no idea how Judge Morgan got his Aunt's address. He tore the Judge's letter open.

"Dear Michael,

By now you should have received the information from my alma mater, Vanderbilt University in Nashville. If not, it should arrive any day.

After a discussion with Miriam and Jim, we decided that the very least we could do to thank you for saving the lives of our precious girls was to make sure that you had a chance to use your intellect and solid character in an academic endeavor. Supporting your college education was the perfect solution.

I have arranged to be on the Vanderbilt campus for your arrival in January to help you navigate what can be a confusing process. I serve on the advisory committee for the School of Law there and a visit to the campus in January will kill two birds with the proverbial single stone.

We all send our love and I look forward to seeing you in January. The Bursar's Office will call me at the Law School when you arrive.

Sincerely, George Morgan"

Michael sat back against the side of the bunkhouse and tried to wrap his mind around what was happening. He was numb.

"I'm for sure to hitch to Indy now," said Bert to no one in particular.

Michael finally read the letters from Aunt Elizabeth and his mother, but his concentration on the mundane reporting of everyday life wandered. At least their news was newsy, not bad. He soon realized that he needed to write to his family right away and tell them. He realized that he should also tell Mother Daniel that he wouldn't be going on the road next spring to help spread the gospel.

***

As often happened during the stay in Tallahassee, Bert and Michael were included in the family's evening meal that night. And that night, after the droning offer of thanks to the Lord by Brother Daniel, Bert announced that he had some news and explained that he was taking some days off to go mend his relationship with Linda Adams in Indianapolis.

"You mean that lady with the neat-o car?" asked Petey.

"The very one," said Bert.

"How long will ya' be gone?" asked Brother Daniel. "We don't give paid vacations ya' know.

"Maybe a week or so. Depends on how long it takes me to get there back using my thumb. But, after the pile of money you paid me during the summer, I can afford the trip."

Michael suppressed a laugh and covered his mouth.

"Mr. Boone, can you take care of repairs and painting by yourself?" asked Mother Daniel.

"Yes, Ma'am. Bert is going to leave me a list of chores."

"When will you be leaving, Mr. Gilbert?" she asked.

"Tomorrow morning early."

"Well, you should try and get hitched to that gal," said Brother Daniel. "At least she has a real job."

"Harlow," Mother Daniel interrupted the flow of the conversation that was headed in a bad direction.

"I wouldn't be the first fellow to hitch his star to a woman with means, would I Brother Daniel?" Bert voice was slippery with sarcasm.

"I have some news," Michael broke into the tension. "I'm going to college in January."

His comment hung over the table like an apparition.

The Daniel family each processed the information in light of how it would impact them personally. Bert looked from face to face for tell-tale reactions.

Brother Daniel just kept forking in the creamed corn, as did Petey. Michael's life didn't much concern them.

Rebecca said, "Which one?"

Mother Daniel, whose face was impassive, looked at her daughter and then back to Michael.

"Vanderbilt," said Michael. "It's in Nashville. Judge Morgan and his family have arranged for everything because of the fire and all."

"Harlow," said Mother Daniel, "Maybe you should have saved those girls instead of being on your knees praying for their souls. We could use a college education in the family."

"If ever a family needed prayin' for it's that godless bunch from Martinsville," he responded.

"Yet another observation that might not please Jesus," said Bert. "

"Your blasphemy, Mr. Gilbert, will be repaid in the hereafter," Brother Daniel said as he rose from the table and headed for the evening breeze on the porch. The others at the table remained silent for a few seconds.

"Can you work through December?" Mother Daniel asked Michael.

"Yes, Ma'am."

"But you'll come back and work for us in the summer, right?" Ruth's question was almost a plea.

"Probably not," said Michael, "I'll have to attend summer school the next two summers to catch up with my class; maybe after that, if there's a job."

"That's too far in the future to know," said Mother Daniel. "Besides, we need help who don't come and go on a school schedule. In any case, congratulations Mr. Boone, I understand that Vanderbilt is very good university."

Ruth got up and disappeared down the hall to her room, saying nothing else.

The next morning, Bert woke early, made a couple of peanut butter and jelly sandwiches, filled a jug with water, packed a small canvas duffel and headed down the driveway to Highway 90.

Later, when Michael finished his breakfast, he began sanding the piano in preparation for applying a new coat of black paint. Mother Daniel had arranged for a man who tuned pianos in his spare time to work his magic, but she wanted the banged-up piano and bench painted first.

At lunchtime, Mother Daniel came to the bunkhouse with two bacon and tomato sandwiches, sliced boiled potatoes, coleslaw, and peach cobbler. Michael enjoyed the break and sat outside in the shade to eat where it was cooler. The cold milk was sweet and creamy. He wished that Ruth could have brought the lunch so they could talk, but she was back in school now. Mother Daniel checked the refrigerator and told Michael that she would have one of the kids bring more milk later this afternoon.

The relationship between Mother Daniel and Michael was confusing Michael. Their intimate relationship didn't seem to impact her as it did him. Except when she was in a position to seduce him, her attitude seemed pleasant but remote and disinterested.

That evening, Michael wrote letters to his parents, Aunt Elizabeth, and Judge Morgan. He wondered how his family would react to his news. The letter of "thanks" to Judge Morgan felt inadequate, and he wished for a more sophisticated way with written words.

Before bed, he settled in the chair beside the floor lamp and opened his latest reading pleasure. This book was one that Ruth had brought him from the house. It was a history of the Battle of the Marne. Ruth's father had been in that battle, but being a lowly rifleman, he wasn't mentioned. The book raised Michael's interest in military history, and he promised himself to read more non-fiction. Maybe he would read something about the various religions of the world.

A small electric fan stirred the air as he read, and when Michael finally turned out the lamp, he unplugged the fan and took it with him to the bedroom. He positioned it pointing toward his bed and plugged it back in. The drone of the electric motor and whir of the three metal blades soon put Michael to sleep. Pure luxury.

The following day was a dull routine of sanding and painting. At noon, Mother Daniel called from the back of the house, "Come in and have some lunch, Mr. Boone."

Michael did a quick wash at his sink and went to the house. The Lincoln was gone from the drive, and the kids were at school. There was one place set at the small table in the kitchen and Mother Daniel directed Michael to it. She had made egg salad sandwiches to go along with a side dish of sliced tomatoes, cucumbers and onions that had been soaking in sugared vinegar all morning.

"Aren't you going to eat?" Michael asked.

"I had a bite while I was fixin' the egg salad. You go on," she said. "Milk or lemonade?"

"Lemonade, please."

While the lemonade was cold, it didn't go well with the vinegary vegetables.

Mother Daniel poured herself lemonade and sat across from Michael.

"I have a question, Mr. Boone." Michael's breathing quickened a bit and he looked up at her. "We're going to the Lion's football game tonight, do you want to go?"

Michael could feel the air go out of the anxiety bubble that was forming in his chest. "Well, uh, that sounds fun but I'm more a basketball fan. Besides, I really want to get that piano project finished and it'll probably take me until after supper to do that."

She got up and took Michael's empty plate to the sink. She stood there staring out of the window. Without turning she said, "I've missed your touch, Michael. Your passion is so refreshing. You make me feel desired. Have you missed me?"

The anxiety bubble began to form once more. He took a deep drink of lemonade before answering.

"Yes Ma'am," he finally said. "But I think that what we did was wrong, and I don't feel good about that."

She turned and looked at him.

"Of course I was wrong. Many things that I've done in life have been wrong. You are just one more lapse into wrong, but being made to feel desired is a drug that's hard to resist. As for you, Michael, you've done nothing wrong. You shouldn't think of that way."

"But it's adultery."

"No it's not," she said. "I'm not married to Harlow. I'm just wedded to his talent for getting country-folk to put money in the offering plate. The money feeds and shelters my children, that's all. Besides he doesn't desire me: he pictures young girls and then uses me. I want to be desired for who I am, not what I feel like in the dark."

Mother Daniel's voice cracked as she made this revelation, and she buried her face in the tea-towel she was holding. Her sobs were quiet. Michael went to her, unsure of what to do. Finally, he put his hand on her shoulder and she turned into him, held him tightly and softly cried into his chest. They stood there embracing for too long.

She finally pulled away, letting one hand drop to his. She looked up at him, her eyes red and wet, "I want to be desired in the daylight, Michael."

Holding his hand, she led him to her bedroom where a slender streak of noonday sun illuminated a nearly vertical column of dust motes in the air. She left him standing by the door and went to the window and pulled down the rolling paper shade behind the lace curtains. The room dimmed but there was plenty of light for Michael to appreciate the smooth skin of her breasts with peach fuzz hair that caught bits of reflected light as she came to him, shedding her blouse.

"But Brother Daniel?" Michael whispered hoarsely.

"He won't be home 'til supper."

His earlier resolve was admirable, but his will wasn't. He helped her out of the denim skirt and then fumbled with his own clothes as the desire she sought made itself obvious. There are few nineteen-year-old males who can be a patient lover during the initial rush of lust. Michael was not in that small, perhaps non-existent, group. Annie Maypearl, however, was patient, and she waited for her own pleasure, knowing that Michael would soon recover his desire for her body after his first shuddering release.

When Michael finally heaved himself out of the bed, Mother Daniel gathered the sheet around herself and watched him dress. As he started toward the closed door, she spoke to him.

"I know that Ruth is sweet on you. Don't encourage her."

"Yes Ma'am, I mean no Ma'am, I mean yes Ma'am, I won't."

Mother Daniel laughed softly at his flustered response as he closed the door behind him.

Late on that early November afternoon, the wind shifted, the sky greyed and the temperature dropped into the fifties. Compared to the heat that had been dominant through the summer and fall, the shift to cool felt cold.

Michael, working on the piano project, stopped and retrieved his one long-sleeve shirt from his limited stack of clothes. He saw the school bus stop near the mailbox, and all three Daniel children headed for the house, clearly underdressed for the change in the weather. Ruth waved at him and then disappeared into the stone house. At suppertime, earlier than usual because of the football game, Ruth came to the bunkhouse with a tray of food.

"I wish that you would go to the game with us," she said.

Michael had trouble looking into her eyes, the smells of the afternoon tryst still clinging to him. He kept his distance for fear of what the scent of lavender and the musky smell of sex would reveal. He should have showered.

"Yeah, well," he said, "like I told Mother Daniel, I want to get this piano finished. The tuning man is coming Monday."

Ruth stepped toward him and he took a step back.

"Don't you want to kiss me?" she asked.

"Sure, but I'm pretty stinky right now; maybe tomorrow when I get cleaned up."

"I don't care if you smell a little," she said advancing.

Michael froze as she slipped her arms around his back and raised her face to his. He cautiously pressed his mouth down on hers and she responded with a much more passionate version, slipping her tongue along the inside of his upper lip. Michael responded in kind, and his heart rate increased, perhaps because of passion, perhaps because of the anxiety.

"You smell like mushrooms," said Ruth. "If that's what you consider 'stinky' then you don't know what stinky means."

"Maybe not," Michael said pulling away. He realized that Ruth smelled of lavender and that the fragrance was always with her. It would never be a suspicious clue as long as she and her mother dabbed from the same bottle.

"See you after the game," she said as she headed for the door. "It'll be cold in those bleachers."

The family, layered up in winter clothing, piled into the Lincoln about 7:00 pm and drove off. Michael returned to the painting and kept at it until the Lincoln pulled back into the drive around ten-thirty. He had heard the faint noise of the crowd on the westerly breeze from time to time.

"Hey Mike," yelled Petey, "We beat that Catholic School in Panama City. Those fish eaters had a nigger on their team and we clobbered him good."

"Peter," Michael could hear Mother Daniel, "Don't use that word, say 'Negro'."

Petey yelled back to Michael, "They had a niggergro and we clobbered him good."

Michael could hear Brother Daniel laugh.

Michael finished his clean-up and went inside. He poured a glass of milk and took an apple from the counter. Finished with his snack, he went and showered the mushroom smell from his body.

The next day, Saturday, Ruth came to the bunkhouse mid-morning where Michael was replacing one of the metal tips on a tent pole, the very same pole that had blown through the church window during the storm in Indiana.

"Whatcha doin', Stinky," she said as she let herself in the screen door.

"Just fixin' the tent pole that got damaged in that storm," Michael looked up and found that he was pleased that it was her, not Mother Daniel.

"I'm going to the movies tonight with some friends. Want to go?" she asked.

"I'd better not," Michael replied, "I don't think that your mom would be too keen on that idea."

"She doesn't have to know. You could meet us there. It's only a few blocks away, downtown. Besides, I told mom that I'm spending the night with Pauline Hill, so I won't be expected home until tomorrow afternoon."

"I don't think that sneaking around is a good idea," the hypocrisy of that statement struck Michael as he said it.

"If we don't sneak around a little, I'll never have an escape plan," Ruth's voice had an edge, "Especially with you going off to college."

"You need to talk to your mother about your graduation wishes. You might be surprised by her response."

"So, I guess you're not planning to help me, then?" Ruth's voice grew soft in defeat.

"I guess not," said Michael. "I wish I could, though."

"Does that mean that you love me?"

"I don't know, exactly," said Michael, "But I know that I care for you a lot and I think about you all the time. If that's love, then maybe so. It's confusing."

Ruth stepped over and kissed Michael on the cheek.

"See you tonight," she said as she turned to leave.

"But I'm not going to the movies," Michael responded to her retreating form.

"I know," she called back.

The paint on the piano was nearly dry, and Michael took pride in the way the old trooper looked all spruced up. If the piano tuner could get the rusty pegs to turn and fix the flat notes, next year's music would be a bit better. Although, he realized, if Ruth wasn't there to play, perhaps it wouldn't get played at all.

Michael finished the tent pole repair and slipped it back into the stack of poles in the storage area. Rebecca came to the bunkhouse with lunch a few minutes later, grilled cheese with dill pickles, canned peaches, and white rice laced with green bell pepper and onions. Through the afternoon, Michael worked on repairing several tears in the canvas on the edges of the tents. He couldn't get to all of the damage without Bert's help unfolding the heavy material. He used a large needle and repair cord made of hemp twine.

He ate dinner in the house that evening. Ruth was already gone to her friend's house. The conversation included some football game highlights and questions and answers about what Michael had accomplished that day. Before he left the table, Mother Daniel handed him his pay envelope, a Saturday night ritual. With little to spend money on through the summer—although he did buy a new pair of work gloves and two pair of overalls—Michael had accumulated a sizable boodle of cash, about $250 last he counted. He never gave its security a thought. He put his week's pay into a larger envelope with the rest of his cash, and stashed it in his canvas duffel among his cleaner clothes.

After a nice long stretch of reading, Michael took a shower and went to bed. He found that he missed having Bert around and wondered when he would return from Indianapolis. Maybe he wouldn't return at all.

Michael was dreaming. *He was in tall grass searching for someone who was hidden there. He could smell lavender and he parted the grass, left and right, expecting to see Mother Daniel. It was Ruth. She pulled him down to her and kissed his mouth.* The kiss caused his eyes to flutter and he realized in seconds that he was no longer dreaming but kissing a woman who was sitting on the edge of his bed. He strained to break though the fog of sleep. Before he could say anything coherent, she whispered, "It's me, Ruth."

He tried to sit up but she gently put her hand on his chest and kept him prone.

"What are you doing?" he finally croaked.

"I'm proving that I love you," she whispered.

"Maybe you shouldn't," said Michael, his breathing started to quicken. "We could get into trouble."

"No, we won't," her sotto voice seemed assured. "I'm not due back until tomorrow afternoon."

Ruth stood beside the bed and slipped off her dress, then reached behind her and released the bra clasps. In the dim light filtering into the room from the distant yard light, Michael could see the outline of her form. In this faint light she looked much like her mother. Similar breasts, hips, the same triangle of tangled hair below her navel. As she slipped into his bed and he pulled her against his chest, he realized that Ruth was, however, lighter and tauter.

Suddenly, Michael panicked. He pulled away.

"Is this your first time?"

Ruth put a finger to his lips, "No." Her answer jolted him physically and she felt him tense. "It was last winter with a boy from school. We tried it three times at his house but it didn't go well; at least not for me. He's got a new girlfriend now."

Michael pulled her close again, her breasts pressing into his chest. While his desire for her was almost frantic, he took deep breaths and tried to check his instincts. "Let's go slow," he said, his voice husky.

She answered by running her hand down to his pelvis and taking him in her left hand. "Oh, my," she murmured.

They made love twice that night. Ruth was a compliant accomplice, but somewhat anxious based on her earlier experience. Michael, who had learned his lessons well, made sure that her pleasure was attended to in both gentle and, eventually, more aggressive ways. Her response was that of a student introduced to a new and fascinating activity. The second time, Ruth woke Michael from deep sleep by exploring his body with her hand. She was amazed that his penis, once so sturdy and serviceable could become floppy and very unimpressive, only to come alive again at her touch. These acts of love thrilled Michael, and he found himself nearly overwhelmed with feelings of benevolent possession.

The sound of the Lincoln belching to life Sunday morning woke Michael. He eased out of the small bed and walked to where he could look out of the bunkhouse door. With Brother Daniel behind the wheel, Petey slipped into the passenger side, and Rebecca got into the back seat. Without Mother Daniel, the trio drove down the drive and turned left onto the blacktop, headed to Sunday school and the ten-thirty worship service.

Michael stood there processing the situation, turning the information over in his mind and beginning to feel anxious.

Mother Daniel was home alone. Michael was by himself in the bunkhouse, or so she thought. There were at least two hours of time before church was over and the family home. If she wanted sex with Michael, she had the opportunity. He found that his mind now worked in the devious way that any secret lover's mind works. And, why wouldn't it?

He went back to the bed. Ruth was smiling and blinking up at him. She reached out to touch him but he grabbed her hand.

"Your mom didn't go to church. She's still in the house. If she comes down here . . ." his voiced trailed off as the picture formed in his head.

Ruth shook her head slightly and continued to smile up at him. "She won't come down here. Sunday mornings are your time off. She can't ask you to work."

Work wasn't what worried Michael.

Ruth pulled her hand free and stroked the top of his penis with her fingertips. The blood in his brain seemed to redirect to his loins, and he knelt beside the bed and caressed her breast, flicking the nipple with his tongue until it was erect enough to suck. Again, with full passion but not great speed, Michael worked his recently obtained knowledge to provide both of them with a loving experience. They lay side by side for several minutes and began again, youth being what it is. He was coming into her from behind, her trusting bottom willingly raised for a new experience. His view of the process below him was certain to hasten his finish. Ruth was making short gasping sounds with each thrust.

What was that? That sound? Michael stopped mid-arch. A door shutting, maybe?

Michael looked back over his shoulder and through the front

window. Mother Daniel was striding toward the bunkhouse. She had a robe pulled around her, her legs bare.

"Christ!" Michael spat the word out. He pulled back, breaking contact and in nearly one motion, stood up, put an arm around Ruth's waist, and pulled her to her feet. She grunted as he nearly drove the air out of her.

"Quick, get in the shower room and stay quiet. Your mother is here."

Ruth looked toward the door and could see Mother Daniel three or four steps away, her robe partially open. She scurried into the shower room and pulled the door shut.

Michael, completely nude, kicked Ruth's dress, shoes and underwear under the bed, a sliver of hemline still peeking out. He got into bed, reached down and flicked the hem out of sight and pulled the sheet and light blanket up to his neck.

Mother Daniel stood at the door and called through the screen, "Knock, knock. May I come in?"

"Better not," croaked Michael, trying to sound croupy. "I'm not feeling well and it's probably catching."

Mother Daniel opened the door and came in.

"Sick?" she cocked her head slightly, looking at Michael's face peering out from the bedclothes.

"Yes Ma'am," Michael worked to hoarsen his reply.

She came over and sat on the edge of the bed. She put a hand on his forehead. With that motion, the robe opened revealing one of her breasts. Michael had no doubt now about her Sunday morning intentions

"You aren't feverish."

"It comes and goes," croaked Michael. "I'm a little chilly right now."

"Can I do anything for you that would make you feel better?" her hand left his forehead and wandered down on top of the covers to his crotch.

"No, no. I'll be fine. It's probably just a twenty-four-hour thing." Michael found that intense anxiety might possibly be the cure for unintended erections. Besides, most of Michael's blood was coursing to his face.

"Well," she said, removing her hand, "You do look flushed."

She stood up, facing him. She opened the robe just enough

to reveal her nakedness and said, "If you feel better in the next half hour or so, come to the house and I'll have something nice for you for breakfast."

She pulled the robe closed and tied the silk sash.

"It smells like mushrooms in here. Maybe they made you sick."

She walked to the door and turned before leaving, "I hope you feel better very soon."

Michael lay very still until Mother Daniel shut the back door.

"Come out?" Ruth stage-whispered through the cracked door.

"Yeah," Michael's reply was quiet.

Ruth came out as Michael pushed the covers off and stood up. Their nakedness embarrassed them both. He reached over and found his cotton undershorts and quickly pulled them on.

"Where are my clothes?" Ruth asked. She folded her forearms across her breasts and turned slightly sideways to hide her pubic hair.

Michael, on hands and knees, retrieved her clothes and then slipped into some dungarees and his long-sleeved shirt. When he finished, Ruth was putting on her shoes.

"Now what? You can't walk across the backyard and just innocently walk in the door," Michael said.

"I'll stay here awhile and then go through the back pasture. No one will see me. The bunkhouse will be in the way."

"You want something to eat?" said Michael.

"Whatcha got?"

"There's those apples on the table," Michael said waving his hand in the general direction, "I've got milk in the ice box and some cereal."

"Refrigerator," said Ruth.

"Refrigerator."

"Can you make some coffee?" she asked

"Sure."

With hot coffee in hand, they sat down opposite one another at the table and said nothing until their cups were nearly empty. They avoided eye contact. Michael was turning the events of the past few hours over and over in his mind. As he did he felt wonderful, he felt terrible, he felt guilty, he felt stupid, he felt invincible, he felt smitten. Ruth was imbedded in his consciousness at all levels, now that they were lovers. He felt nothing like this regarding Mother Daniel. For her, he recalled only the lust, the feeling that she was giving him no option but that he was too…too what? Needy? Normal? Complicit?

"Would you marry me?"

Ruth's question jarred him.

"Wha, What?" he sputtered.

"Would you be willing to marry me? It would be a way for me, for us, to get away from this crazy family."

"You're not ready to be married and neither am I. We're too young," his answer lacked the tone of conviction. He knew several classmates from Calhoun who planned to marry right after graduation. It was a very normal progression and he knew it. The prospect of Mother Daniel being his mother-in-law sent a brief shiver. He certainly couldn't offer that excuse.

"I promise, after college, I'll come back and if you still want to marry me, that's what we'll do," Michael rose, went around the table, and put his hands on her shoulders. She leaned her head over, putting her cheek on his hand.

"You won't come back here after college. You'll meet a smart, beautiful girl there. You'll marry her," her voice was soft, as if imagining the girl while forming the words. "I wonder why mother came out here in her robe?" she asked in that way that suggested thinking aloud.

Michael immediately tensed and considered the danger of an unlikely answer. "Yeah," he finally said, "That was strange. Maybe she had some breakfast leftovers and came out to see if I wanted them. She did mention breakfast."

Ruth looked out the door, her profile revealing nothing of what she was thinking.

"I can probably go now," said, standing up and smoothing her simple dress.

"Okay," said Michael.

Ruth went out through the storage area and between the parked trucks. She walked straight to the back fence, keeping the bunkhouse between her and the stone house. Michael watched her slip between the wire strands and disappear behind a row of evergreen trees. From there, she would go out to the highway and circle back to the drive as if walking from town. She probably took her time, Michael thought, so as not to get home too soon.

***

For the remainder of his time in Tallahassee, Michael's impressions of and attitude toward Mother Daniel were dramatically altered. Neither was positive. He considered how she had seduced him and realized what she had realized, that he wouldn't be able to say no to the lust that she inflamed, while the power dynamic was clearly lopsided.

November was nearly half gone. He had about six more weeks before he would pack his meager belongs and stick his thumb out, looking for rides that would take him to Calhoun, Kentucky.

During that time, Bert returned with stories of plans that he and Linda Adams made for when the revival came to Indiana next summer. Bert confided to Michael that he might abandon the Brother Daniel troupe next summer, look for work in Indianapolis, and take up with Linda permanently. Such are lover's plans.

Ruth, being the clever young woman that she was—and Michael, being the besotted idiot that he was—managed to steal away alone several warmer nights and make love in the back of Michael's truck. Such are lover's risks. Bert pretended not to notice Michael's absences, fearing that he might be trysting with Mother Daniel. With Michael's imminent departure, Bert decided to keep his own counsel regarding Michael's love life.

During his last few weeks in Florida, Daniel had several opportunities to talk with Ruth about their future. They discussed his planned visits during school breaks, possible bus trips for Ruth to come to Nashville and even where they might eventually live once his college studies were complete. Certainly, they would be married. They agreed that it would be a test of their love, having Michael away in Tennessee. But, as young love always does, it convinced them that anything was possible if they did it together.

Michael left Tallahassee on December 22, earlier than planned. He had decided to be in Calhoun for Christmas. He received a letter from his mother in early December. She and baby Nell, now five years old, were taking the train from San Francisco to Chicago, and then a bus to Louisville where Mr.

Berryman and Aunt Elizabeth would pick them up. They planned to arrive in Calhoun on December 20. Michael's heart leapt as he read the news. The sting of leaving his beloved Ruth was eased, but very little.

He promised to write her often as they tearfully said goodbye on the driveway. He also promised to stay in touch with Bert but only the latter promise turned out to hold true, but not because Michael didn't try.

Ruth, occasionally sobbing, and Bert, remaining stoic with cigarette in hand, stood on the front porch and watched Michael position himself on the far side of the highway. Behind them, standing at her bedroom window, was Mother Daniel. Within a few minutes, a soldier in a black Chevy sedan stopped. Michael gave a wave over the top of the car and hopped in. The car lurched into gear and sped off to the west.

Chapter Nine
College Then War

MICHAEL ARRIVED IN Calhoun on Christmas Eve. Baby Nell didn't know who he was. Very shy, she hid behind her mother every time Michael tried to engage with her for most of that first day. His mother, who looked markedly older than he remembered, cried and cried when Michael first walked into the farmhouse and she saw that her skinny fifteen-year-old boy had become a sturdy young man, looking very much like his father. Michael cried a bit too, thinking about all the time gone by without his family.

By the time Michael took the bus to Nashville in January, Nell had become his constant companion, following him around jabbering about her trip from home, about her big brother Mathew, about how she could feed the chickens and they didn't even scare her anymore, about how her daddy would carry her on his shoulders when she got tired, about how he, Michael, was her other big brother because her mom told her so, about how her bed was kind of 'lumpy' here at Aunt Elizabeth's, about how Aunt Elizabeth's kids were her "cushions", or something like that, and all manner of information that she thought would interest Michael. He absolutely adored this little shadow.

***

The bus from Owensboro to Nashville arrived mid-morning on January 9, 1934. Michael, carrying two cardboard suitcases, which Aunt Elizabeth found stored in the tool shed, asked a colored porter how to get to the university.

The porter explained which city bus would take him there. It would be the one with a cardboard sign in the front glass that read *21st Avenue South*. "Cost ya a nickel, Mista," he said.

Michael got to the campus in a wheezing bus that left a trail of blue-black smoke as it left each stop. He found the Bursar's office in the main administrative building as instructed, and told the lady at the counter that Judge George Morgan was expecting him. He sat down while she picked up the phone and asked the operator for a number. In maybe ten minutes, Judge Morgan walked in as if he owned the place.

Their reunion was heartfelt, and Michael was exceedingly glad that the Judge was there to help him through the process. They spent the remainder of the day acquiring the necessities of academic life, including a dorm room assignment, textbooks, student ID card and the like. That evening, he and the Judge went to the "Incoming Student's Reception" where he felt like a complete bumpkin. Judge Morgan introduced Michael to the dean of the Law School, the Provost, whatever that meant, and the President of the student government association, a senior student from Atlanta.

"You'll need some college clothes, Michael," Judge Morgan said when he picked him up at the dorm the following day. Michael assumed they were going to lunch. "I know that your wardrobe is a bit spare and primarily work clothes, so let me get you some basics.

"I'm fine wearing the clothes I have," replied Michael. "I don't care if I look different. I am different."

"I admire your attitude, young man, but college students are notorious for making shallow, snap judgments about classmates based on how they dress. Having a few essentials will make your life easier. Trust me."

Avoiding the gaudy western wear popular among the locals, the Judge bought Michael two pair of pants, khaki and charcoal;

two shirts, white and blue; a pair of cordovan shoes, a cordovan belt, two neckties, four pair of grey socks, one navy blazer, and a grey pea coat. Michael insisted that he use some of his summer earnings to pay for the clothes, but that argument didn't last long and Judge Morgan prevailed.

"Use your money to start an investment account," said the Judge. "And, don't forget, the bursar's office has a fifty dollar monthly stipend for you. It will accumulate until you start spending it on pretty coeds or fancy clothes."

Judge Morgan left the following day, and Michael was launched into his college career alone, but with a loving boost from a warm-hearted family in Indiana.

Michael's roommate was a 6'6" basketball player from Corbin, Kentucky, named Michael Sanders. He was in college on a full basketball scholarship. They soon became known on campus as "Little Mike" and "Big Mike." Although both preferred "Michael," it was clear that college students rarely get their way regarding names and nicknames. On their floor of the dorm there was a "Jersey Joe," a.k.a. Joseph Cavaletti, "Okie", a.k.a. Billy Carver from Tulsa, "Skeeter," a.k.a. Harold Ball, and "Moochie" a.k.a. Lloyd Stotts, who always needed to borrow something. One goes through life remembering these friends thus.

Once classes were underway, Michael found his stride, and he absolutely loved the academics. Most of the other students were engaged in the subjects being taught, and it made for stimulating class discussions, nothing like his high school.

Michael and Big Mike bonded at first meeting, two small town boys negotiating unfamiliar territory. Michael kept Big Mike morally supported throughout the last half of the '33/'34 basketball season. Big Mike, a high school star, spent most of every game warming the bench, backing up an all-conference senior and a junior strong forward. With access to the basketball facility, Big Mike took Michael for exhausting one-on-one sessions to sharpen his skills whenever there was time—whether at midnight or on Sunday afternoons. In the process, Michael regained his skills, pumping in two-handed set shots from long range, and refining his new jump shot from in closer. His ball-handling and defensive footwork skills were superior to Big Mike's, and he held his own against the taller man.

"Where'd you learn that shit?" Big Mike said as Michael faked a move to the basket, and then suddenly backed off to drain another shot from outside.

"Footwork," said Michael.

"Show me," Big Mike asked, and so it went.

Big Mike wanted to perfect a hook shot, both left and right handed, so Michael spent long hours feeding him the ball in the foul lane until most of the attempts found their target, and the net snapped sharply as the ball went through clean.

Michael kept up a steady stream of brief letters to Ruth and hers came weekly for about a month. Then they stopped. Her last letter was dated February 14, Valentine's Day. It was a classic Valentine letter, with professions of love and undying devotion and XXXX's and OOOO's. Michael wrote several times after her letters stopped, but there was never a response. He mailed Bert to see if he knew why Ruth stopped writing. Bert wrote back and claimed ignorance. After that, Michael stopped writing to her. Michael's heart was shattered. He found it difficult to concentrate on his studies. Each time he decided to stop feeling sorry for himself and move on, the lump in his throat returned and he sank into a funk.

"Another boyfriend," Big Mike said solemnly as he stared at a letter in his hand. "She's dumping me for that sorry-assed Mitchell jerk. He was always sniffin' around her last year. He knew that I'd be gone to college this year. I ought to kick his ass."

"Maybe it's her ass that needs kickin'," said Michael from where he sat on his bed. "He's just doin' what we would do I suppose. Hard to blame the guy. He doesn't owe you. She's the one who promised loyalty."

"Advice from the lovelorn," Big Mike snorted. "You mope around for weeks and then suggest that I go back to Kentucky and whup a girl. Some advice."

"It wasn't meant literally, Ichabod," Michael replied.

"Yeah, actually you're right," said Big Mike. "Sorry-assed Mitchell is almost blameless."

Somehow, the fact that Big Mike was now suffering the same pain of rejected love as Michael made Michael feel better. His funk gradually lifted. Eventually, so did Big Mike's.

Winter merged into spring, and Michael's first semester

came to a close. His grades were good, not sterling. He vowed to manage his time better, because he knew that it was extracurricular activities that stole time from the study required to be a Dean's List student.

Summer school was very different. The campus was lightly populated and there were far fewer distractions. Big Mike had gone home to Corbin to work in his uncle's southern fried chicken restaurant. Michael had the room to himself and by the end of the summer session he had posted A's in every class except statistics where he felt fortunate to get a B. Statistics was a bear.

Michael received a letter from Bert during the summer. The Brother Daniel Good News Revival was back in Martinsville, Indiana, when Bert posted the letter. Things had changed. Neither Mother Daniel nor Ruth was with the caravan.

Mother Daniel had announced that she was pregnant in February, and that she would not go on the annual pilgrimage to save souls. Ruth, she said, would stay behind with her, finish her senior year and graduate with her class. Mother Daniel hired a truck driver/stagehand to replace Michael. Not coincidentally, the man also played piano. The piano-accompanied hymns would continue in spite of Ruth's absence. Rebecca was schooled in money collection, counting, payroll, and accounting procedures. Brother Daniel was saddled with the job of being nice to and coordinating with the local host congregations, a responsibility for which he had, to date, proven exceptionally ill-suited, much to Bert's delight.

Bert reported that the Judge Morgan's new house was not completed. The workers were just putting the bricks in place. The Judge came out one day during the revival week, and visited with Bert for part of an afternoon. Bert, Rebecca, and Louisa, Mattie's granddaughter, used the rope swing twice during their visit. Petey was always invited, but declined when he learned that Louisa would be there. Michael had a little touch of nostalgia reading Bert's letter.

Bert also told Michael that he was planning to leave the troupe once they completed the week at Green Fork, east of Indianapolis. He and Linda had agreed that he would join her in the city. He didn't mention marriage, but the move had the sound of permanence.

Bert intended to tell Brother Daniel when they completed the Sunday evening service in Portland. It would be hard for Brother Daniel to rashly fire Bert on the spot with the drive to Harrisville due the next morning. Bert indicated that he trusted Michael's replacement, an effeminate bachelor named Willford Velpen, who went by Will. Bert had explained the issue of Brother Daniel, his predilection for young girls and the challenge it presented with Rebecca's presence. Will promised to intercede should anything happen to indicate that Brother Daniel was trying to do anything inappropriate. Bert would have to assure Rebecca that Will would look out for her when Bert left the troupe. Whether Will was the right guy to be sharing an intimate camp environment with a ten-year-old boy probably never crossed Bert's mind.

Michael's summer semester ended mid-August, and he took the bus to Calhoun. To his delight, his father and brother were both there. His little brother looked very different than the pre-adolescent who had waved to Michael from the old Ford as it headed off to Oregon five years ago. Matthew had their mother's fine features and straight blond hair, nothing like Michael's tangle of red-brown hair passed down through his father's Irish mother.

His father's face, like his mother's, reflected the recent years of hard work and struggle on the West Coast. He was still robust, but the lines around his eyes and across his brow were proof that outside labor took a toll. Robert Boone was clearly amazed that his oldest was in college, and proud of the circumstances that led to that opportunity. He insisted on having Judge Morgan's mailing address as well as that of the Benefields. In years to come and until he returned to Kentucky in retirement, Michael's father sent a case of the vineyard's annual vintage to both the Judge and the Benefields—it was the most he could do to express his appreciation.

Before Michael headed back to school, his family boarded the bus in Louisville and headed for Chicago, where the train would deliver them back to San Francisco. Michael had driven them to the bus depot. Baby Nell and Michael's mother went all blubbery when they said goodbye and, emotions being contagious, Michael joined in the red-eyed sniffling. Even his father and brother were misty. It would be nearly four years until he saw them again. Then, he would be wearing his cap and gown.

The fall semester of 1934 started up in mid-September, and Little Mike and Big Mike swapped stories of their respective summers and prepared for their classes. Big Mike checked in with the basketball staff and began practices even before classes began. Again, he pressed Michael into extra work, and quickly recovered the progress on his hook shot and Michael enjoyed the activity. Things looked up regarding Big Mike's position on the team now that the senior center had graduated.

One evening in early October, Big Mike came back to the dorm after practice and informed Michael that "Coach Cody wants to talk to you."

"Why," said Michael, "Did I do something wrong by being in the gym with you?"

"I don't think that's it," smiled Big Mike. "He saw you working with me a couple of times, and wants to know if you have time to be on the practice squad."

And that's how it came to pass that Michael, the pride of the Calhoun Cougars, became a lowly practice scrub on the Vanderbilt Commodores varsity basketball team. Basically in a state of shock, Michael wrote to his father, Bert, and Judge Morgan explaining this new development. He heard back from all three within two weeks with congratulatory praise and expressions of pride.

At the end of the Commodores 1934-35 season, Coach Cody informed Michael that he was moving him onto the varsity team the following year. For Michael's final two years at Vanderbilt he was a valued seventh man off of the bench, averaging eight points and four rebounds per game. He was small for a forward, but his set shot from the corner was nearly automatic, and his aggressive rebounding set a standard that Coach Cody often cited and encouraged other players to emulate.

When the Commodores played Kentucky in the fall of 1935, Aunt Elizabeth, Mr. Berryman, and two of his sports-minded friends drove to Lexington to see the game. Kentucky won handily, but Michael had a good game off the bench, and he enjoyed having family and friends share in the college basketball experience. Aunt Elizabeth had her Kodak Brownie and took several snapshots. She sent reprints to Michael's parents. His brother, Matthew, now a fifteen-year-old baseball star for the

Healdsburg High Greyhounds, tacked a picture of Michael and Big Mike onto his wall above the bed.

During the '36/'37 season, Vandy played Indiana State in Terre Haute, and the Morgan clan was in attendance. Michael recalled that John Wooden was the Indiana hometown hero in Martinsville and in spite of the fondness he felt for the Benefields, who had both attended Indiana State, he was delighted that Vandy won in the final seconds, Big Mike swishing two hook shots over his opponent. Michael always took some pride in Big Mike's hook shots.

As could have been predicted, Ruth had been correct that Michael would meet a girl at college who was smart and pretty. In fact, he met two. Katherine was a music major who he met in a Greek history class. She was from Knoxville, Tennessee. Their romance, which managed to get sufficiently steamy toward the end, lasted for just over a year. It fizzled out when she transferred to a music school in Boston for her final two years.

Early in Michael's junior year, his dorm buddy, Jersey Joe, set Michael up on a blind date with Martha Lindstrom, a sophomore from Minnesota. Martha was the quintessential Norwegian girl: lithe, blond, and athletic. Among Martha's other considerable charms was a healthy desire for sex, something that she made very clear on their third date. Martha owned her own car, and apparently had lots of money. She and Michael often spent weekends away from campus at various Nashville hotels and motels, refining their skills of lovemaking. Martha always paid for these excursions, knowing Michael's financial situation. One thing was certain; Michael wasn't her first intimate companion, although she claimed that he was the "best." Of course she couldn't have known that he had had an excellent, experienced instructor. On an emotional level, their relationship wasn't deep, however, and by late winter of that year, Martha informed Michael that she was also seeing a fraternity man who wanted her all to himself. With little or no heartbreak, their affair ended—and Michael's grades improved.

Another summer came and went, and with no more summer classes to take, Michael returned to Calhoun and helped his aunt with the farm chores. His cousins were getting big enough to take on various tasks, and Mr. Berryman was often there to help with any heavy projects. Still, it was a hardscrabble life, and the money from selling fruits, vegetables, eggs, honey, and milk was barely enough. Everyone seemed to be poor in Kentucky; economic envy was rare.

Michael's final year at college was probably his favorite. He had completed most of the required courses, and was concentrating on his major, electrical engineering. He was fascinated by electricity and how it flowed like water through conductors, wires, and other mediums. At the same time, with a handful of elective classes available, he also studied literature and comparative religion. The latter often made him recall Bert's distinct distain for much of Christianity's dogma, especially the fundamentalism preached by Brother Daniel. Michael's mind was pried open and cracks appeared in his belief system. He would spend the remainder of his life examining the good things and the bad things inherent in organized religion.

The '36-'37 basketball season ended. It hadn't been a championship year, but the overall experience and friendships were lifetime markers. Big Mike had become an all-conference star his final two years, and Coach Buford, who was new that season, encourage him to attend graduate school and become an assistant varsity coach. He consulted Michael for advice. Big Mike admitted that becoming a college basketball coach would be his "dream job," and Michael encouraged him to take the offer: a graduate degree in education and a shot at coaching at the college level.

Michael talked with a career guidance counselor and decided that the military could be a good place to apply his knowledge. His degree in electrical engineering helped him qualify for the Naval Officer's Training program in Rhode Island. He decided on the Navy in spite of the fact that Michael had never seen a body of water larger than the Ohio River.

"Why is it," his mother had asked him at graduation, when he announced his post college plans "that boys from farm country want to go to sea?"

"Well," Michael explained, "There are other places and people beyond those seas that I want to visit, and if the Navy can get me there, all the better."

His entire family plus Aunt Elizabeth, his cousins, and Mr.

Berryman all came to Nashville for his graduation. He knew what a sacrifice it was, and the serious money it took to get everyone there. He also knew that it did no good to discourage them from coming.

Judge Morgan and the entire Benefield family also attended. Michael, always popular around campus, especially once his famous corner set shots started to swish, had quite a cadre of vocal well-wishers when his named was called, graduating with honors. Even lovely Martha Lindstrom sought him out at the graduation reception to wish him well. The goodbye kiss that she gave him was of such intensity and duration that it had his family and friends sharing glances with each another. Eyebrows were raised.

Judge Morgan hosted the entire group for dinner that evening. Toasts were made and good wishes expressed. Michael's father, not a man of flowery words, struggled to express his deep feelings of appreciation to the Judge and the Benefields. Judge Morgan rescued him from his sincere but tortured comments by interrupting,

"While I understand your feelings, Mr. Boone, it is we who are grateful to have Michael enter our lives when he did. It's an additional pleasure to meet the very people who raised such an exceptional young man." Michael was embarrassed but raised his glass of wine, for which he had acquired a taste under Martha's tutelage, and accepted the compliments.

Within forty-eight hours, after more goodbyes, additional tears and promises of letters, Michael's fairytale college experience ended. Big Mike put him on a bus to Atlanta where he would catch the green and gold Southern Crescent to New York and then the New Haven RR to Newport to learn to be an officer and a gentleman in the US Navy.

* * *

Navy Officer's School was a combination of education, training, hazing, and physical activity that led him to the point of exhaustion. The unfit, either mentally or physically, were weeded out as the weeks wore on. The Spartan sleeping quarters, initially crowded cheek by jowl, eventually opened up as officer candidates dropped out of the program to finish out their active duty obligation as regular seamen.

Michael, at first shocked by the seemingly cruel and demanding regimen, eventually accepted the process as a challenging but necessary initiation into Navy culture. Although he was college educated, Michael was still a Kentucky country boy when it came to things naval. *Fore, aft, above, below, starboard, port, rigging, bridge deck, gun deck, head, close to the wind, bringing about, chop, bow, stern, heavy sea, becalmed, fire control, piped aboard,* and a myriad of *ranks and grades* were just a few of the terms and descriptions that were initially mysterious but essential.

Some of the officer candidates were already experienced seamen, and so the flat-landers in the class were subjected to unrelenting mockery for their ignorance. It was mostly good-natured ribbing from classmates, however, as they were all in the trial by fire together.

The mockery from the training cadre, however, was often biting and mean-spirited. Some of the staff were Naval Academy graduates. These "ring knockers," a term that referred to Academy graduates habit of knocking their graduation rings against a hard surface to call attention to their status, often wore their disdain for these unworthy candidates on their well-pressed sleeves.

By the time graduation finally arrived, almost a year after Michael entered the program; the attrition rate had reached 50 percent. His graduating class, receiving their ensign's brass and uniforms in June of '38, numbered but sixty-three. The clouds of war were gathering over Europe, and the US Navy was preparing for the worst.

After extensive training in fire control, the aiming and firing of onboard guns, Michael received orders to report to the *USS Breckenridge*, an aging, four-stack destroyer mothballed in Philadelphia. He was piped aboard and reported to the ship's Executive Officer, Commander Hollingsworth, in September of 1939, when the ship was re-commissioned in anticipation of a war that was just being initiated in Europe and had been going on in the Far East and North Africa for several years.

In spite of being a ring knocker, Commander Hollingsworth

was an easy-going, friendly man who treated all of his officers with respect, regardless of how they earned their rank. His demeanor was decidedly different from that of the ship's captain, a humorless man who seemed perpetually angry. Some said that Captain Wellbourne had been passed over for the captaincy of a newer, sleeker ship and that his general mood reflected the snub. Of course, no one dared ask.

The *Breckenridge* was assigned merchant marine convoy escort duty for ships plying the waters of the Atlantic. With Germany's invasion of Poland that fall, the threat of German submarines and U-Boats became a lurking menace all along the eastern seaboard, and the merchant ships, often filled with war supplies, were being sunk at an alarming pace.

The destroyer was sent to Boston for retrofitting and additional submarine defense training. Michael learned the art of dropping depth charges on suspected enemy submarine activity, a very different skill set than plotting and firing the deck guns. In 1939, submarine warfare, both offensive and defensive, was a very crude affair.

Throughout 1940 and most of '41, with the US an official noncombatant, the *Breckenridge* provided convoy escort duty for ships leaving the east coast headed to northern European ports. The US Navy handed off the convoys to British Naval forces for the second half of each convoy's voyage east and took them over for the ships headed west to the US

The German Wolfpack's, squadrons of U-Boats, targeted the merchant ships throughout their journey, but mostly avoided attacking the US Naval ships. Hitler didn't want to incite the Americans to declare war. In spite of that, the *Breckenridge* crew saw several of their unarmed wards sunk within a few thousand yards. The American ships did what they could to ward off the attacks, but often found that search and rescue efforts became their ultimate fate.

The crew pulled merchant seaman from the water, some alive, some stone-cold dead from hypothermia, and a few charred bodies, somehow still floating. The crew of the *Breckenridge* quickly learned the brutal, grim reality of combat. Michael became numb to the destruction and death and, as it usually does, the experience changed him in profound ways.

In the summer of '41, he was promoted to Lieutenant Junior Grade and reassigned to a heavy cruiser, the *USS Quincey*. He had made close friends on the *Breckenridge*, and when his transfer orders came through, the ship's officers held a special farewell dinner for the young and well-regarded officer. Even Captain Wellbourne attended, although the real merriment didn't commence until after the captain retired for the evening.

Commander Hollingsworth, a favorite among all of the younger officers, had already been transferred by then. He had been assigned as Executive Officer on a battleship, a plum job that was a stepping stone to captaining his own ship. He was sent to the *USS Arizona*, based in Pearl Harbor.

Michael came aboard his new ship as an assistant gunnery officer on July 18, 1941 in Norfolk, Virginia. Ten days later, the ship set sail for the Straights of Denmark on neutrality duty. These early years of serving with the Atlantic Fleet took Michael to places he had only heard about: Newfoundland, Trinidad, South Africa, Iceland, and, eventually, New York, where the *Quincy* underwent an overhaul and Michael was introduced to Broadway Theater, exotic food, and sophisticated women who smoked, drank martinis, and took handsome young naval officers to their beds. Michael was acquiring the kind of worldly experiences of which Bert would have approved.

Of all his new experiences, however, Michael was most fascinated by the sea. Its changing face and personality were forever a wonder. It was a living thing that, on a dime, went from a silvery serene friend into a raging dark foe bent on the destruction of the interlopers in their flimsy boats. Michael marveled at the changing moods of the water and sky. He began to understand the early warning signs that sailors looked for to prepare for the next personality that would invariably appear.

When possible, he would read naval history and learn of warfare at sea, and how the tactics and strategies had changed as the navies of the world adapted from the time of oar power to wind to steam and now diesel engines. As the method of movement changed, so too did the weapons. But some things were timeless: the need for early detection of the enemy, the primacy of position, the advantage of surprise and the ability to adopt new tactics as the battle was joined. The enemy, on the sea or land, always reacted in ways that required creative and often counter-intuitive response from a talented leader. Sticking with a losing tactic was usually a route to the sea floor.

When news of the Japanese attack on Pearl Harbor reached the *Quincy*, the ship was headed down the West African coast to Cape Town for convoy escort duty from there to Trinidad. The captain addressed the crew via the ship's PA system on the afternoon of December 8, 1941.

"Gentlemen," he said, *"Yesterday morning the Japanese launched a surprise attack on our base at Pearl Harbor. There have been heavy losses of men and material. We have received communication from Norfolk that President Roosevelt will, today, ask Congress to declare war on the Axis. There is little doubt that we are, or soon will be, at war with Germany, Italy and Japan. The Quincy will be asked to serve her country in all-out combat, and I have no doubt that the men and officers of this ship will prove capable, willing and ready to give all when asked. Our immediate objective is to escort a supply convoy from Cape Town to Trinidad as ordered. We will now be targets for U-boats, along with the supply ships, so be alert as always. If we get the chance, let's sink two or three of the sons-a-bitches. That is all."*

Unlike many in the American public, the officers and crew of the *Quincy* were hardly surprised by the news that the US was finally entering the war. They were, however, surprised and saddened that the precipitating attack came upon their fellow sailors and ships, which were enjoying a Sunday respite on the beautiful Island of Oahu. Michael immediately thought of Commander Hollingsworth. Word of the Commander's death on the ill-fated *Arizona* wouldn't reach Michael until weeks later. The sting of losing his friend was just the first of many such bits of sad news that trickled in during the next four years.

After the New York overhaul, *Quincy* headed for the Panama Canal and the war in the Pacific. Once again, Michael was seeing new places while living with the sobering reality that he would be directing and firing guns in anger. The enemy would do the same.

Just after midnight on the morning of August 9, 1942, near the South Pacific island of Savo in the Solomon Islands, the *Quincy* was ambushed by a large Japanese Naval force. Suddenly,

Japanese flares and searchlights illuminated the ship as if she were the featured performer in a Broadway show. Not prepared to fire back or make defensive maneuvers, the ship suffered murderous damage immediately. The flashes of the Japanese deck guns, tracer rounds, and blinding searchlights indicated that *Quincy* was in a withering crossfire. There was controlled chaos as the fire control team stumbled into action. They finally managed to fire a few main gun salvos, one of them destroying the Japanese command ship's chart room. Only twenty feet away and unscathed stood Admiral Mikawa, binoculars in hand, on the bridge of the *Chokayai*. However, as *Quincy* turned toward the eastern Japanese column of ships, she was struck by two torpedoes, and soon another. The deck guns were silenced as the ship listed heavily to port. *Quincy* was sinking.

The fire control room could not get a response from the bridge regarding orders, so Lieutenant Commander Hollis sent Michael down to the bridge. The trip down the heeling ladders and exposed stairwells was perilous. The ship continued to take heavy – weapons fire from two Japanese warships, and the rounds pinged and dented the heavily armored areas, and easily penetrated the more lightly armored metal skin. Michael carefully watched the course of the tracer rounds, and made his progress accordingly. Fires were burning along his route, and as he circumvented the flames, the heat and smoke took him back to that early morning of July 5, 1933. The scars on his arms seemed ready to burst into flames and consume him. Eventually, he made it to the bridge deck. The scene was complete carnage. He could have been standing in a slaughterhouse. The deck was slippery with blood.

In the Official After-Action Report, Michael's written summary of what he found is as follows:

"When I reached the bridge level, I found it a shambles of dead bodies with only three or four people still standing. In the Pilot House itself the only person standing was the signalman at the wheel who was vainly endeavoring to check the ship's swing to starboard to bring her to port. On questioning him I found out that the Captain, who at that time was laying (sic) near the wheel, had instructed him to beach the ship and he was trying to head for Savo Island, distant of some four miles (6km) on the port quarter. I stepped to the port side of the Pilot House, and

looked out to find the island and noted that the ship was heeling rapidly to port, sinking by the bow. At that instant the Captain straightened up and fell back, apparently dead, without having uttered any sound other than a moan."

What his report did not include was that when Michael saw the mangled bodies and body parts scattered across the bridge, he puked, and then trembled uncontrollably for several minutes. These were men he knew, with whom he had shared meals, card games, midnight watches, and family stories. Now they were shredded pieces of meat on a blood-soaked, steel-platted deck. Soon, the deck and the meat would be consumed by the shallow waters near Savo Island. This patch of the Pacific became known as "Iron Bottom Sound" as subsequent naval battles here littered the ocean floor with additional ships and aircraft.

The *USS Quincy* was not the only American ship to go down that dark, pre-dawn morning. Two other American heavy cruisers, the *Vincennes* and the *Astoria*, went to the bottom, and an Aussie heavy cruiser, the *Canberra*, was so heavily damage that it was scuttled later that day. Officially, 1,077 Americans were killed, while the Japanese lost fifty-eight men, and none of their ships sunk or were heavily damaged. The battle of Savo Island is still known as the worst naval defeat in US history, and Michael had played a minor if undistinguished role. After jumping into the water from the bow, now nearly at water level, he was among the lucky 270 surviving *Quincy* crewmen pulled from the sea that day.

Survivors from all of the doomed ships were parceled out to various ships headed back to the West Coast or Pearl Harbor. There, the seaman would be medically evaluated and re-assigned. Michael was the guest on an oiler, *USS Platte*, headed to Pearl for repairs.

It hadn't been quite a year since the devastating attack on Pearl Harbor, but the base was fully active and, although the scars were clearly visible, Michael was surprised by the good condition of the massive facility upon his early September arrival.

He was debriefed regarding his experience at the Battle of Savo Island, and turned his After-Action commentary over to a Naval Intelligence Captain. He was medically fit, and he expected that he would receive orders for a new ship assignment very soon.

He did receive some paperwork about three weeks after he

had settled into the Bachelor Officer's Quarters—or "BOC" in military jargon—but instead of new orders it was notification of his promotion to Lieutenant. At the time, he was reporting to Commander Yellis, who was in charge of a new and very secret radar project. The Commander had seen Michael's college degree major, requested the promotion, and asked that Michael be assigned to his unit. When Michael's new orders did come through in October, Commander Yellis had gotten his way; Michael was going to help perfect the new radar technology, and wouldn't be going back to sea duty just yet.

One morning at breakfast, just after he had arrived in Pearl, Michael heard someone call his name from across the room. It was Lieutenant JG Alvin McMasters, a shipmate from the *Breckenridge*. Michael and Al had become friends on that initial deployment and now Al was working as an aide to an Executive Officer who reported to an Admiral, a situation not to his liking, but which was considered beneficial for an ambitious young career officer. Alvin was living in the same building as Michael, one floor up.

"I see that you now outrank me, sir," Al said.

"Strangest thing," said Michael, "If you have a ship blown out from under you, the Navy gives you a promotion as long as it wasn't your fault."

"Where and when," said Al.

"Savo Island."

"Man, that was bad I hear."

"You hear right," said Michael. "Good men gone from a great crew, and the *Quincy* was a peach. I want to get back there and do some payback but they've got me working shore duty until they can find me a fire control spot."

The next weekend, Michael and Al talked a Seabee into letting them borrow a small dinghy. They rowed out to the *USS Arizona's* resting place in the harbor along Ford Island. In the clear, shallow water, the main deck of the battle ship was visible. Fuel oil continued to leak, and as the drops reached the surface, they spread their oily rainbow sheen. Much of the structure above the water line, heeling to port, was being dismantled by the Seabees, and the sight of the charred destruction brought memories of the *Quincy* ordeal to mind.

Michael was silent, fighting the lump in his throat. Finally he said "Here's to you, Commander Hollingsworth, and the men there with you." He saluted the listing hulk.

"We've got your back," added Al, snapping off his own salute.

They took a small tour along Ford Island, where evidence of the raid's destruction was still evident. There wasn't much conversation, just the occasional motion to point out some especially gruesome tangle of metal or gaping hole.

They returned the little rowboat and walked over to the Officer's Club to sit in the shade of an awning. They ordered drinks and talked of their shared past and their prospects for the future. In this peaceful environment, the feather-soft Hawaiian breeze keeping the temperature mild, it was difficult to realize that war raged across East Asia, the South Pacific and North Africa. People were dying premature and brutal deaths, even as these young officers took their leisure on a Sunday afternoon. War is a strange brew of boredom, relaxation, terror, and death.

Michael and Al eventually walked back to the BOC. Michael had some technical reading to do before reporting to the radar project office at 0700 the following morning.

"I don't know much about this radar project yet," said Michael, "But even when I do, I probably won't be allowed to tell you about it."

"Not to worry, old chap," said Al, using a very bad English accent, "I already know all about it. Your boss—Yellis, right?—reports to my boss."

"Great," said Michael, "That takes some of the cloak and dagger pressure off when I'm around you."

"Speaking of cloaks and such," said Al, "There's a formal reception Wednesday evening at Admiral Tisdale's quarters for Halsey. He's come back from his Frisco sick leave. It's an open house. Let's go and snap up some quality food and drink. What say?"

"Sure," said Michael, "I can break out my dress whites and practice being a gentleman."

Michael first saw her standing next to her father, a dapper man in his fifties, who was chatting up Admiral Halsey. Michael's mouth fell slightly ajar and he simply stared at this young woman in her emerald green, floor-length cocktail sheath. Her complexion suggested Polynesian heritage, and the sheen of her onyx hair, swept up so that her shoulders and neck were revealed, reflected the overhead lights.

"She's turned you into a mouth breather already," Al said, as he thrust a glass of red wine into Michael's hand. "Charlene Castle or Charlie as she is known by most. If I hadn't already met my soulmate," he said, referring to his steady island girlfriend, "I'd make a pass myself."

Michael closed his mouth self-consciously and took a sip of wine. His eyes, however, were riveted on the woman.

Commander Yellis spotted Michael, broke off his conversation with another officer and walked over.

"Gentlemen," he said, "You both clean-up very well. After we kick some Japanese ass you will have a larger collection of salad on those dress uniforms. Works wonders with the ladies."

"Salad," Michael had learned at Officer's School, is military lingo for awards and ribbons.

"Come with me Lieutenant Boone. I want to introduce you to Admiral Halsey."

With that, Commander Yellis turned and walked directly to the trio on which Michael had been concentrating. Lewis Castle stepped back a bit to make room for the Commander as he approached. Halsey broke into a smile at seeing his friend, and introductions were made. Commander Yellis looked over his shoulder and motioned for Michael, who had held back, to join them.

"Miss Castle, Admiral Halsey, Mr. Castle, I'd like you to meet Lieutenant Michael Boone, the newest and final critical piece of my project team. We're going to shorten this war and save thousands of lives. Lieutenant Boone is a graduate of that great Tennessee University, Vanderbilt, my alma mater."

At that nugget of information, Michael turned and looked directly at Commander Yellis.

"That's right Lieutenant, we're both Commodores, and we aren't even Limeys."

The group broke into polite laughter at the reference to college mascots and English naval rank.

"Lieutenant," said Admiral Halsey, "Commander Yellis is briefing me tomorrow about the project. What background do you have that makes you critical?" Michael observed that the painful skin condition that had sent the Admiral to the hospital several months ago was still in evidence on parts of his face and neck.

"Well, sir, I have a degree in Electrical Engineering. I guess that must be it." Michael could feel his face flushing and the sound of his voice seemed strange.

"You will pardon us for not discussing this project in more detail," said the Admiral, looking at the Castles, "But Washington wants the Japanese to be totally surprised when we introduce this new capability. I know you understand."

"Absolutely," said Mr. Castle. "My daughter is great with secrets but I'm not. Best that I am kept completely in the dark."

Michael felt that Charlene's gaze had settled on his face and he did a quick glance to confirm it. She was smiling and, indeed, looking directly at him.

"Lieutenant Boone," said Admiral Halsey, "Might I suggest that you introduce Miss Castle to some of your peers and their ladies. She's been quite patient with our conversation but I suspect not riveted."

"Excellent idea," said her father.

Michael didn't move, and for a brief and slightly awkward moment, everyone was quiet. Then, Charlene stepped toward Michael, looped her hand under his arm and said, "I'd like a glass of that wine."

"Of course, Miss Castle," Michael's words seemed rushed and too loud.

"Please," she said as they were leaving the group, "Call me Charlie."

Admiral Halsey looked at her father. "Charlie?"

Lewis Castle just smiled and shrugged his shoulders.

Michael managed to regain his composure within a few minutes of their initial meeting. Charlie was self-effacing, funny, and sharp enough to know that asking a young officer about his service career was the surest way to put him at ease. She was the one to suggest that they share contact information, before Michael could work up the courage. In later years, he often said that he was just a clueless fly and that Charlie simply let him blunder into her trap. Charlie never objected to this characterization; she would just smile and shake her head slightly as if to indicate that Michael hadn't been all that clueless.

By Christmas, Michael and Charlie were nearly inseparable. When Michael received his orders to report to the battleship *USS North Carolina* for deployment back to sea in March of 1943, he made it official and presented her with a modest diamond ring. She accepted without hesitation.

Charlene Liliuokayalani Castle was the great-great-granddaughter of Samuel Northrup Castle, co-founder of Castle & Cook, Hawaii's largest company. Her father, Lewis Castle, had married a native Hawaiian beauty whose family traced their roots to Queen Liliuokayalani, Hawaii's last monarch. If there were such a thing as royalty anywhere in the American democracy, Charlene Liliuokayalani Castle was surely it. The fact that she was called Charlie by friends and family provided a hint that she didn't take her heritage all that seriously.

At twenty-two, and a freshly-minted graduate of UCLA, she was now teaching English in a rather seedy neighborhood of Honolulu. Her junior high school students called her Miss Castle until rumors of her nickname were substantiated and then she became Miss Charlie.

Commander Yellis's secret project dealt with improvements to the RCA CXAM-1 radar that had been installed on several battleships. As a fire control officer with an electrical engineer's degree, the relationship between more accurate radar and targeting was in Michael's career sweet spot. The *North Carolina* was scheduled back to Pearl for installation of the new fire control and radar gear. Commander Yellis recommended to the Navy that Lieutenant Boone be assigned to the *North Carolina* fire control team when it redeployed to the South Pacific that spring. And so, with his fiancée, and her mother and father, waving farewell from the dock, Michael resumed his role in warcraft.

The *North Carolina*, with its new radar, thanks to Commander Yellis's team, was a major asset throughout the war in the Pacific. It provided defensive screening for aircraft carriers and their complement of sister ships, bombarded Japanese shore facilities with their newly more accurate main guns, and sank opposing ships. As the allies hop-scotched across the ocean, the *North Carolina* did heavy lifting in all of the infamous island chains: Gilberts, Ellis's, Marshalls, Marianas, and eventually the Japanese home group. Michael was a small but important cog in the gears that eventually ground their way to victory.

Michael was back in Hawaii for a few weeks that fall of 1943 as the ship needed repairs prior to the Gilbert Islands operation. His reunion with Charlie was appropriately torrid, and their commitment to one another was confirmed. However, on the 10th of November, the *North Carolina* steamed south from Pearl Harbor, and Michael watched from the deck as anxious family, friends and lovers became indistinguishable dots of color on the quay. Not until the following May did Michael hold Charlie close again in the afterglow of making love, but this return to Hawaii was desperately brief, necessitated by a balky main rudder.

Their brief reunion was much darkened by news of Al's death. He had finally gotten a sea duty assignment—and a promotion to Lieutenant—but after boarding a cargo plane flying to Majuro to board a destroyer, he disappeared. The plane never made it and nothing was ever found. Al McMasters was added to the long list of those "missing in action, presumed dead" whose families kept thinking that any day now that their boy would walk through the door. Most never did.

By June 6, 1944, as American, British, and Australian troops were slogging ashore in France, the *North Carolina* was back with the aircraft carrier, *USS Enterprise* group, headed for the Marianas.

News from home was steady but often delayed, as the Navy did its best to get mail to tens of thousands of homesick sailors and Marines as they moved about the warm waters of the South Pacific.

Besides letters from Charlie, his parents, Aunt Elizabeth, and— by-then— Mrs. Berryman, Michael also got the stray missive from his brother Matt, Bert, Big Mike, and Judge Morgan. His cousins and his little sister sent hand-decorated cards on holidays. When he turned twenty-nine in July of 1944, he received just such innocent handmade cards and he carefully taped them to the collection that he maintained on the bulkhead of his tiny quarters.

His brother Matthew had joined the Army in the summer of 1942, just after he finished his junior year at the University of California, Berkley. Matt's college opportunity came from the fact that he had been an All-State baseball star for Healdsburg High. His decision to enter the military and finish his college later was reflective of the mood of the country after the attack on Pearl Harbor. Try as he might to get into harm's way, the Army assigned him to a military intelligence unit, and sent him to England in late 1943 to play a role in deciphering intercepted German radio messages. His most dangerous assignment was bicycling to a nearby manor to deliver daily reports to the staff of General Eisenhower. He never got used to England's screwy traffic rules. He was sent to Berlin, after it fell, to be part of the team that interviewed suspected Nazis and government bureaucrats. The sheer destruction and pathetic situation of the German civilians left a permanent impression on Matt about the conflicting morals inherent in war.

Bert, who had kept up a correspondence with Michael through college and during his brief naval career, had left the revival troupe late in the summer of 1934, just as he had planned. He eventually married Nurse Linda in 1937. His initial work in Indianapolis was teaching English literature at a Catholic school. He noted to Michael the irony of his association, once again, with a religious operation. By the time America became involved in the war, Bert had parlayed his teaching talent into a tenured position at Wabash College in Crawfordsville. Linda was happy to be back in her alma mater's hometown, and her nursing skills were her job security once their twins started school a couple of years later. Nowhere in his correspondence did Bert mention any specifics about what became of the Brother Daniel's Good News Revival or its members. Michael brought it up a time or two but the fact was, Bert had mostly lost contact, except for what little he learned from Judge Morgan.

News from home dribbled in as the war lumbered along. When he had time, Michael sent replies but avoided news that would suggest that he was ever in any danger. Of course he was. The Japanese fought ferociously even though it was clear that their surrender was inevitable. Earlier in the war, before Michael came aboard, *North Carolina* had taken severe damage from an enemy torpedo that blew a thirty-two foot hole in her port side, killing five sailors. After that, the ship had been mostly damage free. Michael was aboard, however, in April of 1945 when, in a flurry of anti-aircraft fire from several allied ships trying to down Kamikazes, hit the *North Carolina*. The friendly fire killed three, and wounded forty-four. Burials at sea are sobering for any crew. The enshrouded dead would never have a permanent gravesite where family and friends could gather to honor and remember. The living took note.

Survivors from all of the doomed ships were parceled out to various ships headed back to the West Coast or Pearl Harbor. There, the seaman would be medically evaluated and re-assigned. Michael was a guest on an oiler, *USS Platte,* headed to Pearl for repairs. Michael spent most of the journey in the *Platte's* sick bay with second degree burns on his arms and hands. The pain was familiar.

Michael was on duty in Tokyo Bay that September, when the Japanese unconditionally surrendered. His anti-aircraft gun crews were on full alert for rogue Japanese pilots who were, reportedly, planning to strike the *USS Missouri* where General MacArthur was accepting the Japanese surrender. The only fighters in the air that day turned out to be American and Australian.

Michael spent a week ashore in Tokyo as part of the preliminary occupation force. Like his brother, seeing the destruction of the largely firebombed city was unnerving. The civilian population of Tokyo was traumatized. Their homes, businesses, schools, and official buildings were mostly charred ruins. People in the rubble seemed to walk in a daze.

"Where are they even going?" Michael commented to his driver. "There doesn't seem to be anywhere worth going."

"Beats me, sir," replied the young seaman at the wheel of the jeep. "Maybe they're looking for what used to be their houses."

These people weren't soldiers or seaman, Michael said to himself. *Why the hell did we do this? We're supposed to be the good guys.*

He found that what he saw and heard caused him to questioned humanity's underlying moral fabric. He had no empathy for Japanese civilians until he came ashore to what was left of this once grand city.

Official word came down that the *North Carolina* was headed home. It went east through the Panama Canal on October 8, 1945, and steamed into Boston on the 17th. Charlie was there, having left Honolulu almost as soon as the telegram arrived with the news. She had stopped in Los Angeles to visit college friends and talked one of her sorority sisters into making the cross-country train-ride with her. As noted by some of his cracking wise crew mates, he was met by *two* beautiful women while many of the rest had to settle for sisters, mothers, aunts, grandmas, or worse, no one. Michael made no apologies. He did, in the spirit of the event, introduce Charlie's friend Margo to Lieutenant Don Belknap of Fort Worth. Don's lanky cowboy frame and Texas drawl had a certain charm, and for the next few days the four of them enjoyed the rock-steady ground and historic ambience of Boston.

Charlie was now an encyclopedia of wedding plans and particulars. All she needed to start the process was a groom who could be in Honolulu by April. So, Michael applied for re-assignment to Pearl Harbor but the best the Navy could do was San Diego, and not until early in 1946. With plenty of unused leave time, however, the couple married in Honolulu in April. All of his family (except Matthew who was back in school and playing ball) and Judge Morgan were there. The newlyweds had a four-day honeymoon in Palm Springs where they shared the hotel pool for two days with Humphrey Bogart and Lauren Bacall, along with other Hollywood types. Bogart had just bought a new pair of extra-long swim fins and he cut a particularly ridiculous figure, flapping along beside the pool before jumping into the deep end, flippers first.

For the next two years, Michael worked with pilots and fire control officers in the best use of new radar technologies, which were constantly emerging from the Southern California defense industries. Twenty months into their marriage Charlie gave birth to a tiny, six-pound girl, Kalani. Her skin was just like Charlie's, but she had her daddy's tousled hair.

Four months later, Lieutenant Commander Boone and his little family were transferred to the Navy Air Station in Pensacola. They settled into very nice Officers Quarters there in the summer of 1948.

Chapter Ten
The Good News Radio Hour

TIME PASSES SLOWLY when you are a kid. Everything is new and requires examination and thought. Time is something of which there is plenty and it meanders along at a childhood pace. New experiences, however, soon become routine and not much time is taken ponder that which is no longer unique, and so life seems to speed up.

Michael's life had surely sped up. He had matured through his college years and then, with direct contact with war and its brutality; he was shoved hard into adulthood. He certainly wasn't the only kid who went off to war and came back more mature than his years would suggest.

Michael was one of those whose life experience prior to the war protected him from the emotional damage experience by some. He found comfort and purpose in the structure of military life, if not always its routines and politics.

He was sometimes aware that his life seemed to be going faster. One day he is a college freshman then suddenly an Ensign. Then he was jumping into the waters of the Pacific to save his life only to turn around and have a wife and infant daughter.

He sometimes asked himself. "How did I get this far along this fast?"

Of course it wasn't any faster for Michael than it was for any adults who eventually asked themselves the same question. And time always changes things. In Michael's case, the past fifteen years had been valuable and formative. Compared to the Kentucky farm boy who spent his first independent summer puttering around Indiana and points south in a 1931 flatbed Ford truck, Michael was sophisticated, polished, confident, and grounded. He had grown in ways that he could never have imagined when doing the chores on Aunt Elizabeth's farm in the spring of '33.

"Commander Boone," the ensign came onto the bridge of the carrier, anchored and languidly bobbing in the Gulf of Mexico just a few miles from the Pensacola Air Station. "I have a message from Admiral Prescott," he said, handing Michael a sheet of paper ripped from the ship's teletype.

TO: Lieutenant Commander Boone

FROM: Admiral Ernest Prescott

SUBJECT: Special Request

DATE: 3 NOV 1949

Nav Muni Comm snding xprmtl Lark, Sparrow and Hawk for demo/eval off J'ville, 7 NOV – 11 NOV. Pent brass/Raytheon execs req your pres. Trsprt POV. Be sure to eat at Joe's Crab Shack while there. Raytheon gets the tab.

In civilian-speak, this note meant that Michael was driving himself to Jacksonville for a five-day demonstration and evaluation of Raytheon's latest missiles. Michael had made a reputation as one of the Navy's best ordinance and weapons guys, so the Admirals at the Pentagon wanted him to be in on the evaluation. There were lots of new weapon systems being developed as the Cold War progressed, but some of them weren't practical and all of them were very expensive. Lt. Commander Boone was practical and didn't mince words about what he saw as good or bad for the men who would depend on new weapons systems.

"Charlie," he called as he came through the back door. Before he could track down his roundly pregnant wife, Kalani came barreling toward him down the hardwood hall on what looked like a tricycle but it didn't have pedals. At seventeen months, Kalani was faster on her "tri-tri" than she was afoot and a whole lot steadier.

"Poppa!' she squealed as she headed for his shins.

Having been subjected to this wheel-bound greeting for several days now, Michael knew enough to reach out and apply fatherly handbrakes to the little handlebars. He scooped her up and they both puckered up dramatically for a loud "muwaa" smooch.

"Hello, Commander Poppa," Charlie called from the front stairs as she waddled her way down carefully. Actually seeing the stairs over her belly had recently become nearly impossible. She basically came down sideways.

"Hello, beautiful," he said and gave her a kiss that required no puckering and didn't end right away.

"Yeah, right," she snorted. "I'm a blimp with paint in my hair."

"And attractive paint it is," Michael offered. "A yellow room for the baby will be perfect, regardless of gender."

"She's a boy," said Charlie.

"Well, that pretty much covers the options," he laughed.

Because Charlie had been painting for most of the day, while keeping track of Kalani on her roadster, Michael suggested that they go to Mario's Pizzeria.

"This is why I married your Poppa," Charlie said to Kalani, who clearly had no idea what her mother was talking about.

Over sausage, bell pepper, and onion pizza, Michael told Charlie about his trip to Jacksonville. Neither was worried that the new baby would decide to come early so the timing seemed right.

"Anyway," Michael said, "It's only an eight-hour drive at the most, so I could be here if need be."

"Not to worry," said Charlie, "I'm not letting this little bugger out until the room is done."

"Mo pitsa," said Kalani, pointing to the round metal platter.

"Mo pitsa it is," said Michael, placing a second slice on her high chair tray and carefully picking off the bell peppers. "Eat the crust, too, it's good."

Very solemnly, Kalani slowly shook her head, "No," she replied.

* * *

Michael headed for Jacksonville late Sunday morning, November sixth, in his almost new 1948 Studebaker sedan. It was the first car that he had owned and, in spite of the fact that Charlie thought it looked like a torpedo, Michael loved the modern design and the way the front and rear door handles came together at the center post.

Michael realized, as he planned his trip, that Highway 90 East would take him through Tallahassee, and right by the Daniel's family home on the east side. About two thirty that afternoon, he went through downtown Tallahassee and headed out the stretch of road where he expected to see the stone house, expansive yard and out-building that he had briefly called home. Except it wasn't like that.

The city had grown, and nothing looked remotely as he recalled. He slowed and scanned the right side of the road for anything familiar. About where he thought it could be, there was a plain white cinder block building near the road. Beside it was a radio tower. A large sign was anchored to the roof of the flat, windowless building. There was a picture of a grown-up Petey, smiling his gaped-tooth grin, and the lettering read, "Brother Peter's Good News Radio Hour . . . WGNR 820 on your dial"; in smaller letters, "Saturdays and Wednesdays at 4 pm."

Michael eased the car to the shoulder and stopped. He had passed the driveway to the building and from that vantage point he saw the stone house he remembered sitting well back from the road, but it looked different, bigger. There was an addition to the rear of the house that wasn't there before, and it looked like there was a swimming pool. Where the bunkhouse had been, there was a three-car garage with a second story, and beyond that were horse stables.

Looking back at the cinder block building, he could see that the sign atop was replicated for viewing from either direction.

"Well, damn," he said. "Damn."

He sat in the car for a few minutes and thought about those summer and fall months, fifteen years ago—about Ruth and their budding love affair, about Mother Daniel and her skilled and urgent instructions in bed, about feeling wonderful, guilty, lustful, tender, and confused.

He tried to concentrate on the job ahead but his mind kept wandering back to the summer and fall of 1933 as he bore down on Jacksonville. Maybe, he thought, he should stop by on his way home next weekend.

The task of watching at-sea demonstrations and then officially reviewing the performance of three new Raytheon missiles went relatively smoothly. These at-sea tests were usually beset with logistics problems because they require great coordination between several large vessels and towed targets, both air and sea. On top of that was the reviewing of specifications for range, guidance system accuracy, speed, explosives payload, tactical issues, personnel training requirement, and estimated costs.. There were slightly contentious conversations with Raytheon salesmen who stood to gain enormous commissions if the US Navy decided to buy any one or all three of these weapons systems. Back in Port Jacksonville Friday, a group of Navy officers and Raytheon execs went to dinner at Joe's Crab Shack at Michael's suggestion. One of the Raytheon fellows paid the check out of a wad of cash in an envelope that he pulled from his suit pocket. The defense industry had fattened up on the war, and had no intention of letting the spigot be turned down. Many in the military felt the same, although Michael knew that waste and abuse was epidemic. He had eaten the crabs anyway.

Michael headed home early the following morning. He talked with Charlie several times during the week, and promised that he would be home in time for dinner Saturday evening. With a seventeen-month-old that meant no later than 6:00. He had decided to stop in Tallahassee and visit Brother Peter's Good News Radio Hour.

The Studebaker tires crunched on the gravel drive as he pulled in. It was just after 9:30 in the morning. The entrance to the cinder-block building was in back, facing the stone house. On this side of the building there was one double window with wooden Venetian blinds, and a metal-framed glass door. Lettering on the door read: "WGNR 820 Radio," and below that, "Brother Peter, God's Messenger." Before turning off the car, Michael turned the tuner knob to 820, and there was a nice strong signal carrying religious music. He listened for a few seconds and then shut down the engine.

Wearing his summer white uniform, Michael tried the door. It opened and a bell announced his arrival. There was a desk, two side chairs, and a Naugahyde sofa. Otherwise, the room was empty. A door at the back of the room was open. Above the door was a sign that, when lit, blazed "ON THE AIR" in red letters.

Michael went to the door, "Hello," he called into the darkened room.

Through another doorway toward the back of that room came a woman's reply, "Just a sec."

Michael retreated to the center of the reception area. Presently a woman emerged carrying a coffee cup in one hand and a spool of typewriter ribbon in the other. Her fingers were smudged black from the new ribbon. She set the mug and spool on the desk and turned to greet her visitor.

She took in only the uniform initially. Then her gazed lifted to study Michael's face. Michael had been studying her as well, expecting to see someone familiar, given the circumstances.

"Officer?" Her voice trailed off as brain synapses started to connect.

Michael pointed to the plastic nametag above his right breast pocket. "Boone," he said.

"Oh my God," said Mother Daniel and she clutched the back of one of the chairs. Her other hand came up to cover her mouth as she repeated a now muffled, "My God." She left a small dark smudge of ribbon ink where her fingers touched her cheek.

"No, not God," said Michael, "Just me, Michael Boone. I thought you might be looking for a driver and stagehand, Mother Daniel."

As her eyes welled, she managed a smile, which squeezed out one tear. "We're not hiring right now, officer," she said.

Michael was beaming. "I'd like a hug anyway if that's okay"

Mother Daniel took three steps and pressed her cheek against his chest, wrapping her arms around his waist. He circled her shoulders with his arms and gently patted her back, her head just under his chin.

She pulled away after half a minute, and Michael wiped the smudge off her cheek with his thumb. She reached up to where he had touched and gave it another wipe and let out a little laugh. "I must look a sight."

"You look fine," he said. "It was just a smudge of typewriter ink."

"Can you stay and visit?" she asked.

"Ninety minutes, tops. I've got to be back in Pensacola by six."

"Sit, sit," she insisted motioning to the sofa.

"Would you like some coffee?" she asked as she retrieved hers from the desk.

"Maybe later."

She pulled one of the chairs around to face the sofa and pulled it close. When she sat down, her knees almost touched Michael's.

"Tell me everything, Mr. Boone. Oh, sorry, Officer Boone," she corrected herself.

"We actually use the term Mister in the Navy when speaking to another officer so it's quite familiar to hear Mr. Boone," he replied. "But Michael is even better."

"I want to know everything, Michael," she said, taking a sip of lukewarm coffee, "And it's 'Annie' now—please call me Annie."

Michael gave her a very brief review of his life after he set out, hitchhiking from just across the road to Calhoun in the late fall of 1933. If he skipped too much, she would stop him and demand more detail. She never took her eyes off of him as he recounted the high points of college, the early Navy days, his war experience (much glossed over), his marriage and his growing family.

"The baby is due month after next in January. Kalani is especially excited to be a big sister," Michael finished up as he put the picture of Charlie and Kalani back into his wallet.

"What do you hear from Bert and George Morgan?" she asked. "I've lost touch."

Michael told her what he knew from their latest letters.

"Good, that sounds good," she said.

"What about all this?" Michael said, circling his hand indicating the interior of the radio station? "And the rest of the Daniel's clan, what about them?"

Annie took a deep breath and exhaled through partially open lips, as she decided where to begin. Michael processed how she had changed since he left. She was probably fifty now, and her hair was streaked with grey, especially at the temples. Her figure was still trim, although slightly thicker at the waist. Her blue jeans still flattered her bottom. Smile lines had deepened, and her eyes looked weary, but their blue-grey color wasn't faded. She had a hint of two chins, which disappeared when she looked up. From being a "looker," she had become a handsome woman, although she wouldn't have taken that as a compliment.

The radio station had been Rebecca's husband's idea. Her husband, Mark, was a graduate of the University of Florida. He and Rebecca met in school. They were married in '41, he joined the Army early in '42, broke his leg so badly in Ranger School in the Georgia mountains that he was given a medical discharge. He came back to Florida pretty much mended but still limped because the broken leg was shorter.

Mark was fascinated by the potential of radio to reach thousands of people to whom one could sell things. "Why not sell them salvation for tithes and offerings?" he had asked. "Instead of traveling all over the damned countryside and sleeping in tents, for God's sake, why not broadcast to those same people from one spot and let them mail you money?" Annie said that Mark had a head for business that surpassed anyone else's in the family. Mark was the station's business manager, and he and Rebecca had two children, three and five. They lived in a new house on the west side of town.

"Those grandbabies wear me out," said Annie, "But they are my darlin's."

"How come Petey is the face of the ministry and not Brother Daniel?" asked Michael.

Annie shook her head slightly and took another sip of coffee before answering.

"Harlow's in prison over in Raiford," she said.

Raiford State Prison took in Harlow Eugene Daniel in 1942. He had been convicted of Statutory Rape, Indecency with Minors, and Sodomy. Brother Daniel's lust for the younger girls had caught up with him during the troupe's winter stay in Tallahassee in 1941. He was serving thirty years to life.

Harlow had created an off-season job for himself, counseling "wayward" children, sent to him by several local fundamentalist churches. Each child garnered him a small stipend for instructing these waifs on the proper way to lead a "Bible-based" life. It was the perfect way to have access to youngsters, one-on-one.

"He convinced two different under-age girls that the engorgement of his penis was a sign of the risen Lord, and that if she would take it into her body that the spirit of the Lord would eventually gush into her. He convinced them that they could get the 'holy spirit' in several different ways," Annie's flat-toned delivery was reflective of her utter disdain for the man.

"The girls bragged about their 'special' relationship with Brother Daniel, word spread and that's that."

Michael sat stunned and silent.

When he finally looked up and met her eyes she nodded and said, "Sign of the risen Lord." The corners of her mouth began to twitch and she pressed her lips together but it was no use. She burst out laughing.

Michael briefly recoiled, but the very idea plus her mirth was too much. He couldn't contain it. They laughed like slightly mad scientists until Annie caught her breath and said again "The risen Lord" and they doubled over one more time.

Finally, Michael regained some composure, although his eyes were watering he said, "Well, Bert predicted it; either in jail or dead."

"Bert, bless his heart, saved my girls from the son-of-a-bitch," she added. Annie Maypearl had clearly been roughened from a life lived by her wits and the circumstances attendant to that.

"Speaking of the girls," said Michael, "You haven't said what Ruth is doing."

Annie picked at her lip for a moment and stared out the windows. Finally, she turned and looked at Michael.

"I have no idea."

"What does that mean, exactly?" said Michael.

"It means that I have no idea what Ruth is doing. She stopped contact with me just after she finished the Women's College," Annie said.

"Why?"

"I'd rather talk about something else," she said.

Michael was puzzled by her reticence to talk about Ruth but an Officer and a Gentleman did not push into uncomfortable topics.

"Okay. How is Petey doing as the front man for the radio show?"

Annie looked at the ceiling, apparently deciding how to couch her response.

"Peter has his father's gift for oratory, a good radio-friendly voice, and several of his father's less endearing qualities."

"And the radio business?" he asked.

"The money flows like a waterfall from heaven. Small donations, but thousands of envelopes a month," she said, with no indication of pride or hubris. "The people who can afford it least send the most. Peter tells them that supporting his ministry paves the way to heaven for those who sacrifice and send offerings to help keep him on the air. At least when we were on the road the tithes were collected as part of a regular church service. It seemed more legitimate somehow."

"Well," said Michael, "People are free to spend their money however they see fit, selling them salvation may be just as proper as some of the other promises made by the clergy."

"Have you lost your faith, Michael?" she asked.

"Sorta," he replied. "Things I saw and did in the war plus some of the study I've done has caused me to question my faith. I see a lot of hypocrisy in those who say that they are 'good' Christians, Jews, Muslims or, especially the 'good' Shinto Japanese leaders."

"Welcome to my world," she said. "It is, however, paying the bills, and Peter likes to spend the money—mostly on Peter."

The glass door swung open and a boy, probably fourteen or fifteen, came into the reception area.

"Oh, good," said Annie, "you're here. Gene, I want to meet Commander Michael Boone. He worked for us many years ago as a truck driver."

"And stagehand," said Michael as he rose and extended his hand to the boy.

Like most boys his age, Gene's handshake was neither firm nor floppy, just barely there.

"Hello sir," Gene nearly whispered.

"Gene is my youngest," said Annie. "He's been cleaning horse stalls this morning. It's part of the Saturday routine."

"Mom," said the boy in a voice now more normal, "Peter won't pay me. Says he has to inspect the work first. I need the money now so I can go to the movies this afternoon."

"I'll give you movie money now and I'll speak to Peter after Commander Boone has left." Annie retrieved her purse from under the desk and pulled a five dollar bill from her wallet. Michael studied Gene as the boy turned to watch his mother search briefly for the cash.

He was probably 5'8", maybe taller, but not by much. It struck Michael that the boy hadn't stopped growing, given his loose-limbed walk and movements. His hair was the same dusty blond that Michael associated with a younger Mother Daniel, Ruth and Rebecca, but it was a tangle of curls.

"Poor kid," Michael thought to himself, recalling his own adolescent self-consciousness about his mop of unruly hair.

Gene's profile suggested that he had inherited his mother's nose and high cheekbones. His eyes, however, were dark brown, nothing like Annie's of pale blue.

"Thanks Mom," said Gene as he took the money. He turned to Michael and said, "Nice to meet you, sir," and made for the door.

"Nice to meet you too," said Michael to the boy's back.

Michael sat down.

"Is he named after his father?" asked Michael. "As I recall, Brother Daniel's middle name was Eugene."

"Something like that," said Annie.

"Now I recall. Bert told me that you got pregnant right after I left. He wrote that you and Ruth were going to stay here when the revival left the next spring," Michael said, staring at the far wall trying to remember the details. "Ruth was going to finish high school with her class and go through graduation ceremonies, then be with you when the baby came."

"Something like that," said Annie.

"If my math is right, Gene is about fifteen, right?"

"As of July twentieth," said Annie.

"Well, he seems like a nice boy," Michael said. "He has some of your features, especially the nose and facial structure—but not your blue eyes or hair, except for the color of course. I don't recall that Brother Daniel had brown eyes."

"He doesn't," said Annie.

"I'm trying to picture Brother Daniel," said Michael. "All I can see is lank, dark hair and a nice looking but acne-scarred face. Where'd Gene get that hair?"

"From his father," said Annie, "Same for the brown eyes."

Michael rolled her comments around in his brain, trying to connect whatever dots were there. Annie sat silently, watching his face.

"I'm confused," Michael said as their eyes met.

"No you're not," said Annie. "I imagined that when you first saw Gene that you might recognize that he is our son."

Michael's head rolled back and rested on the back of the sofa and he stared at the ceiling. He made a fist with his right hand and brought it to his forehead. There was a rushing noise in his ears and a tightening in his chest. He closed his eyes.

"I wanted to tell you many years ago," said Annie. "But I didn't have the courage, and I decided that I would never see you again anyway. I convinced myself that it was better that way."

Michael slowly brought his attention back to the present.

"I'm sorry," he said, his voice nearly a whisper.

"Why, on earth, are you sorry? I'm the one who should be sorry. I seduced a nineteen-year-old boy. I'm no better than Harlow when it comes to robbing the cradle," Annie said. "I knew that your hormones and job security would give you no choice."

"Maybe," said Michael, "But I wanted the relationship once it started, and you taught me a lot. I didn't want to refuse your attention. It was basically a teenager's dream come true. At least I was of age."

Annie smiled. "Yeah, I guess they couldn't put me in jail next to Harlow, huh?"

"Does Gene know that Brother Daniel is not his father?" asked Michael.

"He suspects—heck, everybody, including Harlow, suspects. But I simply don't talk about it," she brushed a strand of hair away from her eyes.

"Are you going to tell the boy who his father is, eventually?" Michael sat forward, looking at her.

"That's your decision, Commander," she said. "You have another life now, a family and all. Admitting to having another child by a different woman could put that at risk. You are the only one who might know how—Charlene is it?—might react to the news."

"Yeah," thought Michael, "How would Charlie react?" He sat back and tried to collect all of the jumbled thoughts in his brain into some coherent string of logical next steps.

"Look," said Annie, "Things are fine as is. Gene suspects, probably hopes, that the creep in prison isn't his father. Our life here is secure, thanks to the radio ministry. Gene has ambitions to attend West Point because he is huge Eisenhower fan, so he is a good student and stays out of most trouble. Revealing who his father is won't change that, but it could be a problem for you."

"I owe the boy something," said Michael. "He's growing up without a father around. I know what that's like."

"Michael," her voice slightly exasperated, "Even if Gene knows that you are his father, he's not coming to live with you. That simply won't happen, so the circumstances would be the same either way."

They sat in silence for a minute or two. Finally, Michael, his hands on his knees, stood.

"I should be going."

He reached into his hip pocket, removed his wallet and took out one of his Lt. Commander calling cards.

"Here," he said, "It has my work phone and address. Until I decide about telling Charlie, you can contact me at work if you need to."

Annie took the card and said, "Good, I'll write down my phone number for you too. My phone rings in the garage apartment where Gene and I live."

Michael gave her a puzzled look.

"Oh, Petey decided that since he was the star of the operation that he should take over the house. He and his boyfriend added a wing in back and installed the swimming pool. He kindly built the apartment over the garage to get Gene and me out of his love nest."

"Boyfriend?" said Michael.

"Something like that," she said.

"Now I wish I had more time," said Michael, shaking his head slightly.

Annie walked him out to the car. Before he opened the door, he embraced her and picked up the faint hint of lavender.

He pulled away and said, "Are you still using mayo as a skin lotion?"

She stood tiptoed and kissed him on the cheek.

"I can afford the store-bought now," she smiled, "But I still like lavender. Let me know what you decide. Rebecca will be thrilled, Petey won't care, but I'm really glad that you came."

"Me too, I think," said Michael as he slipped behind the wheel.

Annie stood in the parking lot as he backed out and then headed up the drive to Highway 90. She waved as he turned onto the blacktop. He beeped the horn twice and was gone.

The rest of the drive to Pensacola was a distracted mess of happily-ever-after followed by end-of-the-world scenarios as Michael tried to predict how Charlie would react to the news that he fathered a child years ago. Michael argued aloud with himself as he drove,

"Of course I need to tell her."

"No, that's a bad idea."

"We have a good life and one little secret won't hurt."

"Well, it's not exactly a little secret is it?"

"She'll love the boy as her own; she's that kind of woman."

"Yeah, but she has a temper too and pregnancy hormones make her a bit unpredictable"

"Maybe I should wait until after the baby arrives and she gets back to normal."

"Naw, she'll know something's wrong because I'm lousy at hiding my emotions."

"Better talk about it right away, you're a brave guy."

"No I'm not, especially when it comes to Charlie. She's had my number ever since that first glass of wine."

He pulled into the drive about 5:30. He wouldn't be late for dinner.

Kalani was upstairs playing with her model aircraft carrier and fighter planes. Her planes never missed the flattop, although sometimes they came in backwards or upside down. The captain of the ship was often her Raggedy Ann doll, an immense presence who had to sit alongside the smaller model boat.

Charlie heard the car and came out the back door, standing on the stoop, she waited for Michael to negotiate the steps and take her in his arms. Following a long and suggestive kiss, Charlie said, "Welcome home, Commander Poppa."

Michael pulled away a bit but stayed connected with his arms and his stomach, which pressed against her ripe pooch.

"Charlie," he said, "I have something to tell you."

Their family dinner plans had to be adjusted. He didn't want to start the conversation when Kalani would be vying for their attention.

"Let's get Kalani fed and in bed and then we can talk," suggested Michael.

"Sounds serious," Charlie said. "Are you getting shipped out for a long float?"

"No, that's not it, but it is important."

"Okay," said Charlie. "Kalani," she called out, "come down for dinner. Poppa's home."

Michael heard Kalani running down the upstairs hall. "Poppa!" she screamed with delight as she butt-scooted down the stairs.

They had a somewhat truncated family dinner. Kalani was full of news about her adventures while Poppa was gone. She and Momma had gone to the playground and the PX. They had made brownies and eaten them all even after they agreed to "save some for Poppa."

Charlie grimaced a guilty grin at this bit of news.

Michael finally got Kalani to finish her macaroni and cheese and then he whisked her upstairs for a "bathie."

He read her the *Horse That Turned Purple* for the umpteenth time and she nodded off to sleep during the third reading of the evening.

Michael came downstairs and helped dry the rest of the dinner dishes.

"I'd like a glass of wine," he said. "You?"

"If you need wine to tell me whatever it is that you have to tell me, then I should have one too," Charlie replied.

They carried their wine to the living room. Charlie sat in the wing chair, which was easier to negotiate in her condition. Michael sat on the sofa.

Michael told Charlie the story of his summer driving the truck for Brother Daniel's Good News Revival. She had heard bits and pieces over their time together but never the version that included being seduced by Mother Daniel. Now, he was revealing not only that secret but also the fact that their coupling had created a child. This part of the story was fresh for him as well.

"Does the boy know that you are his father?" she asked, her voice flat.

"No, but Annie says that he suspects that Harlow isn't his father and she's not discussing it with him for now," Michael offered. They sat in silence for at least a minute. Michael assumed that Charlie was trying to sort out her own feelings.

Finally, he said, "Charlie, I love you and I don't want you to be mad or disappointed in me. That would be too much."

She broke into a broad grin.

"Does this mean that I have to reveal all of my pre-Michael love-life secrets too? Why would I be disappointed or angry? You were, what, eighteen or nineteen?"

"Nineteen, by the time it started," Michael was still wary of her reaction.

"Look," she said. "From what you've told me so far, it doesn't seem that Gene is in a bad situation. It's his mother's decision regarding what she tells him. If you're thinking of approaching the boy without her approval, that's a bad idea. In the meantime, you can keep up with his life through Mother Daniel. If you can play a positive role in the future, you've got my backing. Until then, let's raise Kalani and baby he/she as best we can."

Charlie reached over and pinched Michael's reddening cheek as if he were a toddler.

Michael stood and pulled Charlie to her feet. He grabbed her face in both hands and kissed her hard.

"I guess that you still love me."

"Hey," she said, "Who wouldn't love a good lookin', slightly bad boy."

Of course, Michael's tale of summer romance didn't include the details of his romance with Ruth.

About five weeks later, Charlie's water broke and Michael rushed home to take her to the base hospital. The delivery was faster, and some would say easier (although Charlie didn't necessarily agree), than she had experienced with Kalani. It was a "he" baby, and he got Michael's father's name, Robert. His middle name honored Charlie's oldest brother, Scott. Try as he might to change it, Robert Scott Boone, was known as Bobby into adulthood.

On a cool day that January, Michael came home from spending the day aboard the Gulf-anchored carrier evaluating student pilot landings, always an anxiety-producing assignment for all involved. For the new flyboys it was a matter of life and possible death, so "anxiety" might not be a strong enough word for their emotions. More than a few had slid off the carrier after failing to engage the tail hook or crumpled the landing gear by basically belly-flopping a crash landing on the deck. Most were successfully rescued, and some never tried it again by choice or by executive decision.

He and Charlie had talked several times about the situation with his son in Tallahassee. Michael felt a sense of obligation but Charlie reminded him, more than once, that his responsibility was to stay out of the boy's life unless or until Annie made the decision that Gene should know about Michael. Otherwise, Michael would be inserting himself into a family dynamic that he didn't understand.

"You're right, you're right," he would say.

Charlie was giving Bobby a bath in the kitchen sink when he came in that afternoon.

"Any excitement today on the high seas?" she asked as he smooched her cheek from behind.

"All hands present and accounted for," he replied. "This class is pretty strack, and the flying weather today was perfect for students." Michael reached down and grabbed one of Bobby's toes and gave it a shake. "Woogie, woogie," his insincerity regarding baby talk always apparent.

Bobby gave a wide toothless grin when Michael's face came into focus and he heard the deep voice.

"Kalani is upstairs practicing her landings; mail's on the hall table," said Charlie. "Dinner's at six thirty."

Michael could smell roasting chicken. He hoped it was the Hawaiian-style that Charlie considered a specialty and was his favorite.

He stopped in the hall and picked up small stack of mail and continued to the living room and plopped down on the sofa. As always, there were two or three third-class mailers, which he pitched aside. There was a letter from Bert, who wrote three or four times every year, and to whom Michael still felt close, although they hadn't seen each other for nearly eighteen years. Bert's letters were always a joy of catching up news and wonderful writing. Just under that letter was one addressed to "Michael Boone," with no reference to his Navy rank, as was usually the case. There was no return address. The postmark was Seattle.

Curious, Michael opened the letter. The neat script tickled some distant familiar memory. He read the entire letter without making a sound, except for the blood pulsing through his ears. When he finished, he put the letter down by his side and stared blankly across the room.

Charlie came down the hall from the kitchen, Bobby swaddled in a bath towel, his little face the only visible skin, which had Charlie's Polynesian hue.

"Anything of interest, Commander Poppa?" she asked.

"Here," he replied. "Give me Bobby."

Charlie, smiling at her baby boy, placed Bobby in Michael's lap.

"No diaper yet." It was a warning.

"Read this," he said handing her the letter. "Maybe sit down first."

Charlie gave him a little frown and sat in the armchair. She began reading the neat cursive message.

Dear Michael,

I thought this day would probably come. There were too many variables that might reveal the consequences of your time with us. Keeping big secrets forever is a fool's game.

Rebecca called me several nights ago and told me that you had re-discovered the family salvation scam and learned about Gene. What my mother told you is a lie. Gene is our son. There are four of us who know the truth, me, Rebecca, mother, and now you.

When I suspected that I was pregnant and told mother, she went into protective mode and concocted the story that she was pregnant, couldn't go on the annual trip and wanted me to stay with her and finish high school. Needless to say, I didn't finish high school that spring. Mother and I lived like hermits that spring and summer. When she went out for groceries or whatever, she padded herself enough to be convincingly pregnant.

Gene was born in August at home. Mother brought in a mid-wife from over by our old dairy farm. This woman had helped mother deliver both me and Rebecca. After the delivery, Gene became mother's baby. By the time Brother Daniel and the rest got home in the fall, mother had sent me to live with her cousin in Atlanta. I finished high school in Decatur. Mother told everyone that I was working in Atlanta.

I went home in February and I told Rebecca everything. Mother found out and was furious. She was so upset that she told me about her relationship with you. I guess it was her instinct to get even for my betrayal. That's when I decided that I wanted nothing more to do with my family, except Rebecca with whom I'm close, although not geographically.

I went back to Atlanta that spring and applied for scholarships at Emory. Thanks to Bert and his insistence on classical learning I qualified. Between waiting tables and scholarships, I graduated with a degree in literature in 1940.

I met my husband there. We got married in the summer of '41. He became a Navy pilot and served in the Pacific until Easter of '44, then he came back and taught student pilots on the West Coast. We have two sons, 4 and 7. The oldest is Michael. My husband doesn't know that I'm Gene's mother and he doesn't know about you.

Gene is a good kid. I keep up with his progress through Rebecca, but I don't have any maternal feelings toward him now. It's just been too long and not enough connection to have had that develop. I decided that if you ever found out, I wanted you to know the truth, not the lie. You were my first real love, but when I found out that I was pregnant, I just couldn't keep writing you. I realized that it would never work out. You had a great life ahead of you and a young wife and baby would have changed all that. My life, too, is probably better as a result.

As it is, the situation with Gene is stable, although Petey isn't doing anything financially to give him hope for college. Rebecca tells me that Gene is dreaming of West Point, but I doubt it's realistic. In any case, I want things to remain as they are. Gene will probably be happier thinking that Annie Foster (that's right, she never married Harlow) is his mother than knowing the truth. I hope that you will respect that decision. You have no responsibility for Gene so your conscience should be clear.

I loved you once but feelings fade with time and circumstances. Rebecca told me that you are a career naval officer and somehow I think that it must suit you very well. I wish for you all good things.

Finally, I think it best that you don't try to contact me.

Warm Regards,

Ruth

With the baby making gurgling noises and squirming in his lap, Michael concentrated on Charlie's face as she read the letter. Her face remained impassive as her eyes darted from sentence to sentence. Finally she stopped reading and seemed lost in thought before raising her eyes to meet his.

"Are there any more sisters from this family who might show up with another of your offspring?" her voice was flat and her demeanor was decidedly negative.

"No," Michael answered softly.

"You didn't mention this relationship when you told me about Gene. Maybe you should have," Charlie's voice quavered slightly.

"Maybe," said Michael. "But what I told you then was the truth, as far as either of us knew. My relationship with Ruth seemed irrelevant. Just one more love life secret from my past. As you said then, you weren't volunteering your secrets."

They stared at one another for several seconds.

"Granted," she said, "But as far as I know, I don't have any father/son relationships to keep secret. It seems that you were a very bad boy and 'boy' is probably the most important word."

"I know it's a lame excuse, Charlie, but I really didn't know what I was doing or how to change it at the time."

"What a lady killer," she said, the corners of her mouth turned up slightly into a rueful smile.

"Come on, Bobby, let's put you in something safer for lap sitting," she said as she rose from the chair. "Go up and see Kalani, Commander Poppa. Dinner is still at six thirty. Most of your immediate family will attend, Stud."

"Come on, Charlie," Michael's tone was exasperated if not pleading.

"You're right," she said, "It was a cheap shot."

She headed down the hall, Bobby on her hip. Without turning around she called out, "You gotta admit, it was kinda funny." Her voice had lost its edge.

Michael sat and nodded slowly. "Kinda," he said to himself.

Epilogue

IN MID-MARCH of 1952, Eugene Foster, soon to graduate from Tallahassee High School received a letter from Major General William E. Bergin, Adjutant General of the Army.

In part it read: *...your acceptance to the US Military Academy at West Point is due in large measure to Florida Congressman Charles Bennett's confidence in you as a deserving and accomplished young man of strong character and ability.*

In addition, a recommendation addendum to your application from decorated Navy officer, Commander Michael Boone, strongly projected your qualities as a potential military leader. This, too, was instrumental in our evaluation process.

You should plan report for physical exams and preliminary training....."

Gene read the letter three times while he stood by the mailbox at the highway. His knees were a little weak. He turned and ran toward the radio station shouting, "MOM! MOM! I'm in, I'm in!"

He rushed through the door, breathless. Annie was coming around the desk to hug him. She had heard his shouts and knew what they meant.

They embraced, his chin nearly resting on the top of her head.

"Oh, sweetheart," she said, "I'm so happy for you."

Gene pulled away and handed her the letter and said, "Who's Commander Boone?"

Without reading the details, Annie smiled softly.

"Someone you should probably get to know."

ACKNOWLEDGMENTS

The first shout out must go to my wife, Frances (Mimi) Breeden, who encouraged me to step away from the corporate world and resume my true soul's code—writing and music. Without her moral and financial support, these creative ventures would have been long delayed. During the writing of this novel I relied on feedback from a small group of test readers to include Mimi, daughter Brooke Yount, Cindy Kesselman, my father, Byron, and my older brother Bill. Thanks to them for suggesting improvements in plot and style, painful as it sometimes seemed. I also thank my fellow novelist Gary Lepper and his wife, Tessa, for encouraging me early in my adulthood to seek out good literature. Clearly, one cannot ignore the writing lessons that soak in when reading a good book. I also want to thank my developmental-line editor, Jennifer Banash of Kevin Anderson Associates, and all of the helpful folks at Koehler Books including John Koehler, Joe Coccaro and Randi Sachs.